Nostalgia Man
in Henley-on-Thames

Without memory, we are nothing.

Paul S Bradley

Paul S Bradley is a pen name.
© 2024 Paul Bradley of Nerja, Spain.
The moral right of Paul Bradley to be identified as the author of this work has been asserted in accordance with the Copyright, Design, and Patents Act, 1988.
All rights reserved.
No part of this publication may be reproduced or transmitted in any form or by any means, electronic or mechanical, including photocopy, recording, or any information storage and retrieval system, without permission in writing from the publisher.
This is a work of fiction. Any resemblance of characters to actual persons, living or dead, is purely coincidental.
Editor: Gary Smailes; www.bubblecow.com
Cover Design and Illustration: Simon Thompson; sthompson01@hotmail.co.uk
Back cover photo: Paul Bradley
Layout: Paul Bradley.
Publisher: Paul Bradley. Nerja. Spain.
First Edition: September 2024
Contact: info@paulbradley.eu
www.paulbradley.eu

PROLOGUE

For as long as I can remember, but only when awake, if I hear or read the word April, a misty outline of a young woman appears in a deep corner of my mind, walking several yards in front of me. My arms are outstretched as I catch up with her, but before I can grab her shoulders, she screams and vanishes into thin air.

I agree, it's weird. Or is it? Because as the years pass by, my memory plays an increasing number of deceptions. At seventy-six years of age, I still muddle through the shopping without a list but have no idea where this recurring daymare originates. Is it pure fantasy, wishful thinking, or maybe the remnants of a drunken event from my youth? Perhaps I'm psychic or inherited it from my forbears? Moreover, what does it mean?

I consider myself a reasonable, regular guy, don't suffer from poor mental health, and as far as I remember, have never committed any heinous acts, so why does my mind wrestle with this convoluted phenomenon? Has my subconscious blocked out the answer, or did my neurons have their knickers in a twist? It would be nice to know one way or the other because, with no accurate memory of my life, I am nothing.

2023

The future loomed ominously over me. The end was approaching. The uncertainty was when and how. Irrespective of current good health and sound mind, inevitably, it couldn't last. At some point, frailty and loss of independence were inescapable. The prospect of death I wasn't too worried about. What concerned me most was becoming a burden on others. The thought of some poor soul having to wipe my drooling spittle or dirty bum was humiliating. Far, far more terrifying was losing my marbles and kissing goodbye to memories. They are my life, which would have become pointless without them.

I could have allowed this heavy burden to weigh me down. I concluded that with such a short time remaining, I should fill it with joy, not negativity. For over seven decades, my solution for lifting spirits was to launch myself into something new. The diversion promoted a degree of sanity and purpose, which should postpone the inevitable depression or at least distract me from it.

I didn't have a wife, children, or garden and, therefore, did not need a potting shed to escape to. Learning new things, such as a foreign language, the guitar, or quantum physics, was too late. The energy and time required would be disproportionate to the knowledge gained. I was a more than capable artist, but the thought of painting three landscapes a week to pass the time was tedious.

After exhaustive reflection, I decided the best way forward was to revisit what memory I had acquired. I could do it from the comfort of my armchair or when out walking and needed no specialist textbooks or professorial assistance.

I could have set off on this retrogressive journey when I retired as Detective Chief Superintendent of the Leicestershire Police. However, at sixty, I was still relishing the prospect of new challenges and adding more memorable moments to my ever-increasing bank. Plus, my regular Sunday morning fourball had other ideas. I accepted the secretary position for my much-loved indulgence, the local Golf Club. Sixteen years later, my patience with increasingly demanding members had all but diminished. My swing had degenerated so much it resembled a lumberjack cutting down trees. My scores were so bad that it was suggested that I use the ladies' tees. Reluctantly, I accepted the not-so-subtle hint. With a heavy heart, I disposed of my trusty bats, binned the garish shorts, and left them to it.

What surprised me most about my newly retired status was that even though I could potter around and not do much, the days flew by relentlessly. Every five minutes, I ate breakfast and wished myself a Happy New Year once a month. Notwithstanding the ever-accelerating minutes, now I had time—plenty of time to think. It didn't take a microsecond to appreciate that too much thinking can be dangerous.

Revisiting my childhood memories, I recalled the horror of losing my mother in a shop, the pain of breaking my arm on a swing, and the joy of boat rides on the Thames despite the disgusting sandwiches. I still grimaced at the guilt of breaking a window playing cricket in the school playground and burning baked beans at a cub-scouts cook-in. Best not to mention my first embarrassing attempt at kissing a girl on a family holiday in Cornwall. Her name was Wendy, or was it Sally?

Half an hour passed, and I failed to resolve her name, but it was an enjoyable experience. I eagerly anticipated more of the same for my teens, but it was not to be. The recurring vision returned with a vengeance.

It had popped up infrequently since my early twenties. Being busy had diluted its significance, but now that I was free of practically all responsibilities, it raised its ugly head more regularly. I found myself examining it from all angles.

Was it me with the outstretched hands? Was the woman an actual person I knew or representative of the fairer sex? Was I stalking her or approaching to ask her something? I had questions, questions, and more questions. The plethora of possible answers was overwhelming. What did it mean?

Which led me to the other matter.

On the evening of Sunday, the twenty-first of April 1968, something drove me from Henley-on-Thames, where I was born and spent the first twenty years of my life. I departed under a cloud the next day with no memory of events to hint at what transpired other than a vague sense of shame.

Even with the benefit of hindsight, I could never fathom why.

With so much thinking time on my hands, these churning elements from my youth evolved into a smouldering powder keg. I switched from one to the other so often they became foggy and confused. Were the two linked in some way or separate incidents? After several months of resisting, I conceded. I had to solve these riddles or risk losing my sanity. I ignored the adage, never go back, and opted to return to Henley. The answers must lie there.

I shared my intentions with the dwindling number of ancient friends who started referring to me as Nostalgia Man because the subject matter of my conversations had become so focussed on the past. I couldn't disagree, but I pointed out that they also had ceased considering their shrinking futures. My solution was to remain silent about my worsening gout or suspicious mole and revisit my youth. They whined about artificial joint performance and bragged about how many tablets they consumed with their breakfast cup of tea. Sorry, but my still sharp as a razor inquiring mind remained thirsty for answers.

Notwithstanding, their advice was to let the past alone; digging it up again would bring heartache and disappointment.

I ignored them. The past was me; how could it be disappointing?

However, I knew returning to Henley would be a difficult and emotional rollercoaster of a journey. Common sense told me it would pass more smoothly with a degree of preparation to toughen up my mental muscle, so I decided to do what any modern adult would: go on a training course.

I spent several months re-experiencing the highlights of my life. Edinburgh for the Royal Military Tattoo, where the wailing pipers squeezing through the misty castle gate never failed to stir a tear. Chelsea Flower Show to treasure nature at its finest, Twickenham, where Harlequins lost to Leicester Tigers, Stratford on Avon to see Shakespeare's *Much Ado About Nothing*, where for the first time I could appreciate what a brilliant comic our famous writer was. Harder, though, for this true patriot was Henry the Eighth's stamping ground at Hampton Court, where my parents instilled in me a love of the royal family and introduced me to this island's chequered heritage. But the most challenging assignment had been Last Night at the Proms. The awe-inspiring architecture at The Royal Albert Hall and straining to croak the high notes while singing Jerusalem had been too much; I'd blubbered like a baby. After returning home to Market Harborough from London, I declared myself ready for my life's quest and booked my online ticket.

The train from Twyford ground to a halt at Henley-on-Thames. I struggled into my overcoat, placed my fedora hat over my bald pate, adjusted it precisely to the correct angle, grabbed my small case from the overhead rack, and, with some trepidation, joined the other passengers waiting for the sliding door to open.

As I approached the exit barrier for my first visit here in fifty-six years, my initial hesitation surged into panic. My emotions were in turmoil, and my pulse was thumping at a rate far exceeding my doctor's comfort level. Was I doing the right thing coming back? Could such an ageing body handle the inevitable mental trauma?

The station had changed since I was there, with only a single platform remaining and the original Victorian ticket hall replaced by characterless 1980s architecture. Was this to be my sole disappointment? I hoped so.

With a population of under twelve thousand, Henley was a small but quintessentially English riverside town steeped in history. It was home to comfortably off middle classes, tourists, hi-tech engineering, ceramics, and the world-renowned Henley Royal Regatta.

The wheels of my case rumbled on the pavement as I headed into town. Outside the enduring Hobbs Marina, with over one hundred and fifty years of catering to boat trippers, I paused to look around. Floating on the river lashed to their winter moorings were vessels ranging from luxury gin palaces to small family-sized clinker-built rowing boats.

Alongside the riverbank were several new shops and cafes, and every other car was a Chelsea tractor instead of a beat-up Hillman Imp or souped-up Mini with a straight-through exhaust. Otherwise, it was how I remembered it.

Canadian geese and Mallard ducks glided regally by in the swirling muddy water as the five arches of the eighteenth-century Henley Bridge came into view. It was a chilly and damp December morning, with a stiff, piercing breeze blasting the few remaining autumnal leaves off the beech hedges. I couldn't resist scrutinising the few passers-by of my age group, probably a tad too closely, searching for any resemblance to long-lost familiar faces. There were none, but I did receive a couple of cordial greetings and an oddball expression as they wrestled with their walking frames or shopping carts on the uneven pavement.

I paused outside the estate agent on the corner, which used to be Crispin's Restaurant and later Tea Rooms, owned by old friends Rod and Edit Newbold. The building was the same, but the sign advertising clotted cream tea and scones in the window had been replaced by property details at eye-watering prices. I visualised Rod in his kitchen whites stirring the gravy for his renowned roast beef and Yorkshire while the smiling Edit dashed back and forth, taking orders and serving. It had been fifty-six years since I last saw them; what a waste of a great friendship. Had I done the right thing leaving Henley, how would life have been if I'd stayed?

On the opposite corner stood one of the most painted pubs in England, The Angel on the Bridge, a listed black timber frame and white-walled building that would never be permitted to alter anything. Distant memories of many a night there with my fellow Henley youth overindulging in local brewer Mr Brakspear's finest ales hovered at the back of my mind. Notwithstanding, revisiting its cosy interiors and the riverside terrace was not why I was here.

It was improbable that my trip down memory lane would progress without assistance. I needed old mates to help dig into the past, but if, as I suspected, they had snuffed it already or dispersed around the globe, my mission was dead in the water. I would need to rely on good fortune or a rare coincidence to move forward, neither of which I was accustomed to. It's why I never bothered with Lottery Tickets and relied on a dogged investigation to solve crimes rather than trust lady luck.

Suspecting that I was chasing wild geese, I trudged across the road with a heavy heart and stood outside my last-chance hotel.

The Red Lion Hotel was and remains today my favourite place on earth. Not because of its forty individually styled bedrooms, gracious red brick Georgian façade, or elegant interiors. That it was by the river was also irrelevant. I adored it because of the people I had met in its Riverside bar. At least three were beautiful women I had fallen madly in love with during 1967/8. These different relationships contributed to the man I became. My memories of them as people had stayed with me all my life as clearly as if it were yesterday. However, the nature of parting with the third and last was a complete blank.

Grace Leo was the designer of the hotel's current adaptation on behalf of the Singapore-based investors who had joined a long line of distinguished owners. They had renamed my place, as I thought of it, Relais at the Red Lion, or in English, Coach House at The Red Lion, which is how it started life in 1732. This pleased me because to have ignored a lifetime of being known as The Red Lion and christening it The Green Jaguar, for example, would have been a travesty. As far I was concerned, they could have called it anything because, to me, and probably thousands of others, it would always be The Red Lion, the one by Henley Bridge. It was also a fantastic coincidence that the designer's surname reflected its feline character. Could it possibly be an omen for a positive outcome?

I shivered with expectation as I surveyed my old haunt. It stood proudly between the riverbank and the parish church of St Mary the Virgin with its sixteenth-century tower. It was home to my grandparent's memorial plaque and the final resting place for some of Dusty Springfield's ashes, who spent her later years in Henley. Her powerful mezzo-soprano voice touched my soul, especially; *I Only Want To Be With You*. Whenever I heard it played on the radio, which was rare nowadays, it reminded me of Inge Lise, the first of the three women and the only true love of my life.

The red-painted statue of a rampant lion stood proudly before a billowing Union Jack over the hotel's entrance archway. The three tall chimneys appeared as solid as ever, but other than a tasteful new sign and a restored Welsh slate roof, the three-floored redbrick building with evergreen ivy almost surrounding the windows had not changed one iota. I crossed the road and noticed a new plaque with intriguing text and an interesting mix of illustrations, portraits, photographs, maps, and diagrams adjacent to the main entrance.

I approached and read every word with avid interest. It was one of several around the town funded by Henley Archaeological and Historical Group and designed by long-time member Vivienne Greenwood. It contained a snippet of history I had failed to appreciate while living here. When James the First, the sixth of Scotland, became King of England in 1603, he commanded the emblem of Scotland, a Red Lion, to be displayed around his new Kingdom. Was this where the hotel name originated? If so, its link to the Royal family reinvigorated a sense of hope.

I strode through the same old glazed timber front door and into the lobby.

The reception desk wasn't where it used to be, which threw me momentarily. I was relieved to spot it a few meters to the left. The walls were decorated in soft tones of contrasting beige and chocolate brown to compliment the dark timber. Large brass wall lamps added warmth and cosiness. The highly polished parquet flooring was still there, and behind the mahogany reception desk, subtly illuminated shelving displayed various ceramics. A young, uniformed woman sat behind the desk studying a laptop. Two traditional visitor armchairs faced her.

To the left of the reception was the old lounge, now the bar, separated from the lobby by Georgian windows. Several middle-aged men in suits were imbibing fancy cocktails and appreciating the low ceiling supported by timber beams. Rowing photos and artwork decorated the white walls. To the right of the lobby was the old bar, now painted white and converted into a chic café. A new passageway was where the reception desk used to be. It led to the Clipper Restaurant at the rear.

"My name is Matthews," I told Leanne, the presentable young lady with a nametag and glasses handling reception. "I have a reservation for tonight and a special request."

"How can I help you, Mr. Matthews?" she said.

"I frequented this hotel during the 1960s and have treasured memories of Room 181. Is it available?"

"I'm sorry, Mr. Matthews, but we don't have a room with that number."

"Perhaps if I describe its location, you might recognise it?"

"Go ahead, please."

"It was on the middle floor at the back, overlooking what was then the car park. It wasn't used much because smells from the kitchen below and car engines starting often generated complaints."

"I know where you mean," said Leanne. "It's Room 118 and is available. Would you like it?"

"Yes, er, please," I said, wondering how I could have confused such an important fact. It worried me. Perhaps other memories were equally as distorted. Leanne probably considered me a complete idiot.

She swiped my credit card and escorted me to Room 118 after I had signed the register.

"I'm ashamed to say I've staggered down this passageway a few times," I said as Leanne pressed the call button of an elegant stainless-steel lift, another modification from the creaky old stairs of yesteryear. "The Riverside Bar at the end used to be one of the most popular watering holes for Henley's youth."

"It's the function bar nowadays," said Leanne. "We wouldn't want to disturb discerning guests with rowdy teenagers."

The lift doors closed, and we zoomed up to the first floor. Room 118 was crucial to my research. It was where my Henley days had abruptly ended on that fatal night. My expectations were high. I was sure that sleeping in its ghostly interior was bound to spur diminishing grey cells into action. From the lift, we walked along a creaky, turquoise-painted corridor through a glazed fire door and paused outside Room 118 while Leanne unlocked it. She breezed right in, but I hesitated on the threshold, full of doubt. Would the room hold the answers I was seeking? When I entered tentatively, I discovered, to my horror, that nothing was the same. My memory remained blank. I hoped the disappointment didn't show on my face.

Leanne handed over the key, showed me how to operate the lights and air conditioning, and left me to it.

The carpet was burgundy with bold white and black stripes. The walls were painted in buttermilk and decorated with abstract art prints. The original Georgian timber sash windows were the same. They overlooked the rear of Chantry House, a fifteenth-century, lemon-coloured timber-framed building with squirrels scampering mischievously along the roof apex. The king-sized bed had a giant headboard. A Japanese-styled wardrobe provided more than adequate hanging space for my one clean shirt and underwear.

I pottered about a bit. Poking my nose into drawers and cupboards and had a pee in the luxury bathroom with a glazed shower and white marbled tiled walls and floor. Bathroom visits were something I was growing accustomed to, especially in the middle of the night. The room's long, narrow, rectangular shape was the same, although it seemed smaller. But the smell was different. Gone were the musty old rugs and furniture riddled with woodworm. The new décor was clean, fresh, and pleasing, but it failed miserably to light any candles from the old days.

I reasoned that old friends would unlikely come to me, especially without warning, so I went out to explore former watering holes, wondering who I could track down.

The streets of Henley Centre, originally laid out during the thirteenth century, were a charming combination of Georgian and Victorian architecture. The older timber frame buildings tended to have white-painted facades and red roof tiles, many covered in moss.

My first port of call was to our former Victorian home on Queen Street. It was a three-bedroom end terrace house in red brick with beige brick corners and a grey slate roof. It was narrow but long, with a small, fenced garden at the rear. The sash windows were topped with cream-painted lintels. A three-foot-high red brick wall protected the house from the street, and the cream front door was set back under a recess. Other than a recent coat of paint, it was as it was. As I stood gawking at the façade, a flashback hit me.

Bodes well, I thought, as I visualised the next-door neighbour, Mr Woodford, repeating his habitual morning greeting to the dozen or so various-aged kids playing football in the street before school. Every weekday morning, on his way to the train station carrying his leather briefcase, he would say, "Ay oop, me duck," having originated somewhere north of the imaginary divide near Watford. I wondered where those kids were now.

Family cars were rare back then, so the street was our playground. At weekends, we were thrown out on our return from Saturday morning cinema and told to bugger off until lunch.

In the 1950s, my dad was the first to have a car in our street. A green Jowett Javelin with a curved back. It came with his job travelling around Oxfordshire and Buckinghamshire, where he sold steel to the many engineering works in the area. They produced parts for the British Car Industry spread around Oxford, Birmingham, and Coventry. My mother taught at the infant's school, so Mrs Woodford minded me until I started there. Most women were stay-at-home mums, and it was accepted practice to help your neighbours. Their son, Barry, was my best mate until they moved away to Ipswich when we were about ten. Where did this old nonsense spring from? I thought, grinning to myself. My plan was working.

I decided to skip Gillot's School, as it was a long way uphill, and I preferred to conserve energy for where old friends were likely to be, in one of the pubs. I did take a turn past The Henley College, where I had studied half an Arts degree, and noticed several new buildings, but none of these stirred anything from the past, so I began my search in earnest.

Henley used to be blessed with a disproportionately high number of pubs per populace, most of which I had known intimately: the pubs, not the people. But after a turn around New, Bell, and Hart Streets, I discovered many had vanished, having been converted into private houses or coffee shops. I knew where the old ones used to be but couldn't recall their names. Those remaining had already decorated for Christmas. Twinkling fairy lights created a Dickensian ambience but without the snow. Many pubs had been built during the eighteenth century with timber-beamed ceilings. Nicotine-stained walls, horse brasses, and pewter tankards hanging over the bar created a cosy atmosphere to sit and chat with the friendly locals.

In the sixties, few pubs served more than nuts or crisps. Patrons ate at home then adjourned to their local for a convivial evening gossiping, debating the inadequacies of the local football team, in this case Reading FC, or arguing the finer points of political manifestos over a game of darts. The engaging community spirit was more unifying when compared to today's divisive social media nonsense. They were also endearing places to meet actual potential partners rather than sorting through manufactured profiles on a dating app.

The Bull on Bell Street had survived this surgical

reduction of traditional hostelries. Externally, it still resembled a private house with a gateway to stables at the rear. However, current owners had added substantial quantities of planting inside and out, including green-painted windows, and with the sparkling Christmas decorations, it was most inviting. It was much brighter and cleaner than I recall, and I appreciated no trace of the typical 1960s pub smell of stale beer and cigarette smoke. My inquiries to the bar person with an unusual accent yielded nought. It seemed that my besties, Ivan, Anita, Sonia, or John Francis, had vanished from this earth.

As my mind flashed back to youthful images of me with my dear friends, sharing a terrible joke around the window table, I had another regret attack. Why had I abandoned these beautiful people I had known since we were babies? Despite the absence of decades, these close bonds will forever be part of me. Whatever had happened on that fatal night to drive me away must have been terrible. What the hell had I done?

Ten pubs later, with no sign of old buddies, I was flagging. Even Norman Shannon and Keith had disappeared into the ether, whom I had always presumed part of the building fabric of the town. Norman, in particular, had been like an older brother. How would my life be now if he and the others formed part of it? Would I still have this annoying vision?

It was amazing that while most establishments had the same layout and appearance, the ambience of yesteryear had vanished. Gone was the jolly landlord with his repertoire of terrible jokes. Where was the camaraderie of a shared second home? These were no longer pubs but dining locations that also served drinks. I was beginning to feel that the past was a foreign country.

If I'd had an alcoholic drink in each of these establishments, I would by now be crawling on hands and knees, but on receipt of no news about my friends, I had left my card and moved on.

After yet another disappointing response to inquiries at the Little Angel, I called it a night. Luscombe's, on Bell Street, was an intimate family restaurant I had discovered while meandering. I took a window seat providing panoramic views of Boots the Chemist and studied the menu. Following a succulent special of duck breast and a glass of Malbec, I returned to the Red Lion for a nightcap and chat with the hotel staff. Maybe they might know something. If not, I would give up and leave after breakfast, a journey wasted, a project failed. At least, I would gain some satisfaction for my attempt. I could live with that.

I perched on a stool by the bar and ordered mineral water from a young man with dark hair whose nametag described him as Antonio. After taking a sip of my drink, I asked.

"Would any staff remember the hotel from fifty-odd years ago?"

"Unlikely," he said in accented English. "We are too young, and most are from other countries. I am from Spain, for example."

"How about elderly regulars?"

"We are a hotel providing wedding receptions, conferences or retirement parties. People your age tend to stay home or go to their favourite pub, such as The Angel on The Bridge opposite. I see several senior citizens popping in and out at lunchtime. You should try there."

"Thanks," I said, feeling down.

I finished my drink and went upstairs. To my delight, it was a squeak-free, luxurious bed that didn't sink in the middle as it had in my day. I switched off the light and settled into my usual dropping-off routine, sad about the lack of success but happy I was once again in the room haunting me for all these years.

It was rare for me to dream, let alone remember the content, but when I dropped off for the second time after the inevitable water closet break, some weird stuff started flashing before my eyes.

The first was a bright light outlining the shape of an angel with short blond hair. The second was a brief misty glow of a gelatinous woman. The third was a dark circle containing an old hag's face with bloodshot eyes. Though I failed to interpret their significance, these ominous images kept rotating through my mind as I shaved and showered. I dressed and headed down to the Clipper Restaurant with a deep sense of foreboding.

Was the dream a message from the past or my subconscious attempt to fathom the mystery? I wondered as my pallid and tired reflection stared back at me in the lift mirror. Thankfully, my rumbling stomach was signalling attention. At my age, when food calls, an instant response is vital to maintaining an even temper. The diversion enabled me to shove the confusing garbage of the night to a distant recess in my brain.

The restaurant was a light and airy space where the kitchens used to be. To associate the hotel with the river, boating, and the famous Henley Royal Regatta, the designer had incorporated a clinker dinghy hanging over the central bench seating from the double-height ceiling. I sat near the window and enjoyed views of the terrace.

Having savoured exquisite Eggs Benedict, I looked around the room, reflecting on my failed visit over a pot of tea. It seemed unfair that my vibrant youth in Henley had left no legacy. There was not a trace of me or my mates anywhere. We were mere ghosts of the past haunting old buildings now used by a new generation.

After all those years of meaningful life, doing my bit for queen and country, I had surely earned myself the right to a place in posterity. I remembered something I learned back at college. Francis Bacon, the Irish-born painter, once said: "I suddenly realised, there it is – this is what life is like… existing for a second, [then] brushed off like flies on a wall… We are born, and we die, and there's nothing else. We're just part of animal life."

Conversely, I considered the words of American Philosopher William James, who decreed, "The greatest purpose of life is to live it for something that will last longer than you."

Which I considered arrogant and the sort of bullshit wealthy, educated people say who have never experienced a struggle to put bread on the table. Was I bothered if I died leaving nothing? No, because I'd be dead and couldn't take a thing with me except my precious memory. This was why I returned to Henley to complete the missing blanks. I owed it to myself.

I thought back to the final night in April 1968.

I remember arriving at the Riverside bar and sinking a few pints to celebrate the first victory of our football team. The atmosphere had been electric. I tried to envisage who I was talking with. How had I ended up in Room 118? Was anybody with me? But my mind remained blank. I reverted to my police days and applied logic to the occasion. Why was all I recalled about the evening a deep sense of shame? What could I have possibly done to drive me away from my dearest friends and favourite place on earth? I suspected it had something to do with the fairer sex.

Whatever it was must have been dramatic.

Powerful enough to leave first thing the following day for Hartley Wintney in Hampshire to enrol at the police training college. My parents badgered me incessantly over breakfast and were mystified by my lack of explanation. But I couldn't give them one because I didn't know myself.

I completed my training and was posted to Nottingham as a bobby on the beat. Mum and Dad sold our house in Henley and headed north to be near me. They purchased a massive house off the Derby Road near the rugby club on the city's west side. My dad became the area manager for the Dunlop Company, and my mum started at another infant's school. They bugged me progressively less about the reasons for my departure and began a new campaign of blatant hints that I should marry and produce grandchildren. I didn't have the heart to tell them I had vowed to drink little and remain celibate. I wasn't aiming to become a hermit, but a desire for self-flagellation burned within me. I had to punish myself for whatever shameful deed I must have committed. It seemed the least I could do.

Despite a few close calls, I had lived a pure life. Consequently, our line of the Matthews tribe was about to disappear from this beautiful planet.

My decision not to reproduce had been a continual source of depression. I loved kids and enjoyed the patter of tiny feet on the rare occasions I visited parental colleagues at home. I'm sure I would have made a good father, but I had made my choice and clung pathetically to my decisions like the stubborn old fool I had become.

I nagged myself to stop mourning the life I had missed and celebrate the one I had. Shaking my head, my eyes filled with tears. While I couldn't disagree with such logic, it didn't prevent my sadness levels from plummeting to rock bottom. If only, I said to the empty restaurant, sniffed, and wiped my eyes with my fingers. This wasn't healthy.

I peered around my surroundings, trying to spot something that might distract me from this downward spiral. The various mirrors hanging on the walls were intended to create spaciousness, but all I noticed were the numerous reflections of my miserable ageing features.

Seeing my face never ceased to confuse me. Every morning when I shaved, I saw this progressively older person staring back at me, yet the voice in my head never aged. I was still my parent's boy.

This constant inner chatter occasionally manifested itself in lengthy diatribes or misty images. Logically, it ought to communicate with wisdom gained from the benefit of experience. So, why did it chastise me for not maximising my potential in love and life? Why did I still feel like a child demanding love and attention? After seventy-six years, I ought to have grown out of self-doubt. But the silent voice was relentless in its arguments and suggestions; it never left me alone.

I was too miserable, fat, or ugly for others to engage with me. It categorised women on my behalf into possibles, probables, or definites. It had an opinion on every aspect of my life, whether I asked for one or not. As I suffered through these nagging monologues, I could understand the usefulness of escapism through religion, hobbies, alcohol, substances, or anything to shut the damn thing up. Perhaps it was why I became obsessed with golf and solving crimes.

However, sometimes, it spoke with reason and positivity. Now, it interrupted me from nowhere and suggested that I play what-if games to distract me from wallowing in self-pity. For once, I couldn't disagree; perhaps they would lift me out of this debilitating self-analysis.

What if one of my relationships in Room 118 had produced a mini-Matthews? Could this fantasy child be a member of the hotel staff? I glanced at the pretty dark-haired girl flitting between kitchen and servery. No matter how I appraised her, she bore no hint of family resemblance and was young enough to be my granddaughter.

I mulled over my relationships.

There had been three I could recall. Any offspring were improbable but possible. I thought long and hard about each girl and concluded that only one was a maternally minded miss. The odds on my paternal prospects were, therefore, remote. I shook my head, scolded myself for being pathetic, took my leave, and returned to Room 118.

I packed my case, used the facilities, and paused on my way out. I had a final look around, but what caught my eye was a repetition of the weird images from the strange dreams: a bright light, a misty blob, and a dark, menacing circle blinking at me from the walls. The images vanished when I shut the door behind me, leaving me shaken and crestfallen. I headed to the reception, parked my hat and coat on a lobby chair, and waited in line to check out.

While the receptionist discreetly handled a difference of opinion about room bar consumption with a bleary-eyed middle-aged man, it dawned on me how to reignite the events of that distant April night. I needed to relive those days.

The facts had to be buried somewhere deep in my subconscious. I dug some of them up when returning to the old family house. If going back had worked for my childhood, it could do the same for my youth, preferably on April 21, 1968.

I gazed out the hotel's front window, wondering where to begin, and spotted someone leaving through the front door. He dashed through the downpour to climb into a waiting taxi. From the back, he was a sizeable athletic man in his fifties, with greying blond hair thinning on top. He paused to hand his luggage to the driver and, for a second, turned toward me.

My heart stopped momentarily.

His face was eerily familiar, particularly the ice-blue eyes.

I shuddered as if somebody had walked over my grave.

Surely, it couldn't be. Could it?

"Memories are made of this."

*By Terry Gilkyson,
Richard Dehr, and Frank Miller,
known as The Easyriders, 1955*

CHAPTER 2

1967

If I remember correctly, which could be doubtful after the debacle of hotel room numbers, 1967 was a year of global turmoil. Harold Wilson of the Labour Party was the UK Prime Minister notorious for not being accepted as a member of the European Economic Community and forced to devalue sterling. Lyndon B. Johnson, a Democrat, was the thirty-sixth President of the United States, acceding in 1963 after the assassination of John F. Kennedy. The Vietnam War was raging at its highest peak, with half a million American troops posted there to deter the spread of Communism. Much more important for my cohorts and me was that out of the senseless slaughter in the Far East emerged the peace movement, now referred to as flower power.

I was nineteen, over six feet tall, with light blue eyes and long blond hair. Hey, I was an art student at The Henley College. To my peers, it was how I was expected to look, but my father had a different view. Owing to his military upbringing, he found it difficult to accept my attempts at modernity. Long-haired git was his subtle hint to visit the barbers.

It was Friday night. Motivation night, Dad called it. In return for accompanying him on a five-mile run along the river towpath, I would be given an extra pound, or it may have been thirty bob pocket money for my beer fund. As a pint cost less than ten old pence, it was generous. Despite being in his mid-forties, Dad loved to stay fit and ran alone most nights after work, but Friday was his fitness test. Could he beat me on the final sprint up Queen Street? I had the edge but needed to push hard to earn my money. After showers, we shared a light supper and gossiped around the kitchen table before I headed out to join the gang.

It was one of those rare mild September evenings. The setting sun cast long shadows over the river. Birds were twittering as they settled into their perches for the night. The River Thames gurgled under the bridge as I strode along the bank. I waved at friends drinking on the Angel terrace, crossed the road, and through the side door into our regular meeting place, the Riverside Bar at the Red Lion Hotel.

The battle for the number one hit was between two of several songs exploiting flower in their title songs. My preference, *Let's Go to San Francisco* by the Flowerpot Men, was blasting forth on the jukebox. Cigarette smoke wafted over everyone, and a faint smell of dope lingered in the background. It was a happy and familiar crowd as I paused here and there on my way to the bar for a brief exchange with fellow students, old-school pals, or friends.

Most guys were wearing Levi jeans with Tie-Dye T-shirts and brown brogues. The Mod types differed in the top department, with button-down collar shirts and

V-neck pullovers. Their scooters were parked in the hotel car park. This was not a motorbike bar, so there wasn't a Rocker in sight. They had their salubrious establishments, which we avoided like the plague. Many girls wore long prairie dresses decorated with hemp and had a flower in their hair.

Norman Shannon preferred bright orange hipster tartan trousers. We estimated Norm to be ten years older than us because he refused to reveal his age. Still, at nineteen, anybody over thirty was considered well past it, especially in such eccentric clothing. He was good-looking, below average height, with longish dark hair and brown eyes. Perhaps they were grey; it doesn't matter. Although he was a carefree, flamboyant character considered way out of it by us ultra-fashion-conscious teenagers, we all adored him. He provided a sympathetic ear for our youthful angst, and we cherished his straightforward advice. He had a luxury launch and invited us on board during the regatta. It boosted our low self-esteem as we steamed back and forth among the rich and famous. What endeared him most was his generosity with drinks when we were broke, which was most of the time.

His parents had died young, and he had inherited their enormous three-floor property at the top end of Norman Avenue. Invitations to his monthly parties were highly sought after, where there was an ample supply of free alcohol, weed, and pills. Sofas were scattered throughout the downstairs rooms where partygoers were welcome to crash. Often, lost souls stayed with him, usually young and glamorous women. He was rarely seen without one or two hanging on his arm. The current pair resembled the iconic fashion model Twiggy. Lucy and Linda were extremely young and pretty but petite and skinny with lots of make-up. They didn't say much but gazed adoringly at Norman. He did work, but none of us understood what. Something to do with main-frame computers, he would reply when asked. Whatever it was had earned him enough to afford a bright red E-type Jaguar we all hankered after.

He waved me over. As I approached, he was telling a joke to his surrounding ensemble, including the fair-haired Best twins. We had been in the same class at Gillot's, and I couldn't remember any period of my life without them being around. It was they who introduced me to Norman a few years previously. They were fraternal twins and were easy to identify. However, in a sly attempt to confuse us, they wore identical clothing and had matching mophead hairstyles. I was too late for the bulk of the joke and only overheard the punchline, "Your weekend is buggered, so you may as well do some gardening.

I'd heard it before. It was funny the first time, and those listening howled.

"Hi, Ollie," said everyone.

I grinned, slapped a few backs, and kissed Sonia's cheek. She was Paul Best's girlfriend, a vibrant, fun-loving girl with short dark hair and a trim figure emphasised by her tight jeans and clinging Che Guevara T-shirt. She hung on Paul's arm and gazed lovingly at him through sparkling brown eyes.

"Listen, Ollie," said Norm, pulling me to one side. "There's a party tomorrow night. Bring who you like."

"Sounds cool," I said. "Any theme?"

"No, but Paul and Pete have announced their parents are immigrating to South Africa and are going with them. I guess it's their farewell do."

We returned to the expanding group. Ivan and Keith had joined us. We slapped shoulders. Keith was mid-height with an athletic figure and short, wiry hair; he played scrum half for Henley Rugby Club's third team and studied at The Henley College to become a pharmacist. Ivan was a tall, good-looking, long-haired lad with a round face and lively personality. He could talk the hind leg off a donkey but had no idea what he wanted to do with his life. He worked as a porter in the hotel while he made up his mind.

I looked at the Best brothers and said, "Where in South Africa?"

They both shuffled with embarrassment as Sonia burst into tears.

"Our dad has been offered a lucrative job," said Paul, glaring at me.

"Export manager at a winery in Stellenbosch," said Pete, shaking his head and avoiding looking at Sonia.

"Do I take it you're not going, Sonia?"

"Oliver," said Paul. "Leave her alone."

"Sorry," I said. "But you're avoiding the elephant in the room. We are your lifelong friends, and we are worried we may never see the three of you again. I assumed Sonia would be going with you."

"Her parents won't let her," said Paul. "She's still under eighteen, and they are concerned about how dangerous it is there with Apartheid."

"Aren't you worried about it?" I asked.

"Can't say I understand it," said Paul, sipping his beer and putting his arm around Sonia, who wept into his chest.

"There's a group of exiles demonstrating in Trafalgar Square, London daily," I said. "They are calling for a ban on South African goods until everyone is treated equally. You might find it difficult to export."

"My dad doesn't seem worried about it," said Pete.

"I wish you luck," I said.

Norman stretched out a hand and touched my shoulder. "Please come tomorrow, Ollie," he said. "There are so many au pair girls; we need at least one more handsome guy. Can you handle it?"

"I'll do my best," I said, heading toward the bar.

"Hey, Ollie," said John Francis, leaning against the timber counter. A quiet, athletic type with fair wavy hair, he was waving a half-crown coin at Sara, the bartender, to attract her attention. I edged in to join him. "Fancy a pint?"

"Thanks, John," I said, offering him my Embassy packet. "Did you win the pools?"

"Final Friday of the month," said John, taking the proffered cigarette and whipping out his gunmetal grey Zippo lighter. "The only weekend when I'm solvent. Any plans for tonight?"

"Few beers," I said, sucking hard and blowing a giant smoke ring over the bar. "Before some rich lady takes pity on me and drags me up to Chez Skinners Night Club on Remenham Hill. After dancing until dawn, she'll drive me back to her place and ravage me until breakfast."

"Pigs might fly," said John, holding up his hand.

"Bacon will go up," we shouted, smashing our palms together with the customary high five—something we'd been doing since Gillot's school days. Nobody noticed.

"I don't see any of the girls."

"Bit early," said John. "The au pairs don't finish work until eight, and the others are at the hairdressers."

"No matter, a pint and some sparkling conversation

will help pass the time."

"Sara, the usual for Ollie," said John, as the bartender, also in our class at school, flashed by. She served three customers simultaneously and muttered the separate running totals to herself.

"Are you putting your name forward for the Red Lion football team?" added John. "We are playing the Catherine Wheel on Sunday morning.

"To be honest, I hadn't thought about it. I never was a team player."

"I remember, but we need a goalkeeper. With your height, you would be perfect. You won't have to run around much; however, I suggest you tie your hair into a ponytail; otherwise, you won't see the ball coming."

"We have shirts?"

"Yes, the hotel owner Richard Elsdon has chipped in half, but players pay the rest."

"At least we will look the part."

"Do I take it you'll play?"

"Goalkeeper is fine; with you as centre-half, I'll be leaning against the post most of the time. Can the Catherine Wheel find enough regulars to muster a team? It's a Berni Inn, not a pub."

"Lee Somerville, their assistant manager, has assured us that they will take this first match of the Henley pubs league seriously, but we will see. If they can't drag eleven sober chaps from their bar, we'll lend them a couple of our reserves."

"Here you go, Ollie," said Sara, plonking a pint of Brakspear's on the bar in front of me with a friendly grin. She was a tall, kooky but shapely blonde with a confident, bubbly personality wearing a revealing blouse, micro skirt, her trademark large hoop earrings, and dark red lipstick. At work, she wore her hair with a French plait. Most guys in the bar ogled avidly when she extracted a bottle from the fridge, me included, but she was out of my league. Surprisingly, she looked at me fondly and added, "You fixed up tonight?"

"You offering?"

"One day, hunky, but you should know Inge Lise is interested in you. She asked me to tell you she will be in later."

I pretended with some degree of nonchalance that this was an everyday occurrence, but inside, my pulse was racing. Inge Lise was gorgeous.

"Might be your lucky night," said John.

"I doubt she is that type of girl."

"After a couple of pints, who knows?" said Sara. "Scandinavian girls adore English gentlemen like you."

"Thanks for the, er, tip," I said. But with all the noise, she failed to hear me and moved on to the next customer.

John chuckled as I hopped about, watching the entrance through the crowd. Inge Lise was bound to enter through the internal door. Most girls did, having used the adjacent ladies' room first to fine-tune their appearance.

"Relax, Ollie," said John. "And stick your tongue back in. You look like a lovesick puppy."

"Sorry," I said. "But this could be the big one."

"You mean, you're still?"

"Pathetic. But I have this romantic notion of loving them first. What about you? I have never seen you with a girl. You're not, er?"

"Certainly not. I love Sonia, but she's hooked on Paul Best. Until she dumps him, I'm remaining celibate."

"Unlikely, while he has a fancy Daimler."

"It's an extremely old Daimler, and one day, she'll learn that money isn't everything. Meanwhile, I'll be waiting and pure."

"With your Vespa, good luck, but haven't you heard the latest?"

"What?"

"The Bests are immigrating to South Africa next week, and Sonia is not going with them. There's a party at Norman's tomorrow to send them off. I've been invited. Do you want to come? It could be your chance to make a move on Sonia."

"In that case, I'll be there," said John, looking perkier than he had been for months.

"Good for you."

"Don't look now," said John, looking over my shoulder. "But Inge Lise walked in with her American friend Jenny. They are looking around and deciding where to go. Wait, no, er, yes. They're heading this way."

"I'm cool. You couldn't lend me a fiver?"

"Sure," said John, palming me a note. "Fifteen per cent interest per day."

"You tight-fisted son of a bitch."

"It could fund the way to Inge Lise's heart."

"Agreed," I said, pocketing the money.

"Hey boys," said Inge Lise. "Mind if we join you?"

I turned to see an alluring elfin face crowned by short blond hair with fringe and intense blue eyes gazing at me inquiringly. She wore burgundy, or maybe blue culottes, with a matching roll-neck sweater and a light touch of makeup, which I preferred.

"It's our pleasure," I said, using my bulk to make some room at the bar and squeeze Inge Lise close to me. I breathed in her hair; she smelled delicious. "What are you drinking?"

"A small shandy is fine," said Inge Lise.

Phew, I thought, economical as well.

"I'll get my own," said Jenny, copying my accent perfectly.

"Impressive," I said. "Where did you learn such perfect pronunciation?"

"I can't help myself; I'm a natural mimic," said Jenny.

I often talked to Jenny and Inge Lise but had not determined if they fancied me. As an only child, understanding female minds and gestures was beyond my experience. Jenny was a few years older than Inge Lise. She was also attractive but dressed more conservatively than most of our crowd, with her long blond hair tied in a ponytail. Her soulful blue eyes burned into mine, but with Inge Lise at the forefront of my mind, it failed to register.

I was a member of the Leander Rowing Club based on the riverbank opposite the Red Lion and was in serious training to try and qualify for next year's regatta. I'd often passed Jenny running along the towpath while rowing my single scull back and forth. Lurking under her loose clothing was a killer figure.

My parents were proud that I had followed my father and his father into the world of rowing. They had won many national and international trophies, now displayed in a cabinet in our front room. They were confident I would add more silver to their collection, which I had but only for the Princes Elizabeth Challenge Cup J18s. I was doubtful about winning more. The competition was fierce; I smoked and drank too much for a serious athlete and found golf far more enjoyable than flogging up and down the same stretch of water for hours on end.

Conversation with Inge Lise was proving difficult in such a raucous place. Voices grew louder each time someone turned up the music on the Juke Box. The current number was *The Last Waltz with You*, by Engelbert Humperdinck. It was the top of the hit parade and played repeatedly while everyone sang along in their out-of-tune voices. After I'd bought a couple of rounds, Inge Lise and I attempted to get to know each other better by taking turns to talk into each other's ears. Frustrated by the lack of communication, we agreed to go outside. As I led the way to the exit, Inge Lise whispered something to Jenny, and we headed out to the river.

Jenny scowled as I passed, but I was too focused to guess what might have irritated her.

Inge Lise and I walked hand in hand along the towpath for a while, stopped at an isolated bench, sat down, and watched the water rushing downstream. Twilight was morphing into night. Millions of stars were emerging above us and a new moon.

"How romantic?" she said, sighing and snuggling into my shoulder. We kissed gently at first but with growing passion as we caressed each other. I was in heaven.

"I adore your accent," I said after a while to cool us down. "And your English is perfect. It makes me feel so inadequate. Have you been learning long?"

"There are under five million Danes," she said breathlessly, gazing into my eyes. And we speak with potatoes in our throats. Nobody understands what we say except Swedes and Norwegians, so I understand why foreigners wouldn't consider learning Danish. If we want to do business with the world, we must learn

English, the most popular international language. We start in kindergarten, and many become au pair girls here to polish pronunciation and expand vocabulary."

"Where do you come from?"

"I live with my parents and elder sister in the port of Grenaa. It is halfway up the Jutland peninsula on the bit sticking across from Sweden. My dad is a timber merchant."

"What do you hope to do?"

"I want to study child psychology, but if my boyfriend has his way, I will probably end up working for my dad and handling his exports."

"You have a boyfriend?" I said, trying to disguise my disappointment.

"It's complicated."

"Why?"

"Erik and I have known each other since we were tiny. His parents and mine have been friends since they were at school. There has always been this understanding that one day we will marry."

"Does he visit you in Henley?"

"No, he is at the University in Hamburg."

"Do you miss him?"

"Yes."

"Then why are you here with me?"

"I've been asking myself the same question since we met about a month ago. Out of respect for Erik, I've resisted the temptation, but something this morning told me to follow my instincts."

"Hence the message via Sara?"

"Yes."

"Do you mind if I ask why me?"

"Ollie," said Inge Lise, taking my head in both hands and gazing intensely at me. The distant streetlight reflected in her blue eyes. "Your presence stirs feelings I have never experienced with any man. I've never kissed anyone with so much passion and desire, and nobody's touch has excited me like yours."

"I wouldn't want to come between you and Erik."

"You haven't. He will still be there when I return home, and I can't see my feelings for him changing."

"How would you describe them?"

"We used to have a cocker spaniel that I loved to bits. I guess I feel the same way about Erik."

"Woof," I said.

"Don't you dare," said Inge Lise. "I cannot compare you with Erik or the dog. They touch my heart while you reach deep into my soul. Is that how you feel?"

"I've never felt so excited in my life."

"Don't let Erik bother you," she said, snuggling into me and kissing my neck. "I'm not."

"You sure?" I said, tingling as her lips brushed my ear.

"Absolutely."

"When do you go back?"

"In four months."

My heart tumbled to the floor.

"But I've just found you."

"Er, no," she said. "I found you."

We laughed and hugged tightly.

We spent the rest of the evening talking about our upbringing in between bouts of ever more passionate kissing. Erik was utterly forgotten.

The family she was working for on Hamilton Avenue insisted she was back by eleven, so I walked her home, and we lingered under a sycamore tree, hugging tightly, neither wanting to part. She couldn't come out on Saturday but agreed to watch me play on Sunday morning and have a drink afterwards. Reluctantly, we parted, and she left me under the tree, already yearning for her touch. As the church clock tolled the first chime, she paused at the half-open door to wave and blow kisses before disappearing inside.

I did a little jig as I walked back home, but nagging away at the back of my mind was the four months before she returned home. What if we fell in love? Don't be daft. You have.

"You're early," said Dad as I crept past their bedroom door. "No Skinners?"

"Not today. Goodnight."

"He never comes home at this time," said mum.

"Must have met a girl," said Dad. "An au pair, perhaps?"

"Probably ran out of money," said mum. "What is it with you and au pairs?"

I grinned and fell asleep in minutes.

CHAPTER 3

2023

I rushed outside the Red Lion Hotel lobby as fast as my feeble frame could carry me in a pathetic attempt to speak to this man with blue eyes. They had left when I reached the spot where I saw him climbing into a cab. I stood in the pouring rain, scratching my head, watching them disappear over Henley Bridge. Within seconds, I was drenched.

Someone tapped on my shoulder. It was Leanne, the kind receptionist carrying an umbrella.

"Forgive me," she said. "But I'd say the same to my grandfather. You shouldn't be out in this freezing rain. A change of clothes and a scalding hot cup of tea is the order of the day." She pulled me out of the rain and, holding my arm, escorted me back into the reception, where I collected my things from the chair and succumbed to her suggestion.

Having not checked out, I returned to Room 118 and had another shower to warm up while my clothes dried by the heating vent.

I made a pot of tea, sat on the bed wrapped in the

hotel robe, and contemplated the familiar stranger. Considering my mental meanderings at breakfast, was this the coincidence I had been looking for? Had my visit to room 118 initiated some strange quirk of fate? I'd never considered myself psychic, but this was way out of the ordinary.

There was no doubt he was a face from the past. One that by rights shouldn't exist, but who was he, and what was he doing here? Perhaps the kind receptionist might reveal his identity? There was no harm in asking.

I dressed again in dry clothes, repacked my case, put on my coat and hat, and headed to the lift. I paused at the door to say a fond farewell to Room 118. Memories of the three women I had loved here flashed before my eyes. Were they still alive?

I longed for one last chance to see them. I had to find answers about that final night and thank them for the part they played in my life. Perhaps it would clear my head of this damned vision. With a tear in my eye, I headed for the lift.

"Thank you for your kindness, Leanne," I said as I checked out. "I know I ought not to ask, but the man driving away in the taxi seemed familiar. If I recognised his name, could you tell me his address?"

"We aren't permitted to give out any information concerning guests," said Leanne. "But seeing his importance to you, I'll make an exception. His name is Chris Jepsen."

"The Olympic oarsman?"

"You've heard of him?"

"I was an oarsman, Danish, right?"

"He is the coach for Aarhus Rowing Club. He was here to confirm training and accommodation arrangements for next year's Royal Henley Regatta."

"Thank you again, Leanne."

"At least you know which room number to ask for next time you stay with us. It's usually available; we use it only during high season."

The rain had eased as I strolled toward the railway station, contemplating how to track down Chris Jepsen. As a police car passed, it hit me. A case I had worked on years ago in Oxford involved Detective Constable John Harker from the Thames Valley Police based at Henley. He was considerably younger, so ought still to be serving. Could he help? I paused under the shelter of a chestnut tree, dug out my phone, and checked maps to see if Henley Police Station was still located on Kings Road.

It wasn't. There was a patrol base on Greys Road, but at least I had the Thames Valley Police number in Reading. I couldn't help but notice my hand shaking as I dialled. Was this Parkinsons or nerves?

"Could I please speak with DC John Harker? " I asked when a woman answered my call.

"You mean Chief Superintendent Harker, sir," she said. "May I ask who is calling?"

"Detective Chief Superintendent Oliver Matthews."

"I'll transfer you."

"I thought you hung up your badge decades ago," said John almost immediately.

"Sixteen years," I said. "I guess you're ready to join me?"

"Next year, if all goes well. How can I help, Oliver?"

"I need to track down the address of a Danish citizen."

"Is it a criminal matter?"

"No. It's personal."

"Sorry, Oliver, but I dare not assist. Times have changed. You can't fart without declaring it on your time sheet."

"How frustrating."

"The Danish Embassy would be your best bet. Can you tell me why you need to find this person?"

"I hadn't thought. I suppose I could."

"Do you have a photo? It would help the embassy should several Danes have the same name."

"I do have a likeness. Do you want a peek?"

"Why not?"

"I'll send it to you now. What is your email?"

I attached the only relevant photo in my gallery and pressed send.

John called me straight back.

"Are you sure you sent the right image?" said John.

"Absolutely."

"But it's a picture of you in your fifties."

"I know."

"What's going on Oliver?"

"This man is a carbon copy of me. I suspect he could be my son."

CHAPTER 4

1967

After closing time at the Red Lion on Saturday, we headed to Norman's house instead of Chez Skinners or home. It was the same crowd, the usual banter and another round of terrible jokes involving unfortunate Scots, Irish or Welsh and borrowed from the enormous number of excellent comedians around at the time, such as Frankie Howard with Bruce Forsyth, Dave Allen, Stanley Baxter, Benny Hill and so many more.

Apart from his terrible taste in trousers, one of the things I had in common with Norman was a love of Moody Blues music. As we entered the spacious lobby of his red brick house with enormous bay windows, *Nights in White Satin* belted out on his superb stereo system with speakers in every room.

John Francis was wearing his latest fashion acquisition, a white shirt with an incredibly long pointed collar and lacy frills on the cuffs. We had walked up from the pub together and helped ourselves to cans of lager from the giant dustbin in Norman's kitchen filled with water, ice, wine, beer, and soft drinks. Spirits were forbidden, but if you wanted a joint or a pill, they were available in the back room. I had enough problems handling beer, so I was never tempted by other substances. Many did, though, and having seen the mess it made of them, often for days, I stuck to my guns.

I liked to know what I was consuming. Substances were unknown entities both in content and self-control. Whereas beer was a familiar bedfellow with whom I was well acquainted. My biggest problem, though, was memory. After three or four pints, I was in la la land. I didn't slur my words, stagger around, or throw up, but when I'd reached my limit, I went home or crashed on any horizontal surface I could find. Because I hadn't drunk much, when I awoke, I rarely had a bad head but couldn't recall a damn thing about the previous evening.

One of the things I liked about our gang is that they weren't judgmental. If you didn't want to get smashed, smoke a joint. Or take a pill; they respected your decision and didn't nag or take the piss. And if you did feel the urge to try a substance, someone with experience would supervise your first experiment.

Norman, for the first time dressed in flared trousers with not a check in sight, had complete control of the music, which meant we had an abundance of Moody Blues, Elvis, Rolling Stones, Motown, and smaller groups such as Kinks and Amen Corner. However, the Beatles were the most requested as we danced the night away until everyone had passed out or a spoilsport neighbour had summoned the police. Thankfully, it wasn't often. As we knew most of the officers, despite the house being full of semi-stoned youngsters and reeking of dope, we were left to our devices.

This Saturday was about saying farewell to Pete and Paul.

Usually, I would be trashed by now, but because of the football and meeting Inge Lise tomorrow, John and I had paced ourselves.

The front room was the dancing area. With the curtains drawn and bubble lamps casting mysterious patterns on the walls and ceiling, we could have been in any nightclub or one of the more modern emerging discotheques. John and I danced nonstop with a range of au pair girls. They came from all over Europe, but mainly Scandinavia.

We danced with Sonia, who looked stunning in hot pants and a skimpy top revealing her toned stomach. Later, I noticed her and John deep in conversation. I'd assumed she'd still be sad about Paul's departure, but she seemed to be holding her end up.

When he was bored with the conversation in the kitchen, Norm joined us with Lucy and Linda for a dance. The girls were dressed in identical long, clingy red dresses with no apparent signs of underwear. He took turns kissing them passionately in front of everybody, then watched as the two girls kissed each other. Nobody took much notice as there were many entwined pairs. Some were not even bothering to dance. When a couple became over-amorous, shouts of *Get a Room* echoed around the lounge. Their response was often a finger, or they would scuttle off to a sofa room to cheers and jeers. Norm even provided condoms.

A tad after midnight, Norm turned off the music.

We laughed when there was a loud cheer from next door.

Everyone crowded into the lounge to see what was happening.

"Friends," said Norm, standing by the fireplace. "Saying farewell is such bittersweet sorrow, but at the end of this week, Pete and Paul are leaving us forever. It will be sad, especially for Sonia. However, we can sympathise with their preference to live in sunny southern climes surrounded by South Africa's finest Chardonnay grapes. I've agreed to buy the Daimler. I've always fancied becoming a vintage car collector. So please raise your glasses, and let's have a toast for Pete and Paul. Have a good life."

"Cheers," shouted everyone.

We stood on both sides of the hallway as Paul and Pete left with Sonia, all three in tears. We hugged them and clapped in time as we sang, *We'll Meet Again,* as they exited.

Norm refused to turn the music back on, so we filtered home.

As John and I passed the Daimler parked under a tree, we spotted the windows steaming up and the springs squeaking. We assumed Sonia and Paul were exchanging goodbyes in the expansive back seat. I wondered where Pete had gone.

"Perhaps you could make Norm an offer for the car," I said as we crept by. "It might encourage Sonia to feel at home."

"And it would be more comfortable than the Vespa," said John.

"Could you afford it?"

"No chance."

We parted company at the main road.

"See you tomorrow, old friend," I said.

"Likewise," said John. "Could be a big day for you."

"Fingers crossed," I said. "And good luck with Sonia."

"She's agreed to a consoling drink," said John.

"There you go, halfway there already."

"You live twice:
once in reality,
the second time,
in memories."

(Honoré de Balzac)

CHAPTER 5

1967

The camaraderie and banter in the musty rotting timber shed described by the council as modern changing facilities at the Reading Road recreation ground was uplifting. Our Red Lion team comprised Ivan and the Heber-Smith brothers from the hotel. Plus, Keith and a variety of enthusiastic but ungainly customers. We were in good spirits as we sprinted onto the pitch to warm up with a surprising burst of energy. Such a keen display of pale hairy legs was rare for a Sunday when we were usually in bed sleeping off the previous evening's excesses.

At the far end of the pitch, our opponents were jumping up and down in unison, doing what appeared to be coordinated callisthenics. To our surprise, they were smartly turned out, had a full complement, and seemed fit and capable. A tiny but shapely woman in a pink tracksuit with big curly hair was running between them, shouting instructions and advice.

After a few minutes of practice, apart from our Captain and organiser, John Francis, we could have been more useful. When the referee summoned us for kick-off, I still couldn't see Inge Lise anywhere in the small but boisterous crowd of Red Lion supporters, which worried me.

We had parted on such loving terms on Friday evening; I was a hundred per cent optimistic she would show up, but perhaps she felt guilty about Erik and changed her mind about seeing me. After we kicked off, I was so busy watching out for Inge Lise's arrival that I forgot to pay attention to the game. I vaguely registered a shout from John but was too late to salvage the situation. The Catherine Wheel scored the first goal. It went straight between my legs. My teammates were not impressed. I blushed like fury. After such a disgraceful display of goalkeeping, I threw myself into the game and concentrated hard.

I sighed with relief when I saw Inge Lise arrive midway through the first half. We were two one down already. She was with Jenny and two older, clean-cut, athletic men in light-coloured raincoats and wearing sunglasses even though it was cloudy. I had never seen them before, which was alarming. Who were they?

My heart soared when Inge Lise walked around the pitch to the goal.

"Sorry, I was late," she said. "I had to wait for Jenny and her colleagues. They have never seen a live football match before."

"Who are they?"

"Chuck and Dwight work with Jenny. They stay at the hotel, so you'll meet them in the bar after the game. They also want to try English beer and would welcome your expert counsel on what they should drink or avoid."

"Ok, look," I said as the opposing centre forward

came racing toward me. "I've already let in one goal looking for you. I'd better concentrate."

She laughed.

"See you at the bar," she said, blowing a kiss before returning to Jenny.

My serious concentration made little difference. Their team was better, and we were thrashed five to two. It could have been more, but I made some reasonable saves, and the team forgave me.

My frantic diving around the goalmouth during the last ten minutes, when we were bombarded by a constant stream of shots from the Catherine Wheel, covered me in mud. I dashed home, showered, and changed quicker than ever before.

"Laundry," screamed Mum as I closed the front door.

"Later," I shouted as I sprinted toward the hotel.

Despite my record-breaking ablutions, the Riverside bar was heaving when I squeezed in next to Inge Lise.

"Here," she said, passing me a pint, indicating Jenny and her two colleagues. "Courtesy of the American Secret Service."

"Are you joking?"

"No," she whispered in my ear. "They are part of an American VIP protection team, but you're not to let on. Jenny told me in confidence."

"Cheers," I said, raising my glass toward the Americans who had removed their raincoats but not sunglasses. "And thanks for the beer."

"This is Ollie," said Inge Lise, turning to look at me with a tender, loving expression. "My boyfriend."

Boyfriend. Wow. I must have grown about ten inches. I'd never been referred to as such. The exhilaration was, well, exhilarating. The Americans remained stony-faced. Or were they? Behind the dark lenses, I couldn't read their thoughts or see if they were looking at me.

"Cheers," said Jenny. Ollie, this is Chuck and Dwight. We work together. They are staying in the hotel for a few days, so be nice to them."

"I'm always nice," I said, reaching out my hand and shaking theirs. "Welcome to our beautiful town."

"Thanks," they said.

"What brings you to Henley?" I said.

"We're checking out the area," said Dwight, a severe athletic type with dark, close-cropped hair. "Before a visit by an American VIP."

"If all goes ahead," said Chuck, staring at Inge Lise. He was almost a carbon copy of Dwight but with sandy hair and freckles. "We'll be back with said VIP and a larger team for Easter."

So, not so secret.

"Including you, Jenny?" I said.

"I'm based here," said Jenny. "I work for the Embassy and take care of logistics."

"I didn't know," I said.

"You never asked."

"Fair enough."

"To be frank, it's not something I broadcast," said Jenny. "Too many Brits object to our involvement in the Vietnam war. To avoid confrontation, I say I'm temping."

"Do you?" asked Chuck, who once again openly admired Inge Lise.

"Object to the war?" I asked.

"Yes," said Chuck.

"As an art student on a meagre allowance from my

parents, my time is fully spent surviving. Would it affect the likelihood of your VIP's visit if I was?"

"Probably not," said Dwight, irritated by Chuck's behaviour and giving him disapproving sideways glances. "Apart from Regatta week, Henley is a sleepy town. Most folks are like you."

"There are a few firebrands at college," I said. "I doubt they would agree."

"Could you tell us their names?" said Dwight.

"No need," said Chuck, glaring at Dwight. "We're here to enjoy this rather tepid beer. Is it always served this warm?"

"Ale should be served at room temperature; cold temperatures mask the flavour subtleties," I said.

Chuck and Dwight each took another tentative sip.

"Sorry, I can't detect any subtleties," said Dwight, rinsing it about his mouth before swallowing. "What should I be looking for?"

"A fine balance of hop bitterness and malty sweetness," I said. "With notes of caramel."

Dwight took another sip and rolled it around in his mouth, swallowing it with a mock ecstatic expression reserved for a robust burgundy.

"It's bitter but slips down nicely," said Dwight, nodding toward the bar. "Which from the row of beer taps would you recommend?"

"I'm drinking Brakspear's Bitter Ale," I said, holding up my pint glass and taking a long gulp. "It has no added carbon dioxide. Many friends mix it with a bottle of light ale, preferring a stronger flavour and bubbles. According to my trainer, gas is bad for my health. He also advises me to drink only a half pint. As you see, I don't take him seriously."

The jukebox changed to *Sloop John B* by The Beach

Boys. The Americans looked at each other and sang at the top of their voices in almost perfect harmony. Everyone paused before joining in and applauded our overseas guests at the end.

"That was awesome," said Chuck with a smug grin. "Singing helps the long, tedious hours on long plane journeys. Oliver, what do you train for?"

"I'm an oarsman, single scull. I'm winding down now, but come February, I'll be on the water every morning bright and early, preparing for next season."

"Sounds like hard work," said Dwight. "Why do you flog yourself to death just to speed up and down a river?"

"It's a whole-body workout that improves posture, cardiovascular fitness, and mental health, but I'm also carrying on the family tradition from my father and grandfather."

"Have you won anything?" said Chuck, returning to his open admiration of Inge Lise.

"Not as much as my father and his dad. I won the under-eighteens championship at Henley two years ago, but nothing since. There is too much amber nectar, and I prefer golf. The training isn't so demanding."

"Have you been to the States?" asked Jenny.

"I don't have a passport," I said. "I'd love to travel, but not on my current budget."

I downed my beer in one and raised my eyebrows at Inge Lise.

"Sorry, guys," said Inge Lise, removing the glass from my hand, placing it on a nearby table, and linking her arm through mine. "I must drag Ollie away; we have a lunch obligation."

Inge Lise hauled me out of there.

"What?" I said as we hit the street.

"Sorry, but I had to escape that awful man."

"Which one?"

"They were both a bit weird, but while watching the football, Chuck insisted he was the perfect man for me, and I should spend the afternoon in his hotel room. And did you spot the way he was ogling me?"

"I did. Hence the boyfriend routine?"

"Did you mind?"

"It made me feel ten feet tall."

"I noticed, and by the way, I feel the same."

"So soon?"

"Crazy, isn't it?"

"Where are we going to lunch?" I asked as we stood outside the hotel's main entrance, watching the customers piling out of the Angel on the Bridge. It was two o'clock, closing time.

"Your house. I want to meet my boyfriend's parents."

CHAPTER 6

1967

I was a tad nervous as I ushered Inge Lise through our front door. I took her coat and indicated she should remove her shoes and park them on the rack at the bottom of the stairs as I did the same. I never understood why my mother insisted on white carpets, but the design style of the times complemented the primary colour curtains and bright prints by Bernard Buffet hanging on the wall.

"That you, darling?" shouted Mum from the kitchen.

"No, it's me," I said, entering the kitchen where she was stirring Bisto gravy powder into the juices from a joint of beef. "Have we enough for my friend?"

She turned and peered over her glasses at Inge Lise, who rushed over and hugged her. "I'm Inge Lise," she said. "Ollie's new girlfriend."

My mother was a tall but slender and still attractive woman in her mid-forties. She had short, permed blond hair and blue eyes and wore a white apron and green dress. She stepped back with a surprised expression and appraised this new addition to my life.

"Well, I never," said mum. "I'm Peggy. He never mentioned you, but you are welcome to join us for lunch. I'll put on some more vegetables, but we'll be short on Yorkshire."

"Please don't go to any trouble," said Inge Lise.

"It's no problem," said mum. "My husband, Chris, will be back shortly. He popped out for a bottle of wine."

My father adored Inge Lise within seconds of his return, brandishing a bottle of Margaux. He wore his customary beige corduroy trousers, checked shirt, and favourite navy-blue cardigan.

"So, you're from Denmark. Are you an au pair," he asked.

"I am," said Inge Lise.

"We would have liked someone like you when Oliver was younger," said Dad. "Wouldn't we, Peg?"

"First I've heard of it," said mum. "But if you say so, dear. We couldn't afford it just after the war and given the national angst against Germans at that time, anyone with a foreign accent wouldn't have been treated nicely."

"Nonsense," said Dad. "Danes would have always been welcome. Their resistance fighters were renowned for bravery. Wouldn't you say, Inge Lise?"

"My parents never talked about it," said Inge Lise.

Why were my parents digging up the war? I wondered. They'd never mentioned it before.

Dad fussed over Inge Lise, ensuring she was sitting comfortably at the table, laying an extra placemat and cutlery, and pouring her the first glass of wine, much to my mother's amusement. Inge Lise was the first girl I had ever mentioned, let alone brought home, so this was as momentous an occasion for them as it was for me.

Lunch was delicious, and as the wine slipped down, the conversation became carefree as Inge Lise battled through the parental inquisition. I watched in awe as she gave as good as she received, and my love for her leapt another notch.

This was how I had dreamed of how it should be with a girlfriend since I drooled over Raquel Welch and Brigitte Bardot as a young teenager.

After we'd all chipped in with the washing up, my parents settled into their favourite armchairs for a nap, so I showed Inge Lise up to my room.

"No hanky panky, mind," said my mother as we thumped up the stairs.

"I'm showing her my model aeroplanes," I said as we entered my tiny bedroom at the rear of the house.

"Where are they," said Inge Lise as we moved to look out the window.

"What?"

"The aeroplanes?"

"I was joking,"

"Shame?" she mocked as we looked at the small, neat garden. "I was hoping to see them."

"How about etchings, or perhaps you prefer an electric train set?"

She grinned, shook her head, and cuddled into my shoulder.

"What is hanky panky?" she said.

"English slang for making love."

She looked up at me with loving eyes. I leaned toward her, and we kissed tenderly.

"Do you want to make love to me?" she said.

"It would be incredible," I said. "And you?"

"Yes, but not here."

"I don't have any experience."

"Neither do I. You are the first man I've ever wanted."

"What about Erik?"

"We fool around occasionally, but unlike you, he never inspired me to go further."

"I feel the same, but I'm sure your employers would object to us using your room, so where could we go?"

"I will speak to Sara at the Red Lion."

"Why her?"

"She's discreet and told me I should ask her if I ever needed somewhere private."

"What time do you have to be home?"

"I'm free until eleven."

"When my parents wake up, shall we talk with Sara?"

"Please," said Inge Lise, biting her lip.

We spent the rest of the afternoon chatting, kissing, and exploring each other. When I heard my parents making a pot of tea, we headed downstairs, tingling with anticipation.

"We're going for a walk," I said. "Afterward, I'll escort Inge Lise home."

"Thank you so much for a lovely lunch," said Inge Lise, hugging my parents. "It was lovely to meet you."

"Our pleasure," said Mum, glowing.

"Any time," said Dad with an appreciative look.

They exchanged hugs, and we headed to the Red Lion, holding hands and pulses racing.

Sara's room was in the staff rooms overlooking the car park. We knocked on the door, hardly able to contain ourselves. Sara opened her door a fraction and seemed relieved to see us. She wore a towel robe that did little to cover her shapely curves. She looked tired and dishevelled, but she was beautiful even without her usual ton of makeup. She beckoned us inside. We didn't need to say anything; she knew what we wanted.

Hers was a tiny room with a single bed she'd just crawled out of. She opened a drawer in the bedside cabinet and handed us a key with a hefty brass tag.

"It's on the first floor," she said. "Tread the rear fire escape quietly, and you will find the emergency door open. Enter and open another door into the main corridor. The room is the second on the right. Once inside, lock the door and leave the key in the lock. It's two pounds for two hours, and don't dirty the sheets, or there will be a cleaning bill on top."

"But what if a guest checks in," I said.

"It overlooks the kitchen and car park," said Sara. "To avoid noise complaints, they only use it during regatta. The key in the door is extra security. If someone tries to enter, it will give you time to exit while they return to reception. Trust me, we've never had a problem."

"How often is it used?" said Inge Lise.

"At least five times a week," said Sara.

"I'll be around for a bank loan," I said.

Sara grinned lasciviously and stroked both our cheeks.

"When you've finished, lock up and discreetly return the key and cash to me in the bar," said Sara. Have fun. Our secret."

She ushered us out and shut the door behind us.

We looked at each other nervously.

"You sure?" I said.

Inge Lise dragged me toward the hotel's rear entrance,

We tiptoed up the fire escape, where the emergency door was ajar as promised. We entered an interior stairwell, opened the fire door a fraction, and peered through the gap. The corridor was empty. As we furtively scuttled along, I glanced at the key tag.

Room 118. It said.

CHAPTER 7

1967/8

I was sure the noise from creaky floorboards in the corridor would attract attention, and as we turned the key, I squirmed like a naughty pupil caught with his hand in somebody's biscuit tin. Satisfied we were unobserved; we slipped inside and closed the door as silently as possible despite an ominous squeak. I locked it and, as Sara instructed, left the key in the lock.

Inge Lise stood at the window, peering through the net curtain. I watched her as if she were a creature from outer space. Was I about to make love with this gorgeous woman, or was she a figment of my imagination? I joined her at the window and put my arm around her shoulder. Yep, she was real. She snuggled into my shoulder, a loving gesture I had become accustomed to in our brief time together.

A grey sky dotted with black clouds scudding overhead threatened a violent rainstorm. The room darkened as sheets of rain hit the car park tarmac and drummed on vehicle roofs. I moved to turn on the bedside light.

"No," said Inge Lise.

"I want to see you," I said.

"Please wait in the bathroom while I get undressed."

"But."

"Ollie, I'm shy."

"Ok, ok," I said, complying with her request.

"I undressed and took a quick shower. I inspected my reflection in the full-length mirror while drying. I grinned like an idiot. This was it, the moment I had been waiting for and fantasised about since my first sex education lesson at school. A flash of lightning outside struck a chord in my head. I could hear the teacher nagging about condoms. I didn't have any. Was I going to ruin this magic moment before it had even begun?

I opened the door.

Inge Lise was lying under the eiderdown. Her blue eyes watched me intently as I strode across the room naked. I slipped in next to her, seeing a brief expose of shapely white flesh.

She threw herself on top of me.

She was freezing cold.

"Yikes," I giggled and rubbed her back to warm her up.

"I don't have any condoms," I said.

"You won't need them," she said. "I started taking the pill the first day we met."

"You knew before we kissed?"

"Of course, didn't you?"

"Yes, but it was wishful thinking."

"Well, now your dreams come true."

"Wasn't it difficult as a foreigner to register with a doctor?"

"Yes, so I didn't."

"How did you acquire the pills?"

"A friend sold me some of hers, enough until I go home in February."

"It's incredible the difference these pills have made to women's freedom."

"Isn't it? But we are here to make love, not discuss women's newfound liberty."

"Yes, but if it weren't for the pills, we wouldn't be in this room without walking up the aisle of a church first."

"True, now shut up and come here."

"Shouldn't we put a towel or something underneath us?"

"Why, oh, I see, good idea."

I fetched a towel, lifted the eiderdown, and spread it in the middle of the bed.

This was it, no further delays or excuses.

We turned to each other and gazed into each other's eyes.

"You sure about this?" I said.

She nodded. After some clumsy fumbling, we kissed and joined for the first time. I pushed myself up on my elbows and admired her beautiful creamy breasts. We smiled.

It didn't take long.

Self-control is something I would have to practice.

Ninety minutes later, after several frustrating attempts at doing what nature intended, we hit solid gold.

We lay in each other's arms as our pulses calmed down.

"What a beautiful experience," I said. "Way better than I expected."

"Me too," said Inge Lise. "Eventually."

We both laughed out loud. She rinsed out the bloodied towel, and we showered together.

She wasn't shy now, and we made the most of exploring every part of each other. We kissed under the warm spray and made love yet again. It was divine, but the rush to dress and clean up after us took the edge off our evening as we hurtled down to the bar to beat the two-hour deadline.

"What about the shower and towel?" I whispered to Sara as I palmed her the key and money.

"No worry," she said, regarding me with a wistful expression, her huge earrings swinging back and forth. "I'll take care of it later."

Christmas and New Year raced by in a blur. For the next four months, most of my allowance was spent hiring Room 118. We were never caught, and as we learned about each other's preferences, we polished our lovemaking to a fine art. The combination of deep feelings for each other with incredible physical harmony brought us closer and closer.

In the meantime, when she wasn't on au pair duty, we would lean against the Red Lion bar holding hands, eking out a pint between us. Our friends envied our closeness and compatibility. We were made for each other and never disagreed or differed on anything. If she had been a man, she would have been me, and vice versa.

Inevitably, the middle of February edged nearer. The weight of sadness at our parting weighed heavier by the day.

"I don't want you to go," I said on our last occasion in Room 118.

"Neither do I," said Inge Lise with a tear in her eye.

"What can we do about it?" I said.

"I could apply for another au pair girl visa in six months," she said.

"I can't wait six minutes."

"I know how you feel."

"We could marry."

"I would marry you tomorrow, but I'm not sure how the visa works with marriage. Another au pair mentioned she had tried the same thing but was informed it would take two years."

"Why so long?"

"To deter people from marrying for British citizenship."

"I could quit my degree course and work for your father. It shouldn't take long to learn how to wield a chopper."

"It took about two hours," said Inge Lise, giggling.

"I meant."

"I know, but my father would need time to get acquainted before handing out a rare job at his precious timber yard. It was hard enough persuading him to fund Erik's business studies course in Hamburg."

"Oh, I see," I said, her reference to Erik plunging my sadness even deeper. Was he still at the forefront of her mind? Soon, they would be reunited. Where would I stand then? I had to find a way to stay in her life.

"M, my parents adore you," I stuttered. "You could stay with us and find some sort of employment."

"I would, but I haven't finished my child psychology degree, and the only job I could apply for would be menial, which would depress me. Anyway, without a visa, I'm not allowed to work; I'd be deported and never able to come back. The best way forward for us to be together is for me to go and find a solution with my parents. They have the money and contacts to resolve this. In the meantime, I will tell Erik I no longer wish to continue our relationship, and you could visit and get to know them."

"I don't have enough money."

"Try working. You finish college at four; you could easily find a job in the new supermarket loading shelves until eight."

"I will."

With a heavy heart, I borrowed Dad's Ford Cortina GT and drove Inge Lise to Harwich to catch the boat to Esbjerg. We waited outside the ferry terminal in the car, weeping and hugging until the last minute before she had to check in.

I carried her case and waited in line, trying hard not to sniff.

When she disappeared during departures, my heart went with her. Would I ever see her again? Was she strong enough to dump Erik?

On the way home, I played the Moody Blues album Days of Future Past on Dad's cassette player. The song *Dawn is a Feeling* had me in tears. It reminded me of the love I felt for my beautiful Danish girl—the love I had just lost, hopefully temporarily.

Valentine's Day 1968 was the most painful day of my life.

CHAPTER 8

1968

I wasn't the best of company after returning from Harwich. A couple of days later, having watched pain and misery wipe out the usual high-octane energy levels of her strapping son, Mum sat me down, and I wept in her arms. Her words of comfort gradually penetrated my brain fog.

"It's comparable to when Grandad passed away," she said. "You're grieving. The pain won't diminish, but slowly, you'll become accustomed to life without Inge Lise."

"It's not as if we have split," I sniffed. "I'm applying for a job loading shelves at Waitrose on Bell Street to save up and visit. The six months of not seeing her don't bug me too much, but I'm incensed by the insensitive immigration policies standing in our way."

"How much money would you need?"

"No idea."

"Ask the travel agent. Find the cheapest way, add some spending money, and make the total your savings goal. It will help you feel as if you are doing something to resolve the situation. What you must not do is loaf around here feeling sorry for yourself. Inge Lise wouldn't approve, and neither would I."

"Nobody likes a wimp," added my dad with his customary sympathetic touch.

I went to the pub.

I didn't have the money to get drunk, which is what my head was yearning for, but one of our circle worked at Waitrose, and I wanted her to tell me about the process for joining their staff.

It wasn't complicated.

Turn up, tell them what hours I could do, and start straight away.

It sounded good to me.

The following afternoon after college, I was interviewed by a gruff man in a brown coat and started three minutes later. I worked four until eight, five nights a week, unloading pallets, loading shelves and general odd jobs. I saved every penny after giving my mum a couple of quid housekeeping, a new experience for all of us.

The job was boring and mindless, but the co-workers were hilarious. I knew many of them, so the exchange of banter and terrible jokes was relentless. Mum appreciated the staff discount.

Upon receiving my first wages, I penned a letter to Inge Lise and enclosed a copy of my earnings. Twenty hours work for four pounds twelve shillings after tax and national insurance contributions. Together with my parental allowance totalled ten pounds a week. Inquiries at the travel agent determined I would need at least fifty pounds to visit Grenaa, and if I cut back on beer and fags, the quicker I could amass such a sum.

I quit smoking cold turkey and resolved to drink

half pints. To everyone's surprise, I restarted my rowing, and my timing improved. The healthy regime was working. Keeping busy also helped the time slip by, and I grew accustomed to living with the pain of missing my love. A few weeks apart seemed an eternity, but I soldiered on. The ends more than justified the means.

I had no idea how long it took for a letter to reach Grenaa or when Inge Lise might reply, but after six weeks, I had heard nothing which concerned me. Why was she taking so long? Inevitably, I assumed something was wrong, or she had gone off me. Perhaps Erik had stepped up to the mark. Whatever, it would have been better to know.

On the Friday night before Easter, I was propping up the bar, nursing a small beer. There had still been no communication from Inge Lise, and I was wallowing in misery. Did I have a girlfriend or not? Was the future we envisaged together still on? The bar was quiet, so Sara stopped for a chat and put her head close to mine. I gazed into her eyes as she regarded me. A spark flashed between us.

"Heard from Inge Lise?" she said in a low voice.

I shook my head.

"Can I discuss something?" she said, moving nearer, her forehead almost touching mine. I loved her perfume.

"Go on."

"Do you remember my dad wasn't around when we were at school?"

"Yes, but you never explained why."

"I was just a kid, and my mum refused to discuss it. The point is, I am unaccustomed to seeing a man and woman openly expressing their feelings for each other.

Watching you two snuggling reminded me of what was missing in my life."

"Surely, you've had boyfriends. What about Terry from the sixth form?"

"I'm no virgin, but I was responding to what boys wanted; I never loved any of them. When I saw you two, it made me think."

"What?"

"If there had been a God, you and she would have been his perfect couple."

"Why?"

"Good looking, compatible, and so in love, nothing would have split you asunder."

"Except for stupid immigration laws."

"Ollie, I was jealous."

"Sara, why?"

"Every time you went to Room 118, I wished it had been with me."

"You could have intimated something before Inge Lise arrived."

"Jenny and I tried to flirt, but you never reacted. Are you blind or what?"

"Sorry, Sara, but I was hopeless at reading signals from girls. Inge Lise taught me how to love and relate to women and what they prefer or detest in a man."

"And it showed in the way you treated her. It was why I envied her. No man has ever done that for me. I'm sexy Sara, the slut behind the bar who hands out keys to lovers but rarely has one herself."

"I never have thought of you as such, but why are you telling me this?"

"I can see underneath your brave exterior that you are hurting. You must miss her dreadfully."

"I do," I said, striving to hold back a tear.

"Don't get me wrong, I am not comparing myself with Inge Lise or trying to come between you, but I'd like to help ease your pain, even until you can get back with her. I want to go upstairs with you and experience your tenderness. If something comes from it, fine; if not, it is also fine. I would have satisfied my burning curiosity and hopefully cheered you up. Oh, and if you mention this to anyone, I will kill you."

"Your secret is safe with me," I said. "I feel privileged you would do this for me. Do you mind if I reflect on it for a day or two?"

"Not for long. When we close at two pm on Sunday afternoon, knock on my door. We can take it from there."

"Take only memories;
leave only footprints."

(Chief Seattle)

CHAPTER 9

2023

"Oliver," said John Harker, finding it difficult to disguise his astonishment at my claim. How do you know he is your son? We all have a double somewhere. Put it down to coincidence."

"I wish I could," I said as the Henley train pulled into Twyford Station. I remained in my seat until the carriage emptied and then transferred to a platform bench to wait for the Paddington train and continue my conversation with John.

I shivered in the cold wind and pulled my hat down tighter. The man beside me started eating a bacon sandwich dripping with brown sauce. Another man joined him from the café in the middle of the platform just behind us with an identical snack. They exchanged glances, nodding with satisfaction as they chewed. Roasting coffee and toasted bread wafted around us from the extractor fan above my head.

"John, this is more than one coincidence. If I don't resolve who this man is, I'll blow a fuse."

"Curiosity killed the cat."

"But satisfaction brought it back."

"I don't see how I can help."

"Imagine you are an assistant at the Danish Embassy, and a kooky old fart arrives waving a photo of himself at fifty-odd, saying somebody in Aarhus looks like him and must be his son. How would you react?"

"I see what you mean, whereas if it was an official inquiry from a senior serving police officer, they might take some notice."

"In one. I appreciate it goes against the rules, but could I report a theft, and you issue an international arrest warrant?"

"If you want me fired and lose my pension rights, we could. Sorry, Oliver, but this is not something we can do through official channels. I suggest you go to Aarhus and make inquiries there. Do you have his name?"

"I do and what he does."

"Have you looked online?"

"Er, no."

"You want me to search?"

"Would you mind? Give me a minute, and I'll email you his name and position."

"Can't you tell me?"

"I don't know how to pronounce his name."

"But you always used to impress us with your Danish phrases. What was it, Jeg..?"

"Jeg elsker dig. It means I love you, but the rest were swear words. Hardly fluent."

"Wait, didn't you have a Danish girlfriend?"

"Inge Lise, she taught me."

"Could she be the mother?"

"Possibly, but she returned to Denmark at the

beginning of 1968, and I'm positive she wasn't pregnant."

"Did you hear from her again?"

"She never replied to my letters."

"So, you can't be sure. Can you spell his name?"

"Chris Jepsen," I repeated letter by letter. He is from Aarhus in Denmark and is a Coach at the Aarhus Rowing Club."

"I see. He is also an oarsman. Now I understand what you mean about more than one coincidence."

"It's not just his looks or being an oarsman."

"What else?"

"His name," I said. "My second name is Christopher, after my dad."

"I always wondered what the C stood for. We always used to take the piss when we saw O.C. Matthews. Officer Commanding, we called you."

"I never knew."

"Your fearsome temper was a strong deterrent. Here he is," said John. "I'll send you the link, but I would turn up at Aarhus Rowing Club. As the son of a champion oarsman, I'm sure they would welcome you with open arms."

"Thanks, John. I will."

"Keep me posted."

I muttered a curse as I accepted reality. I hadn't brought my passport, had no idea how to travel to Aarhus, and needed clean laundry. Now, I would have to train it back to my apartment and squander yet more of my hard-earned pension on this crazy venture. But I had to know one way or the other, and if nothing came of it, I could at least try and track down Inge Lise to say hello. I wonder if she still lives in Grenaa. Perhaps she inherited her father's timber business and is a multi-squillionaire.

I'd have to make further inquiries at home on my desktop.

After climbing the police ladder in Nottingham, I was promoted to Detective Inspector and transferred to Leicester, where I purchased a tiny apartment adjacent to police headquarters. In my occasional free time, I attended Leicester Tigers home games and played golf as a member of Kirby Muxloe. It was on the western outskirts of the city. When the occasional woman agreed to a date, they lost interest when I explained my celibacy. It meant I lived a solitary existence outside my long working hours but remained determined to stand by my decision.

Nearly every time I was due annual leave, a new and absorbing investigation gave me a grand excuse to cancel my travel arrangements. I now had a passport, which I used mainly to watch England's five nations matches in France and Dublin, but going to Grenaa to track down Inge Lise never crossed my mind. What I had often been tempted by was returning to Henley and renewing my lapsed friendships. Perhaps they may have heard something about Inge Lise or could answer what happened on that fatal final night. I must have popped into Leicester train station and bought over a dozen returns to Henley, but every time I was due to depart, another case came my way. I blamed it on fate but accepted that I didn't have the courage to go. I was frightened by how I might be received by those I had abandoned without a word. Eventually, I accepted that remaining ignorant of the past was better for my future. While the visions continued, I learned to push them to one side and not interfere with my supposedly vital and irreplaceable position in the force.

This focused energy on my career did at least generate rewards. I was repeatedly promoted, finally achieving the exalted rank of Detective Chief Superintendent.

In my fifties, my parents died of natural causes within a year of each other. I inherited their house and decided it was time I climbed the property ladder. Not long after, I was posted as station chief to the south Leicestershire town of Market Harborough. It's over twice the size of Henley, but the eclectic mix of red brick buildings and quaint, white-painted Georgian facades reminded me of my place of birth.

Harborough was a smaller station and less demanding despite its adjacency to Gartree, the all-male high-security prison. I hunted around for a place near a golf club with a short waiting list and an affordable entrance fee. I purchased a charming cottage in Great Bowden, a medieval village in fox-hunting country on the eastern fringes of Harborough. I served my final years before retiring to concentrate on golf and was voted in as club secretary.

I had recently moved from Bowden into a brand-new assisted living complex on Fairfield Road behind the Three Swans Hotel in the town centre. I didn't need the assisted living facilities, but it was comforting that they were available without more relocation hassle. The Dunroamin Apartments were not far from the police station, and former colleagues often popped in for my views on complex cases. It was from here that I planned this trip down memory lane experience.

I texted my regular driver on the way up from St. Pancras, and he delivered me to my flat. I threw everything on the bed and started researching Chris Jepsen and travel arrangements for Aarhus.

I sat at my oak desk in the small living room and turned on my computer. It was all there: his life, successes on the water, and photos from his early days as a teenager growing up in a single scull, the same boat as me. It was uncanny to see him mature into the man he is today. I pulled out the family albums and held them up to the screen. I wasn't going crazy. At every stage of our lives, we were practically identical. He had to be my son. There was no other explanation. If so, who was his mother?

In principle, it could have been one of three. If he was Danish, it had to be Inge Lise. My heart swelled with pride. I must be a father, but what of his mother? Was she still alive? Would she see me? Why hadn't she told me about Chris?

I searched for her in Grenaa.

And there she was.

Inge Lise Oleson, Child Psychologist. She was practising in a clinic in the town centre. I clicked through to the staff bios page, and my pulse skipped at least ten beats when I saw her photo. Why hadn't I tried an internet search before?

Yes, she had aged, but she was still beautiful. Her short blond hair was now platinum grey. Her blue eyes were less intense and had a few wrinkles. Who cares about looks at our age? My emotions were running riot. All the love I had bottled up since 1967/8 bounced right back. I translated her description, but it yielded no personal information.

How would I travel?

I preferred the train, a hangover from boyhood toys and my fascination with steam engines, but it was a long and complicated journey to Aarhus. I could have used the Ferry from Harwich to Esbjerg, but it was an overnight trip, and I wasn't fond of rough seas. I opted for a direct Ryanair flight from Stanstead and bought a one-way ticket, not knowing or caring when I might return.

I wavered about announcing my arrival in advance but decided to message Chris at the Aarhus Rowing Club email. Years ago, my father had competed in several regattas there, so I invented an excuse: I was researching to write a book about the Matthews rowing clan.

The reply was immediate. They remembered my father, and Chris would be delighted to meet me. I packed the photograph album. It would be fascinating to watch his face as we flicked through it.

CHAPTER 10

1968

I lay in my bed on Sunday morning, considering Sara's proposal. My mind swirled in confusion. Was Inge Lise still an integral part of my life? I had written half a dozen letters to her expecting something in return, but not a peep. I doubted our future, but was I ready to move on? Should I accept Sara's offer of a long afternoon in Room 118? Irrespective of Sara's motivations and the guilt I was suffering for even considering her offer, this was not something I could ignore. A dear, attractive friend needed me, and I was more than tempted. I decided to let matters unwind by themselves.

The smell of frying wafting up the stairs dragged me out of my pit. I opened the curtains to a beautiful spring day. The trees were bright green, daffodils dying back and tulips bursting forth. I opened the window, and it smelt fresh and clean. I showered, shaved, and joined Mum in the kitchen.

"Bacon sandwich coming up," said mum. "Help yourself to orange juice. How is the money saving?"

"Er, fine," I said. "Hoping this wasn't going to be a grilling about Inge Lise.

"How much do you have?"

"About thirty pounds."

"Have you applied for a passport?"

"Er, no."

"May I suggest you do so. The forms are available from the Post Office. You'll need three copies of a passport photo. You can book a sitting at that shop on Bell Street, and you'll need Doctor Harcourt's signed statement on the back confirming it is a true likeness of you. Have you inquired about tickets?"

"I thought I'd wait until I had the right amount."

"Tell you what. When you reach forty pounds, I'll give you the rest. It should give you motivation. You're still keen to go right."

"Er, yes."

"Nice to know teenagers' conversational skills are improving."

"Yes, Mum," I mumbled, wracked with confusion. While Mum encouraged me to go, I was trying to move on from what I considered a lost cause.

I sat at the kitchen table. Mum served my roll, then pottered about at the sink. Should I say I had given up on Inge Lise when they had been so happy for us? As soon as I'd finished breakfast, and not wanting to face any more difficult questions, I jogged down to Leander, desperate for some physical outlet to relieve my inner tension.

Today was a significant landmark in my training. To measure any improvement, I was attempting to break my mile record. I extracted the boat from the rack, placed it in the water, and climbed in. I checked that the foot stretcher and the rigger were firmly connected.

The gates and slide seat were fine, so I gingerly strapped in my feet, held the blades, pushed gently on the jetty, and eased into the fast-moving current. I rowed downstream toward the start line at the bend before Hambleden lock. The single scull is designed to cut through the water with minimum resistance but is narrow and tips over quickly. Rough water is a nightmare and impossible to row at full pressure. Today was as calm as I'd ever experienced, with barely a ripple on the surface as I zoomed along in the strong flow, warming up for my challenge.

My coach, Rick Phipps, was already on the riverbank wearing his pink Leander tracksuit and riding his bike, holding a megaphone with a stopwatch mounted on the handlebars. His long, fair hair was dangling down his back. He was a tall, muscular ex-oarsman in his late forties and the club's elite trainer. His son Mervyn had attended my school and also rowed for Leander. I reached the start point, turned so Rick was on the bowside, and kept the boat straight into the current as I waited for the go.

As soon as I was ready, Rick shouted, and I was off. As I surged through the water, blades square on entry, I knew I was performing my best. The boat surged through the water, my rhythm and course unfaltering. I judged my position by the distance from each bank and held the centre line where the current was weakest. I glanced over my shoulder every hundred meters to ensure the way was clear.

As I whizzed past Temple Island, Rick shouted, "Three seconds up. Go for it."

I held something in reserve for the closing few hundred metres. These were the real challenges when fading muscles and energy levels combined to slow me down. I managed to sustain my pace and smashed my best time by four seconds. A crowd was cheering on the Leander terrace, yelling their congratulations as I heaved the boat out of the water, wiped it down and replaced it on its rack in the boathouse.

I showered, changed, and had a snack in the upstairs bar, chatting with fellow rowers, my dad included. I sensed how proud he was while exchanging memories with retired members. For the first time since Inge Lise departed, I felt content and decided to take Sara up on her offer.

As I knocked on her door, I had another guilt attack and turned to go. Before I could leave, Sara opened the door wearing her skimpy towel robe and grabbed my arm.

"Sorry," I said. "I can't do this."

She yanked me inside.

"You don't escape so easily," she said. "Ollie, please don't see this as unfaithful to Inge Lise. You are doing me, your lifelong friend and schoolmate, a huge favour by introducing me to something I have never experienced. Warm and tender lovemaking."

"I'm not sure I can live with the guilt."

"Tell me, who was Sally Burton and the gorgeous German blond Christiane?"

"Sorry?"

"You've forgotten already? Sally was last weekend at Norman Shannon's party. Christiane the weekend before. She drove you to her place after Chez Skinners."

"I must have been drunk."

"Ollie, ever since Inge Lise left, you've been smashed every weekend. You need to improve your relationship with alcohol. Three pints, and you behave like a wild man and crash."

"Sorry, but I don't remember a damn thing."

"Are you sober now?"

"Of course."

"Keep this in mind?"

She opened her robe. It was all she was wearing.

"Where?" I said, indicating the unmade single bed.

"Not likely," she said, putting on her slippers. "Follow me."

We scampered up the hotel's rear stairs and into Room 118. "When do you want the money?" I asked, locking the door behind us.

"Don't be silly," she said, taking off her house coat and dropping it on the floor. "This is not a business relationship. She threw her arms around my neck, and we kissed as she squirmed against me. I tried to resist, but my body had other ideas.

Afterwards, when we lay in each other's arms, kissing and caressing, I realised I hadn't thought of Inge Lise. The pain of her parting had diminished. Sara's therapy had worked. She had provided what it said on the tin—inner peace.

"Thank you, Ollie," she said. "It was everything I dreamed of."

"Happy not to disappoint. Does this mean you want to continue?"

"Of course, but don't you dare let anything as soppy as wedding bells enter your head. This was never about us. It was for you and me as individuals. I yearned for what I now know you had to give. And you needed a sweet distraction to help you handle your feelings about Inge Lise and put her in perspective. Was I?"

"Sweet?"

For the first time, Sara seemed unsure of herself.

"It was different," I said, choosing my words. "But as we haven't spent much time together, the emotional connection wasn't as intense."

"Friends with benefits, you mean?"

"Exactly."

"Fair enough. Want to try again?"

"Do we have enough time?"

"No limits today, except I open the bar at seven and need to shower and change beforehand."

Sara and I continued to meet almost every night after she closed the bar. Our physical relationship was incredible, and our feelings intensified, taking us to new heights. In our way, we loved and respected each other but didn't need to express it. We posed as friends in public, but she reminded me occasionally that we would stop instantly and remain friends if anyone came along for either of us. All traces of guilt had disappeared, but whenever I thought of Inge Lise, which I often did, I regretted that the love of my life hadn't become my wife and the mother of my children. Despite my growing affection for Sara, I never envisaged setting up a house with her, and I think she felt the same.

Toward the end of March, I detected a change in our intensity levels. First, it was every other night, which progressed to every other couple of nights. She had business to attend to, she said. I didn't mind. As the regatta approached, it gave me more time to concentrate on my increased training schedule. I accepted that she wanted less from me and wasn't too bothered. When we were together, it was still passionate and fun. We laughed a lot.

A conversation we had one Sunday, though, perplexed me. We were lying in bed sharing a cigarette, and I was conscious that she was checking the time on her new fancy watch almost every minute.

"Nice watch," I said.

"Rolex," she said. "I treated myself."

"Some reward. Room hires going well?"

"Yes, but I have other interests. I don't always want to be a barmaid."

"Care to tell me?"

"Best you don't know."

"You seem anxious," I said.

"Sorry, Ollie," she said. "Bit of business I can't put to the back of mind."

"Must be important."

"It could lead to bigger things."

"Can I help distract you?" I asked, kissing her neck.

It seemed to do the trick, but when we were done, she rushed off, leaving me to tidy up on my own. I didn't object, but was the real Sara starting to emerge? If so, I wasn't sure I liked her.

A couple of weeks before Easter, we were chatting in Room 118. For some reason, she was reticent to undress and looked relieved when there was a light knock on the door.

I froze, assuming we had been rumbled, but Sara crossed the room and unlocked it. She didn't say a word, grinned, and indicated that whoever was outside should come in.

I stared at the door in horror.

What was going on?"

CHAPTER 11

2023

Aarhus is located on the eastern shore of Jutland in the Kattegat Sea and is the second-largest city in Denmark, with an urban population of under three hundred thousand. As the cab driver drove through the town toward the harbour, I was impressed by its cleanliness and blend of modern with historic architecture. Many of the older houses were painted in bright blues, yellows, and reds, creating an ambience different from Henley or Harborough, but it appeared inviting and the sort of place I could enjoy living. The townsfolk were well-wrapped up and didn't rush around pursuing vitally essential tasks. I spotted many groups standing in parks or gathering on pavements to enjoy a carefree chat. The Danes seemed a relaxed and jolly lot. We drove along Fiskerivej, one block from the seafront with industrial buildings on either side accommodating businesses from fish handlers to boat sales and maintenance.

The driver stopped outside the rowing club around one pm. The building was a rudimentary single-floor shed painted in dirty cream with Rowing Club hand-painted in black letters on the front. A biting easterly wind blasted over the marina from Aarhus Bight, and I shivered while waiting for my change. With low grey clouds and white horses whipping off the waves, snow appeared imminent. This was a lot colder than Henley. I pulled my hat down tighter and wished I had brought some gloves. I trundled my case to the clubhouse entrance and went inside.

Chris came striding toward me, hand outstretched as I entered the reception area. We shook hands. He insisted on taking my case and led the way to his office. He was a tad taller than me and in good shape, wearing a club tracksuit.

"We have photos of your father in our international gallery," he said in English with little trace of an accent. It reminded me of my inadequacy when talking with Inge Lise, ignorant of anything beyond the white cliffs of Dover. "We'll have a chat first. Afterwards, I'll show you the superb training facilities and boathouse, followed by lunch in our cafeteria."

We entered his office. He closed the door, relieved me of my coat, and poured coffee from a flask on his desk.

I sat down opposite, and we appraised each other.

"Your face seems familiar," he said. "Have we met before?"

"I saw you in Henley a few days ago," I said. "We exchanged glances as you climbed into a cab."

"I don't remember," said Chris. "But never mind, perhaps it's because you resemble your father. I was not even born in 1959 when he participated in our annual regatta, but I've seen his photos hundreds of times. Did you come with him?"

"No, I was twelve and had to attend school. How did he do?"

"He won the single scull by miles, which was my forte."

"Mine too," I said. "But I let it go in my twenties to concentrate on golf and my career."

"You are no longer working?"

"I was a police officer and retired at sixty to play golf. I became the secretary of the club for fifteen years but quit to research this book. Did you work?"

"I was a trainee police officer for a couple of years, but when my rowing career took off, I have been involved here ever since. Now, I am our club's chairperson and elite squad trainer. I'll still be at it when they carry me out in a wooden box."

"A good life, though," I said, looking into his ice-blue eyes, concluding that even his mannerisms were similar. This is uncanny. "Are you married?"

"Yes, I married Carolyn, an English girl I met at Henley Regatta. We have two strapping sons, Lars and Rikard, both elite oarsmen in double sculls."

"Rowing must run in the family."

"It started with me. My parents were teachers and not sporty at all. They died a couple of years ago. My mother from cancer, and my Dad a broken heart because he couldn't live without her."

"Were you born in Aarhus?"

"I was born in Grenaa, but we moved here when I was a baby. I have lived here ever since."

"I'm going to Grenaa when I've finished here. What can you tell me about it?"

"Other than it's a port and popular summer holiday resort, not much. Why are you going?"

"I'm hoping to see an old friend."

"I see. How can I help with your research?"

"I'm collecting photos and media articles to collate into a history of my father's and grandfather's rowing careers."

"Are you a writer?"

"No, but I have a friend who specialises in biographies as my co-author."

"And you wish to include photos in the book?"

"Yes, it will go into the museum at Leander Rowing Club as a record of successful members."

"That's a Good idea. We should do something similar. When you're finished, perhaps you could send me a copy so we can learn how to produce one."

"A pleasure," I said. Shit, now I will have to write the damn thing.

"So, how do you want to proceed?"

"I'd like to see what you have about my father and photograph it. My co-author and I will decide what originals we need. When ready, I will commission an expert to copy what you have so the quality for printing is good enough."

Chris pushed back his chair, stood, scratched his nose, and said, "Shall we go to the gallery?"

"Fine," I said, conscious of a similar habit when setting up a task. He must be my son, I thought as we walked along the corridor. But how can I broach the elephant in the room?

The cafeteria was empty, but a young man in a chef's uniform waited behind the servery. He thumbed at Chris as we headed to the far wall, laden with hundreds of images and articles.

"We offer a menu of the day in low season," said Chris. "But when the weather's cold, we don't have enough customers to make it worth our while. I asked the chef to come in anyway, and he said he would make something quick and easy when we were ready."

"Kind of you, thanks."

"It's no trouble; the least we could do for the son of such a famous oarsman." He pointed toward the left-hand side of the wall. Your father is there, and various articles were published after his visit. They were only in local papers, nothing national. Rowing wasn't popular in Denmark in those days."

"I guess your Olympic medal must have raised awareness?"

"Possibly."

I took out my phone and snapped away at a dozen photos of Dad and three articles in Danish.

"Enough," I said.

"Good," said Chris. "Now for the training facilities and boathouse."

"Incredible," I said as we stood on the threshold of the gym. Three men were working out on the latest technology rowing machines. Two were racing each other over a virtual Henley mile. I recognised every inch of the bank."

"To make you feel at home," said Chris. "Our elite team is supported by nutritionists, physios, psychologists, and fitness trainers."

"You are better equipped than Leander," I said.

"Jyske Bank sponsors us," said Chris. "Their marketing budget is most generous."

"Leander will have to watch out at the regatta this summer," I said.

"Do you live near Henley?"

"No, but not far away. When I saw you the other day, it was my first trip back for fifty-six years."

"Amazing, the same as my age."

I decided to strike while the iron was hot, whipping out the album from my jacket pocket.

"I have photos of my father and my grandfather. Would you care to see them?"

"I'd love to but let me show you the boathouse first. We can look during lunch."

"The freezing boat house was packed with floor-to-ceiling racks containing every model of inrigger, outrigger, and canoe, plus a few traditional clinker-built boats."

"This was my Olympic boat," said Chris, indicating a yellow single-scull hull perched upside down on one of the racks. "Elite members who beat training targets can use it in their next race."

"What a great idea. You have a most comprehensive range."

"Not everyone fancies the training routine required for peak performance in a rowing boat, so we offer other options to appeal to those who just want to have fun."

I shivered.

Chris put his arm on my shoulder.

"You're feeling the cold. Shall we go to lunch?"

"Thanks," I said, returning the gesture.

Back in the warmth of the cafeteria, we settled on French omelettes and a salad.

While we waited, I opened my photo album. I had loaded Grandfather at the front, followed by Dad and myself.

I handed it over for Chris to browse at his own pace.

He studied each photo and flicked to the next page. The first one of me was as a thirteen-year-old in a single scull on the Thames outside the Leander Boat Club.

"Is this you?" he said, showing me the image.

"Early teens," I said.

He continued, looking even closer than before at each image.

He finished and looked at me hard.

"By our looks, we could be related," he said.

"Indeed," I said. "My second name is also Chris, after my father."

"Is this why you came?"

"After seeing the similarity the other day, I had to know for sure, but there is also a book."

"But it's impossible. My birth certificate clearly states my parent's names."

"I'm sorry for wasting your time. Shall I go?"

"No, of course not," he said as the lunch was served. "Everyone has a double somewhere. You must have another reason for suspecting we might be related."

"The love of my life came from Grenaa. I was hoping she might be your mother."

"What was the lady's name?"

"Inge Lise Oleson. Her father was a timber merchant. She is now a child psychologist practising at a clinic in the town centre."

"Yet another coincidence. My mother, Angelika. Her family name was Oleson."

"Perhaps they were related?"

"Possibly. I never met my mother's family. I was only informed they had a falling out not long after I was born, but I don't know why. Did your friend have a sister?"

"Yes, but I never knew her name."

"Where did you meet Inge Lise?"

"At the Red Lion in Henley. She was an au pair. When her visa expired, she had to return but never responded to my letters. I met another girl, and she faded away."

"Out of sight, out of mind, Carolyn always says. What were you doing at the Red Lion after all these years?"

"I had other outstanding issues in Henley. They happened after Inge Lise left. The reason for my visit was to resolve these. It was a total fluke when I saw you."

"I'm sorry to disappoint you, but I've never questioned who my parents were. However, I never discovered the origins of my Christian name, and I admit you've piqued my interest, so will make inquiries. If you manage to see Inge Lise, and she did have a sister called Angelika, could you do me a huge favour?"

"With pleasure?"

"If Inge Lise is my aunt and wants to connect, we want to meet her. Would you pass on the message and tell me how it goes?"

"Of course," I said, and after finishing my food, I stood. "Thanks for the delicious lunch, and I'm sorry to have taken up your valuable time."

"How are you travelling to Grenaa?"

"On the train."

"I'll order you a cab."

"Thanks."

We waited in reception, and when the cab arrived, I said. "You know the book idea was a spur-of-the-moment thing. But on reflection, it's a good concept."

"It is," said Chris. "If I can help, let me know."

"Thanks again."

Our farewell handshake evolved into a backslapping hug.

He came out with me and handed my case to the

driver.

We gazed at each other as the cab drove away. I was confident we had made more than a warm connection and was sure I detected a tear in his eye. There was indeed one in mine. Despite the evidence on his birth certificate, I remained convinced he was my son. Our inquiries might reveal the truth.

CHAPTER 12

2023

During the ninety-minute journey to Grenaa, I contemplated whether revisiting my past was moving me forward. I rarely suffer from self-doubt, but this step back in time was revealing unexpected results. And I hadn't even begun to explore my original objective. However, I was here and would complete my visit to Inge Lise no matter the outcome. I found the quest therapeutic; at last, I was doing something to unravel the mysteries of yesteryear. Even if I failed, I no longer need to scold myself for not trying. Perhaps the effort might rid me of the vision.

It started snowing as the train pulled into Grenaa station. The small coastal town of some fifteen thousand residents is a popular summer resort renowned for its white sandy beaches. Many log cabins are for hire inland from the shore, and the few hotels I could find were in the same area. On the way up from Aarhus, I'd booked a room for one night at the Hotel Marina. It wasn't the Red Lion, but it was affordable and clean.

It was even colder as I climbed into a cab waiting in a rank outside the station. We headed along Havnevej, the main road out of town providing access to the port. Inge Lise lived on this road with her parents at the timber yard. It was somewhere near the harbour, I recalled from the many letters I'd addressed to her. When I checked on Google Maps, it was now a housing development.

Perhaps she lived there? Suspecting that the love of my life was somewhere nearby, I found frustrating. I dined in the hotel restaurant and spent a wretched night hardly sleeping on a bed too hard and under a heavy duvet that made me sweat.

As I checked out, I inquired about the timber yard. Nobody could recall it. However, I had better luck with Inge Lise. She was a well-respected child psychologist and town councillor.

The main roads and pavements had been cleared of overnight snow, so the taxi had no problems dropping me outside the clinic not far from the station. I was so preoccupied with my emotions running riot that I failed to notice the charming timber frame houses lining narrow cobblestoned streets. I stood before the building, looking up at the windows. Perhaps she was looking out the window and could see me. To think she might recognise me brought on a panic attack. Was coming back into her life doing the right thing, or would we be better off if I left?

No, I'd come this far, I couldn't chicken out now,

I went into the lobby and inspected the rows of signs. They described each clinic's function, name, and floor number. Inge Lise's was on the first floor, so I walked up and entered, my heart hammering.

I had no idea what to expect, but it wasn't much

different from my doctor's practice in Market Harborough, except the furniture was blond pine and chrome, and the décor was light and airy.

"Godmorgen," said a young blond lady behind a reception desk.

"Sorry, I'm useless at foreign languages," I said. "Do you speak English?"

"Of course, how may I help?"

"I'm here to see Inge Lise Oleson."

"Do you have an appointment?"

"No, I've come from England to see her, but it's a surprise. We haven't seen each other for over fifty years."

"Fifty years, good heavens, but I'm sorry to disappoint you. Nowadays, she only comes in for actual appointments and is not due until the end of the week. She has gone to Copenhagen for a few days."

My face must have dropped to the floor because she came rushing around to see if I was ok. She sat me down on the nearest chair and perched by me as I fought back the tears—all this way, for nought.

"Could I leave a note?" I croaked.

"Of course."

"Could I trouble you for some paper and an envelope?"

"Would you like to sit in her office to compose your note? It will be more comfortable."

"May I?"

She guided me across the tidy office into a door near the window.

It was a spacious office with a couch and toys stacked neatly in racks. A whiteboard was mounted on the wall behind a blond pine timber desk. I sat down in the high-backed swivel chair and appraised her workplace. My eyes were drawn to a framed photo on her desk. It was of me and her by the river in Henley. We were outside the Red Lion with the Leander Club in the background. Jenny had taken it.

I picked it up and examined it. A bolt of electricity which had nothing to do with static made me shiver. From my vision, the girl appeared, but this time, she evaded my arms, stopped, turned, and threw her arms around me. It was Inge Lise.

"Jeg elsker dig," she said.

That finished me.

I burst into tears.

The receptionist was beside herself, worrying about me.

"Is it the photo?" she said.

I wiped my eyes with my fingers.

"I often catch her hugging it," she said. "With a dreamy expression. Is it the two of you?"

"Yes," I whined.

"That is so sad," she said and started crying too.

We hugged each other, tears streaming down our cheeks.

"I've always wondered who it was?" she sniffed after a while.

"Inge Lise didn't say."

"No."

"Did she marry?"

"No, and I've never known her to have a date. She works hard at the council and rarely takes a holiday."

"What a time to go to Copenhagen?" I said.

She fetched tissues for both of us and placed several sheets of paper and a pen in front of me.

"Write," she said. "I'm sure you have a lot to say."

I did, but I wasn't about to pen my life story.

"What's your name?" I asked.

"Greta. I'm the receptionist for all the psychologists who work here."

"You are an angel," I said. "Like Inge Lise."

She blushed and said, "Thank you. I'll leave alone."

I thought for a bit and began to transfer my thoughts onto paper.

My dearest Inge Lise

I am so sorry to have missed you. First, thanks to Greta, your kind assistant, for helping me through this trauma. Without her, I'd be a complete wreck. This long story is best not explained in my inadequate handwriting. To cut it short. I want to see you again to clear up outstanding questions. I saw Chris in Henley the other day after staying in Room 118 at the Red Lion. I wondered why he looked almost identical and followed him to Aarhus. He explained he couldn't remember ever meeting you and mentioned a family fallout. I have no idea if you are his mother, but his resemblance to me is uncanny. Chris said his mother was Angelika Oleson, and her father was a timber merchant from Grenaa. There can't be many Olesons in Grenaa, so was she your sister?

Chris and his English wife Carolyn have two strapping sons, Lars and Rikard, also oarsmen. Both parents are dead. If Angelika were your sister, he would love to meet her. I will leave his email and contact details at the end of this note. I appreciate that this will be a shock, and I apologise if my reappearance in your life is upsetting. Our parting at Harwich was such sweet sorrow; it was inconceivable that you never replied to my letters. I assumed you had returned to Erik or something terrible had happened.

You have always been in my heart. Oh, and I never married.
I was hoping to see or hear from you soon.
Your ever-loving, Oliver Matthews xx

"Memory
is the treasury
and guardian
of all things."

Marcus Tullius Cicero
(106 BCE - 43 BCE)

CHAPTER 13

2023

I was so wrapped up in sorrow that the journey home from Grenaa passed quickly. These intense emotional investments were delivering little in return. I was disillusioned with my attempts at unravelling the past and questioned whether I should continue. It was the American writer Thomas Wolfe, whose 1905 novel entitled *You Can't Go Home Again*. So far, he was right.

I could have stayed in Grenaa and met with Inge Lise on her return from Denmark's capital, but I had decided against it. If her reasons for never writing to me were so strong all those years ago, I must respect them. There was no way I was going to impose my pathetic self on her. With my note, she could decide without pressure. If she was to reappear in my life, I wanted her to do so with a willing heart and no obligations or guilt, but it had to be her decision. Meanwhile, I would have to wait to discover whether I was a parent. After fifty-six years, a few weeks more wouldn't matter in the grand scheme.

There was mail waiting for me in my letterbox,

postmarked Henley.

I slit it open with shaking hands.

Dear Ollie,

I dropped into the Angel on the Bridge last week for my weekly constitutional, all I can manage nowadays, and Tomak, the Polish bartender, was complaining about some old fart who had been in the previous week looking for me. From his description, I had no idea who it could have been. Thankfully, he found your card under the till, and here I am.

Forgive me for using more traditional methods of communication. I can't understand this digital nonsense.

I still live in Henley with my daughter Ginny on Deanfield Avenue. I would love to meet. There is so much to catch up on after all this time. You can telephone my daughter at the number below and let me know when you can come. She does a nice lunch, or we can try one of the old watering holes or both, whatever you prefer.

Warmest felicitations.
Your ancient footballing friend.
John Francis.

I called the number straight away, but John was out for a walk. I made an appointment with Ginny for the following day.

It's seventy-five miles from Harborough to Henley, but it takes over three hours by train with three stops. With frost on the points at Bedford and leaves on the line near St. Albans, my connections failed, so it took four hours. I was accustomed to this ongoing British saga of a not-fit-for-purpose transport system, so I built in enough time to arrive at the Angel on the Bridge before John.

I ordered a half of Mr Brakspear's finest, took a window seat, and watched the same geese and ducks I saw last week swimming in what, with the recent arctic freeze covering Britain, must have been even colder water. However, it wasn't as bad as Denmark.

Minutes later, three older gentlemen approached me dressed in thick overcoats, tweed caps, gloves, and scarves with apprehensive smiles. Andy Capp cartoons sprung to mind, but I wouldn't have known them from Adam if we had passed on the street. The smaller one stretched out his hand and said, "Hi, Ollie, you haven't changed a bit."

"Thanks," I said. "You too, Ivan."

"I'm John. I hope you don't mind, but I brought Ivan and Keith. We all have burning questions, but forgive Keith if he asks the same one several times. His memories of half a century ago are crystal clear, but of five minutes, they are a tad dodgy."

"How can I help you?" said the bartender.

"Thanks, Tomak," said John. "Three pints of the usual."

"Put those on my tab," I said.

"There's no need," said Ivan.

"It's my pleasure," I said. "I feel as if I owe you."

"For running out on us?" said Keith.

I studied each one, trying to visualise them as the teenage friends we were back in the 1960s. Through the mists of time, teenage heads morphed into senior models. They were no longer strangers but dear friends with whom I had shared much of my youth.

I could better see their ageing frames with outer clothing and accessories hung on the coat rack. John looked fit, elegantly attired, and well cared for. Keith was not so good with shaky hands, and Ivan had a pallid complexion, heavy jowls, and a huge belly. Both were dressed in well-worn clothing. All three had close-cropped hair and sported a variety of spectacles. Johns included integral hearing aids behind the ear. I was doing well by comparison, considering we were in the same year at Gillot's school.

They regarded me steadily.

"Fifty-six years ago," I said. "We shared our last Sunday night in the Riverside bar of the Red Lion. We played for their football team and, as I recall, were celebrating our first victory."

"Three–two against The Bull," said Keith.

"We were well pissed," said Ivan.

"It's why I'm here," I said. "Because I can't remember a damn thing. All I know is that the following day, I left to join the police. Until last week, I have never returned. I hoped you could throw some light on what happened."

"You need closure," said John.

"I do."

"So, you can go to your maker with a clear conscience," said Ivan.

"Correct."

"It's what we do at our age," said Keith. "Do you remember we beat the Bull, three–two?"

We looked at him with sympathy.

"Trouble is," said John. "We were wanting the same. None of us can recall the night."

"What happened the day after you left," said Ivan. "Created hell of a quandary."

"Go on."

"Can we order sandwiches?" said Keith.

"One moment," I said. "What quandary?"

"Sara was fired," said John. "Never to be seen again. She vanished along with Jenny and the American Secret Service team. Tragically, the Riverside Bar closed forever, and we were never informed why."

"It was the end of the football team," said Ivan.

"We had to find a new pub," said Keith.

"The gang fragmented," said John.

"Many never to be seen or heard of again," said Ivan.

"There must have been rumours," I said.

"Too vague to make sense of," said John.

"Perhaps Sara could throw some light on the mystery?" I said.

"Possibly," said John. "Do you know where she is?"

"No idea," I said.

"I heard she married a guy named Colin and moved to Sonning, but we never saw her again," said Keith.

"Would anyone know her location?" I said.

"Anita might," said John.

"What happened to her," I said.

"I married her," said John. "We had two daughters but divorced over twenty years ago."

"Sonia escaped your intentions?" I said.

"No, we spent about eighteen months together," said John. "Before she married Paul Best."

"Him with the Daimler?"

John nodded, a tear in his eye.

"I thought his family immigrated to South Africa?" I asked.

"Paul came back after a year," said John. "He hated it there and missed Sonia. She dropped me and resumed where they left off."

"Was Anita your rebound?"

"It was a mistake, but we had two beautiful girls, Ginny and Daisy and now three grandchildren."

"How was the divorce?" I asked.

"Amenable and fair. We're still close friends."

Does she live in Henley?" I asked.

"Around the corner," said John. "In her parent's old place."

"Could we go and see her?" I said.

"No need," said John. "She can join us for lunch. My daughter is knocking up a roast dinner. She can't wait to meet you. Before we go, there is something I want to ask. Why did you leave without saying farewell?"

"The following morning," I said. "I woke up at home with my ribs covered in bruises, a sore neck, and a sense of shame hanging over me like a pall. I had no idea why, but some instinct told me I couldn't bear to face you. Because you were the last people I remember being with, I assumed the shame must have stemmed from something that happened between us. So, went off to join the police."

"None of us had bruises," said John. "Just bad hangovers."

"And we've been through hundreds of disagreements together and always resolved our differences without violence," said Ivan.

"It is safe to say," said John. "Whatever the cause of shame, it had nothing to do with us."

"It must have involved a woman," said Keith. "Nothing else can be as infuriating."

"You never said anything about becoming a cop," said Ivan.

"I had been discussing it with my parents as a career possibility but was unsure. The night of shame tipped me over the edge. What did you end up doing?"

"I opened an ironmonger shop," said Ivan. "But when the superstores arrived, I went bust. Overnight, I switched from being a respected local businessperson to a rubbish collector. When the work became too physically demanding, I became the lollipop man outside the infant's school. Now I'm in a council-run old folk's home on Greys Road. Most of my pension covers the cost, but I'm allowed pocket money for the occasional beer."

"I qualified as a dentist," said Keith. "I had a practice on the Reading Road but had to retire early. I've got these feet, you see. I can't stand up for more than a few minutes at a time. Not ideal for peering into serried ranks of rotten teeth. I live with my son and his wife in a council house. Did I say I was a dentist?"

"I worked for the council," said John. "In the housing department. It was heartbreaking at times. Especially when I heard one of the hundreds of sob stories was true."

"Why did you ignore us for all these years," asked Ivan.

"I was wrapped up in my career to the exclusion of everything. I used the work commitment as an excuse to delay our reunion because I was too frightened to learn what I might have done."

"It wouldn't have mattered to us," said John. "We're your best mates and would have supported you whatever. Instead, we have wasted our relationship for fifty-six years. I hate to dwell on those lost moments of our amazing camaraderie."

"Not to mention the terrible jokes," said Ivan.

"And my wedding," said John.

"And your divorce," said Ivan.

"All I can say is," said John. "You must have enjoyed being a cop?"

"I was a detective and found unravelling mysteries spellbinding. Listen, sorry guys if my pathetic behaviour pissed you off, but now I'm here. Can we put it behind us?"

I stretched out my hand.

All three of them grasped it, and we had a mutual shake, exchanging glances through moist eyes.

"We should go, Ollie," said John, standing and breaking the moment's magic.

"We haven't had our sandwiches?" said Keith.

CHAPTER 14

2023

John Francis and I strode along Hart Street toward his daughter's house. We had left Ivan and Keith at the Angel. Their need for more beer was more pressing than my pursuit of old demons, and Keith refused to leave until he'd eaten his sandwiches. We ordered them, and I paid the tab.

When passing the Catherine Wheel, I said, "Did you have any more football matches?"

"Some yes," said John. "But for the Catherine Wheel. Their assistant manager, Lee Somerville, called and asked me to recruit our best players for their squad. We needed a new local, and they had recently opened the refurbished stables at the back for cocktails, so we joined. It remained our pub for years."

We walked up past the old police station, now a council building, and the grand sweeping entrance gate to Friar Park, where George Harrison of the Beatles used to live. We turned left into Paradise Road, which led to Deanfield Avenue. We entered the driveway of a mock Victorian detached property opposite The

Henley College, and John let himself in.

"Finally, the elusive Oliver Matthews crosses my threshold," said a petite lady with auburn hair and a familiar face approaching us as we stepped inside. She was in her mid-forties, wearing tight jeans and a royal blue blouse protected by an apron printed with artistic text and a glass of red wine on the front. It read, 'I love cooking with wine; occasionally, some of it goes in the sauce.'

She was warm, bubbly, and instantly likeable—the petite lady, not the sauce.

"My daughter, Ginny," said John as Ginny and I hugged and exchanged cheek kisses.

"You look like your mother," I said, sniffing a delicious aroma from the kitchen. And by the mouthwatering smells from the kitchen, you cook like her, too."

"Thanks," said Ginny, blushing. "My husband Mike and charming teenage daughters Megan and Melissa never say anything so complimentary."

"Where are they?"

"At work and school."

We removed our coats, hung them behind the door, and were ushered into the dining room, where a beautifully decorated floor-to-ceiling Christmas tree dominated the corner. White fairy lights were twinkling, and carols played in the background.

"Pour yourselves a glass of wine," said Ginny. "Now you're here, I'll put the Yorkshire pudding in the oven."

We sat down as the doorbell rang.

"It's mum," shouted Ginny. "Dad, let her in."

Anita had survived the ravages of time. A tiny woman with a slender frame, still athletic with graceful movement. She wore a fur hat and thick Canadian coat, which she hung with ours to reveal a figure-hugging beige dress. Her outstanding feature used to be her pretty face. Now in her early seventies with a few wrinkles, she had hardly changed. Her petite features were still a delight, highlighted by sparkling hazel eyes and framed by short silver-grey hair. John was crazy to have divorced her, I thought.

We appraised each other, hugged, and sat down at the table. Anita poured the wine, and we raised our glasses.

"To the future," said Anita as we exchanged clinks.

"However long we have left," said John.

"Always with the negative waves," said Anita.

We all laughed. It had been her catchphrase at Gillot's school.

"So, Ollie," said Anita. "To what honour do we owe your visit after all these years?"

"He needs closure," said John. "What can you remember about our final night in the Red Lion bar?"

"Oh gosh, now you are asking me to push the boat out," said Anita. "Especially as I wasn't there."

"You weren't," said John. "But you girls were more up to date with the gossip. What can you remember?"

"Sara was fired," said Anita. "Never to be seen again, and the Riverside bar closed."

"Listen," I said. "Let me make this quite clear. Yes, I am on a quest to find some closure, and if I can find answers, it will be amazing, but the thoughts driving me to take this trip have always been about renewing old friendships. I have treasured my memories of you every single spare moment, and finally, we are reunited, which outweighs everything else. If we discover why they fired Sara or closed the bar, that's fine. If not, also fine."

"The same goes for us, Ollie," said Anita. "There is so much we have shared since infant school. Birthday parties, singing in the school nativity play, scraping you off the playground floor, and tending to your wounds."

"Don't forget when he crapped his pants," said John.

We all roared with laughter. It was true.

"We often talk about you," said Anita. "And speculate why such a dear friend abandoned us without a word. The whole town was obsessed for months. Leander was furious at the loss of a potential star. Your parents were so devastated they were embarrassed when we asked them in the street until they also left town. All kinds of rumours flew about, and we want to clear those up as much as you do."

"Why did the Elsdon's close the Riverside bar?" I asked

"They kept a tight lid on explanations and sold the Red Lion shortly after," said Anita. "They bought a place in Hungerford. Why is all this so important to you, Ollie?"

"Something untoward happened on that final night, and I feel sure I was involved, but other than the first few beers celebrating our victory against The Bull, the rest is blank."

"Isn't it more sensible to leave it unresolved?" said Anita. "What if you uncover something unsavoury? The shame might bring on a heart attack."

"True, but at least I would depart this world knowing what happened. No matter how bad, I would have found closure and could pass away in peace."

"You need to find Sara," said Anita.

"Do you know where she is?"

"No, but I heard she married a guy called Colin and moved to Sonning."

"Can you recall Colin's surname?"

"Marwood or Martin, anyway, something beginning with Mar."

"Did she meet this Colin before she was fired?"

"I don't know," said Anita. "Sorry, Ollie, but the way I heard it, Sara was fired the same night and kicked out of her room. Nobody has seen or heard of her since except for marrying this Mar, whatever he's called, guy."

"I thought she had a boyfriend," I said.

"She did," said Anita. "He was one of the American Secret Service Team."

"Secret Service?"

"He was one of the team staying at the hotel to protect Jackie Kennedy. She used to visit Henley during the late sixties. Her sister, what was her name, er, Lee Radziwill, was married to Prince Stanislas Radziwill. They lived at Turville Grange, a grand mansion north of Stonor. Jackie stayed with them regularly until she married Onassis in October 1968 when she lost her right to secret service protection."

"Turville Grange," I said as it came flooding back. "Of course, it's a grade two listed building with stables in fifty acres of land built in the mid-eighteen hundreds. Sean Connery used to stay there. Jackie always brought the same team of twelve Secret Service guys with each visit. They worked in groups of four, eight hours each, seven days a week. They stayed at the Red Lion; Jenny organised the logistics."

"I'd forgotten about her; didn't you have something going?" asked Anita.

"Short and sweet, yes. It ended a few days before I

left. I've never heard a dickey bird about her since."

"Perhaps she didn't know where you were, like us," said John.

"A letter to my parent's house would have been forwarded."

"Or you could have contacted them," said Anita.

"I wasn't sure how to."

"Did you bother with their surnames?" asked John.

"Sara, I can't recall, but Jenny Leovich was from Washington, D.C., and I never had their telephone numbers."

"Cowan," said Anita. "It was Sara Cowan."

"Of course it was," I said. "It reminds me of the teacher calling the register."

"Canford, Carter, Cowan," said John.

"Dawkins, Downs, and Dudley," said Anita.

"Happy days," said John. "Poor Miss Glasspool having to put up with our motley crew. Ollie, there is still one outstanding item from those days that might help you lift some shadows."

"Go on," I said.

"The Henley stalker," said John.

My pulse went through the roof. My mind churned with flashing images of my recurring vision of the girl walking ahead of outstretched hands. The stalker must have triggered something in my subconscious, but I had no idea why.

"Remind me," I said.

"Between 1967 and 1968, a tall, athletic man in a hoody with a scarf over his mouth and nose followed au pair girls' home," said Anita. "At first, he never touched them or spoke, but he walked right up close, breathing heavily and making obscene gestures with his fingers, implying what he would like to do to their breasts. Eventually, he injured and raped a Swedish girl."

"The Henley Standard followed the case," said John. "They were incensed about catching him and used a female reporter to entice him to follow her, but he evaded their trap. He was only interested in au pairs. You don't remember, Ollie?"

"Sorry, no," I said with a sense of foreboding. "What colour was the hoody?"

"Pink," said Anita. "According to one of the many articles in the Henley Standard, the police suspected it was a Leander Club sports top without the logo, but they never caught him or had any suspects."

"He was also never heard of again after you vanished," said John.

"If I have it right," said Anita. "You had a similar top."

"You have me there," I said. However, all active members had hoodies to protect their heads from ice-cold winds when we were in training. Why?"

"One of the vague rumours was you were the stalker," said John. "Were you?"

"I don't think so," I said. "But in the build-up toward my departure, I was floating so high, I could have done anything."

"Do you still have the top?" said John.

"I have several," I said. "One was my grandfather; another was my fathers. I also have one without logo and one with, although they are all tired. I'm considering writing a book about my father and grandfather and will donate them with the family cups and surviving artefacts to the Leander Museum."

"What a great idea," said Anita. "What inspired you?"

"Do you remember Inge Lise?"

"The love of your life?" said Anita.

"Wow, your memory is amazing."

"Most of us girls were green with envy when we saw you together at the bar," said Anita. "So much love and tenderness on display. It was what we all yearned for."

"Did you hear from her after she returned to Denmark?"

"No, did you?" said Anita.

"Not a single letter."

"Painful?" asked Anita.

"Agony, but I recovered. Anyway, I'd like to share a recent development with you concerning Inge Lise."

"Go on," said Anita.

"The first event in the chain leading me here was in the Red Lion last week when I left my card everywhere. Having not found any old friends, I went home. As I was about to leave the hotel, I spotted a man in his early fifties climbing into a cab. He was the spitting image of me in my fifties. To cut a long story short, he turned out to be Chris Jepsen, the Danish Olympic oarsman. He was here to arrange the accommodation and training facilities for next year's regatta. He is based in Aarhus Rowing Club, so I visited him to research my father's participation in one of their regattas for inclusion in this book. Up close, he was a carbon copy of me. We both said he could be my son, but it turned out he had parents, and guess what? Inge Lise's sister was probably his mother."

"Wow, what a coincidence," said John.

"Did you speak to his mother?" said Anita.

"No, she died a few years back. The family had a significant fallout after Chris was born. He couldn't remember ever meeting his aunt. So, I went to Grenaa to see Inge Lise."

"This is so exciting," said Anita. "Did you see her?"

"She was away in Copenhagen but had a photo of us on her desk."

"Why didn't you wait for her?" said Anita.

"I didn't want to impose myself on her after all this time. I left a note so she can contact either Chris or me when ready."

"I couldn't be so restrained," said John.

"It was tough, I said. "But there had to have been a powerful reason for her not to have contacted me. I allowed her to decide if she was now ready to explain."

"Have you heard from her?" said Ginny.

"Not yet, but she won't have received my note until she returns to her office on Friday. Maybe next week."

"I can't wait to hear the outcome," said Anita. "And now we have rediscovered you; don't you dare disappear again. What are you doing for Christmas?"

"Nothing."

"I insist you join us at my place for my annual bash. Several other mutual friends will die to see you and far too much food and wine."

"You sure?"

"It would be awesome," said Ginny. "Mum has several spare bedrooms."

"It would be my pleasure."

Lunch was excellent, and yet more regurgitations of past foolishness were hilarious. By the time we nibbled at cheddar and oatcakes, it seemed only yesterday we had been together in the Riverside Bar.

My train beckoned, and Anita offered to drive me to the station.

Ginny took a photo of us and added each other to our WhatsApp contacts.

"I'll insert this in my screensaver file," said John. "I'm collecting the various stages of my life into a slide show, which kicks in every time I forget why I turned on the computer. It reminds me of the great people I have known and what fun I've had. This has been another episode I've often dreamed about but doubted would ever happen. Thanks, Ollie, for getting in touch. It's been special."

"It works both ways, John," I said with a tear in my eye.

I hugged John and Ginny while Anita went to collect her car.

On the way there, she had another revelation.

"Marshall," she said. "Sara was engaged to Colin Marshall; you should be able to trace her now."

"Amazing," I said. "Again, well remembered."

She stopped outside the station door. I reached over to hug her, but she took my head in both hands, redirected me to her mouth, and kissed me.

"Forgive me," she said. "For my whole life, I've dreamed of kissing the hunky Oliver Matthews. Now, I can tell our few remaining classmates that I did it. They will be so jealous."

"I can't imagine why, now I'm an old fart."

"A distinguished old fart, but in those days, we all fancied you like mad but were too shy to say or do anything."

"Good heavens, you surprise me. I never noticed a thing. Does this mean the Christmas invitation is because you want something more from this ancient frame of mine?"

"No, Ollie. Keep your wrinkles to yourself, and thanks, but I am happy with my life as a single woman. I adore everything about Christmas. It's my prime-time nostalgia. Your being there will broaden our revival of memorable events and add more joy to my favourite festival. The kiss was a schoolgirl urge; now I have closure. I wish you luck with yours."

"Thanks, who else will be there?"

"Ginny with husband and granddaughters. Daisy won't attend. This year is her turn with the in-laws. My sister Virginia, Sonia and Paul Best, and if he is still up for it, Norman Shannon."

"Wow, most of the old gang."

"The key members anyway. It'll be fun."

We hugged, and I left.

As the train packed with students from Henley College pulled out of the station, I revelled in the warm cosiness of renewing acquaintances with old friends. They had brought back long-forgotten memories to mull over.

CHAPTER 15

1968

Waiting to identify whom Sara might tolerate disturbing our afternoon of passion was nerve-wracking.

It was Jenny.

She entered Room 118, unsure of herself. This was not the educated woman with a ponytail and dressed in conservative loose clothing I had become accustomed to. Her blond hair was loose and cascaded over her shoulders. She wore black hot pants with bare legs, a transparent white blouse, and no bra.

Jenny sat on the end of the bed and gazed at me with big, blue, soulful eyes. Sara stood by the door with a quizzical expression.

"You're looking lovely, Jenny," I said. "Am I missing something?"

"No," said Sara. "Change of plans."

"Go on."

"We said from the outset, should we find someone else, neither would stand in the other's way. Well, I have met a man, and before I explore a relationship with him, it's proper that I end it with you. However, you are forbidden from taking off and finding someone new. If you agree, Jenny will take over from me."

I appraised them both while my mind adjusted to this unreal situation. Would I prefer to be single again? No, but swapping me over made me feel like a prize bull being exchanged by two farmers. Was this my real objection, or did I have a too-high opinion of myself? I mean, here I was with two beautiful ladies, one ex-lover and one volunteering to replace her. Only an idiot would object, but this idiot was uncomfortable with this weird situation. Despite the free love swinging sixties mentality promulgated everywhere by the media, I remained mister traditional. I felt comfortable following the role model of my parents and decidedly uncomfortable being passed around like a parcel. Was this a typical tactic of the modern female? Should I be adjusting to this new form of male-female interaction?

I shook my head to try and banish these old-fashioned thoughts. I regarded Jenny as she posed on the bed with shapely legs crossed. It wasn't that difficult; she oozed sex appeal from every pore. Sara had used the identical pose.

"It's uncanny," I said. "How similar you look."

"We wanted the transition to be as smooth as possible, so Jenny borrowed my clothes and did her hair like mine."

"Amazing. How will I know who is who?"

"Show him, Jenny."

Jenny turned her back and lifted her hair. High on the back of her neck, almost disappearing under the hairline, was a heart-shaped birthmark.

"And I don't need to show you my peculiarity," said

Sara. "You've kissed them often enough. Now, come on, answer me. Do you have a problem with Jenny?"

"Of course not. She's gorgeous, but it's unconventional. Was this your strategy from the outset?"

"Since Inge Lise went home," said Jenny. "We felt sorry for your suffering, and our hearts went to you."

"We wanted to relieve your pain," said Sara. "I was the first to do something about it."

"Please don't compare me with Sara," said Jenny. "I desire to experience what you and Inge Lise had together, especially after Sara confirmed it was everything she anticipated."

"As I said. It's unconventional."

"It worries you?" said Jenny.

"Chopping and changing partners every few weeks is not something I had envisaged."

"We both love you," said Jenny. "In our way."

"Doesn't make it any less weird."

"For our parents' generation, I agree," said Jenny. "But haven't you noticed how social norms have changed with the advent of birth control pills? Now women can be independent from men; the fight for our liberty has become a mainstream reality."

"No longer do we need an engagement ring," said Sara. "Or wait for men to make advances."

"Now we can make love with whoever and whenever we choose," said Jenny. "Without having to worry about finding a man to provide a roof over our heads or joining a queue for diapers."

"Now we can have our careers and make our way through life as independent people, but we have needs," said Sara. "Finding a decent man to share them with is nigh on impossible."

"Until we saw you with Inge Lise," said Jenny.

"Such tenderness is rare," said Sara.

"Most want to grab and squirt," said Jenny. "You hear them in the bar."

"Cor blimey, nice tits," mimicked Sara.

"Summa that," said Jenny in a perfect Cockney accent.

"They have no idea what a turn-off treating us like objects is," said Sara.

"And those awful chat-up lines," said Jenny.

"Hello, darlin', 'ain't I seen you somewhere before?" aped Sara.

"So crass," said Jenny.

"I'm privileged two such beautiful ladies are so interested in me."

"And you, Ollie. Do you love me?" said Sara.

"Not like Inge Lise, but in my way, I guess so."

"I never wanted to compete with your love for Inge Lise," said Sara. "As long as I have a little piece of your heart, I am happy. But how do you feel about Jenny?"

"As I said, it's unconventional, but I'd be a fool to say no. When er do we begin?"

"How about now?" said Jenny.

"Room money in advance?" I asked as Sara opened the door.

"With Jenny, no," said Sara leaving. "Anybody else, the going rate will apply."

"How long do we have?" I asked.

"We have an hour," said Jenny, removing her blouse as soon as Sara had departed. "A colleague needs the room. Fancy a shower?"

Jenny was a dark horse. Underneath the studious and efficient exterior was a woman hungry for love. She wanted more, but her demands were way beyond me. Physically, it was out of this world. But after intense emotions for Inge Lise and passionate weeks with Sara, something was missing. Notwithstanding, Jenny could grow on me. Her looks and animal sexuality might be captivating, but I didn't know her as a person and that needed a remedy.

As we lay in each other's arms, I thought a conversation might yield some rewards. We'd hardly spoken until now.

"Where have you been hiding?" I asked.

"I've been waiting for you since our first drink together last year," she said. "But you never noticed me when Inge Lise was around, and Sara was quicker off the mark."

"I've always lusted after you," I said. "Especially in your running gear on the towpath."

"I almost tripped over every time you passed the other way in your rowing boat."

"Aren't we funny, humans," I said, laughing. "Why can't we be straight with each other and say what we want."

"Civilized women find it hard to ignore the feelings of others," said Jenny. "We don't want to be accused of stealing anyone's man, so hold back until an opportunistic and uncomplicated moment presents itself."

"Whereas men barge in oblivious to the emotional damage they might cause."

"You don't, Ollie. It's why many women around here desire you."

"I wasn't aware."

"It's part of your charm."

"Do I take it we can continue?"

"If I have your total commitment. I'm not

interested in sharing you with anyone, even Sara."

"Suits me, anything more I'd find too complicated. If your colleagues are here, does this mean your VIP has arrived?"

"She is on her way and landing at an Air Force base tomorrow. Our team has checked in and wants to party before beginning work tomorrow. There will be several shifts in Room 118 tonight."

"Who are the other girls?"

"Professionals. The boys gave me a shopping list, and I had to track them down in London."

"Another hard day at the office," I said. "I wonder what the Elsdons would say if they knew their hotel was an American Secret Service knocking shop?"

"They like the money," said Jenny.

"Why choose this hotel?"

"Perfect location for our job, access to the Leander gym for the boys to work out while off duty, and it's so English."

"Who is your VIP?"

"Jackie Kennedy. The former first lady. Her sister lives at Turville Grange."

"The mansion near Stonor?"

"Correct."

"How long is she here?"

"Three weeks during which I will be busy and under unbelievable stress."

"Will you have time for me?"

"Every night, I will need you to help me relax. Can you come to my apartment? I'd prefer not to bother Sara with the keys to Room 118 so late in the evening, and knowing my debauched colleagues, it will probably be in use. You could sleep overnight if you want."

"A new experience for me."

"You're kidding?"

"Never been so serious."

"Wow. I hope to make it a memorable experience."

"Me too."

"Let me deal with my colleagues; I'll meet you at home at about nine."

"Where is your apartment?"

She stretched out to her handbag on the bedside table and extracted a key fob. She slid one off the ring, gave it to me, and said, "If you arrive before me, make yourself comfortable. The apartment is on the first floor above the solicitors on Station Road."

"Around the corner from my house."

"I know."

"How cosy."

We showered again, dressed, and tidied the room. I left while Jenny waited for her colleague.

I ran down the stairs and along the corridor toward the front entrance. I was about to turn the corner by the pay phone into reception when I heard voices from the other end. A female was giggling. It sounded familiar.

I stopped and peeked around the corner. There was only a glimpse of Sara, and she was with Dwight, one of the American guys who had accompanied Jenny and Inge Lise to the football match the previous year.

They headed up the stairs to, I assume, Room 118.

I shook my head.

She didn't hang about. I thought.

Am I jealous? I am a bit, but there is not much I can do about it, and Jenny was an intriguing replacement. At least Sara wasn't with the weirdo who had irritated Inge Lise. What was his name? Oh yeah, Chuck.

I turned and went home.

CHAPTER 16

2023

On my return journey, neither leaf nor frost played a role, and the train delivered me to Market Harborough on schedule. I walked the three-quarters of a mile home to shake down Ginny's excellent lunch, hoping Chris or Inge Lise had sent news. Sadly, not a single letter, voice message, or email welcomed me back. At least I could have an early night.

The following day, I popped over to Milo's café for my usual pot of tea and mulled over recent events.

The Henley stalker worried me; somehow, we were connected, but how could I confirm or eliminate me as the culprit?

I panicked about what else I might have been up to while intoxicated, not realising how low I had sunk. I've always had a low resistance to alcohol, and since I left Henley, had made a point to limit myself to a maximum of two drinks. Perhaps these were the events leading to my decision.

The details of the final night continued to elude me. John, Ivan, and Keith had been no help, but why would they be? After a few beers, they were also out of it. I needed someone sober. Sara and Jenny were the only possibilities.

I needed to trace both of them.

I called John Harker.

"How did it go in Denmark?" asked John.

"Not at all well. I did meet Chris. He does resemble me, but he has parents. They are deceased and are on his birth certificate. Inge Lise was away, so I left a note at her office. It's up to her to contact me."

"What's next?"

"John, sorry, but I haven't been completely transparent. I didn't return to Henley to look for a long-lost girlfriend with potential offspring. My real reason was to uncover what happened on Sunday, April twenty-first, 1968, in the Red Lion."

"Sounds ominous to have stuck with you all these years."

"It could well be serious, John, but I was drunk, and my memory is a complete blank. All I do know is the next morning, the shame was so embarrassing it drove me to join the police and vow to quit booze and stay celibate for my remaining days."

"Sounds like a hell of a party."

"We were celebrating our football team's first victory. I returned to Henley to track down two girls at the party who were the only ones sober enough to remember what happened. One was a bartender; the other worked for the American Government. Also, can you check the old files on The Henley stalker from around the same time frame?"

"There was a stalker in Henley?"

"The local newspaper was obsessed with the case."

"I'll have a word with them and look in police

archives, but something so ancient may not even be digitised. With the amalgamation of stations, the original could be in one of several locations, if anywhere. Tell me more about the girls."

"Won't it be a problem if you're caught using police resources for a personal matter?"

"Yes, but new evidence has come to light on the Henley stalker case; searching for people involved at the time is an inevitable part of the investigation."

"I don't recall mentioning new evidence."

"Neither do I, but being in charge has advantages, and we love resolving cold cases."

"The bartender is Sara Marshall, nee Cowan, aged twenty in 1968. Last heard of in the village of Sonning, married to a Colin Marshall. The other person is Jenny Leovich, aged twenty-six. She was an American citizen working in logistics at the London Embassy. She lived on Station Road in Henley from 1967 until the twenty-first of April 1968, when she and her Secret Service colleagues protecting Jackie Kennedy departed unexpectedly. Does this help?"

"Jackie Kennedy was in Henley?"

"Her sister lived nearby."

"Listen, the computer power we have nowadays is incredible compared to when all this occurred. My concern is that it could have been too long ago, and no details were entered into the database. Concerning the girls, there may be more modern events such as buying a house, a traffic violation, or unpaid debts. Any of them might lead to their current whereabouts. You only want to talk to them, right?"

"Of course, what else?"

"You don't hold any grudge?"

"Certainly not."

"All right, Ollie. I'll see what I can dig up, but please keep this confidential."

"Sure, John, and thanks."

"My pleasure, but it will take a few days, and I can't promise anything."

CHAPTER 17

1968

Back home in my room on Queen Street, I stared out the window, thinking about my new predicament. I'd woken that morning with one girlfriend only to be spending tonight with a new one. While my loins were relishing the attention, my head spun with confusion. Images of Sara and Jenny alternated with Inge Lise. As each girl morphed into another, my emotions changed. With Sara and Jenny, I grinned at the debauchery, but with Inge Lise, they switched to a lovely house with children running around. I conceded I was more content with that picture than the other two. I shaved, trimmed my split ends, changed into a pink Leander hoody and clean Levis, and joined my parents for supper.

Inquisition, I thought by their serious expressions.

"Do I take it Inge Lise doesn't feature in your plans?" asked Mum.

"Sorry," I said. "I know you liked her and had visions of a daughter-in-law, but she hasn't replied to a single letter. If one arrives in the next week or two, perhaps," I said. "But I'm kind of acclimatising to life without her."

"You have another girlfriend?" asked Mum.

"I do, but she's more of a girl who is a friend. Her name is Jenny."

"Are we going to meet, er Jenny?" asked Mum.

"It's not that serious. Later on, maybe if we click, I'll spend the night at her place, so don't wait up for me."

"Another au pair?" asked dad.

"Er, no, she's American."

"Is she on holiday?" asked Mum.

"No, she works for the Embassy in London. Now, she's handling the logistics for Jackie Kennedy's protection team. They are staying at the Red Lion."

"Most international of you?" said Dad. "Shame she's not an au pair."

"Broadening my horizons," I said, wondering what it was with Dad and au pairs.

"Jackie Kennedy," said Mum, who seemed beside herself with excitement. "What an amazing woman. Will you meet her?"

"No, but Jenny will."

"How exciting. I wish I could?"

"I'll ask," I said. "But don't hold out your hopes."

"Can we stop this frivolous nonsense," said Dad, looking at Mum with an irritated expression. "We'd agreed on a serious conversation. How's it going with college?"

"To be frank, I'm not enjoying the course. I love art but prefer to explore creativity at my own pace rather than be taught how to pass an exam."

"What would you prefer?" asked mum. "Languages, sciences?"

"Architecture or Law?" added Dad.

"Too academic," I said.

"Everything at University involves studying," said mum. "I had four years of it before graduating as a teacher."

"Did you enjoy it?" I said.

"I loved it."

"And your job?"

"Initially, yes, but it was more of a vocation when I started during the war. I taught many of those poor kids who were evacuated from London. Many lost their parents in the Blitz, and I was the only adult there for them."

"What about today?"

"The job has changed dramatically. Education has become politicised. Everyone, except the rich, has the same education regardless of ability. I must teach a set curriculum to all and prepare them to pass exams even the dumbest can scrape through. Today's Leaders don't want the masses to have more than a basic level of education to ensure they slot into all the tedious jobs they need to fill. The consequence is that kids show less respect than we did. Mainly because the future we paint for them is dull, which makes them bored, so they misbehave. Plus, whatever bad things they do have no repercussions. We wouldn't dare disobey our parents or the authorities, but the attitude some of my pupils show toward me is horrendous. They have no sense of patriotism or belief in God and can't be bothered to help anybody less fortunate than themselves. One boy called me a bossy cow the other day."

"We would have been thrashed for such disrespect," said Dad.

"In your day, fear of the cane kept the adults in

control," I said. "And made sure yet another generation toed the Queen and country line. However, it did nothing to encourage kids to discover themselves or push themselves harder to succeed at their passion. We baby boomers aren't in the least bit interested in toeing anybody's line, and you can forget fighting wars and slaving in mines or car factories for a pittance so the wealthy can stay in power. Why do you think we are breaking free from those shackles? We want a better world, not a carbon copy of your mistakes. Listen to our music, see how we dress and wear our hair; we are trying to smash convention, not submit to it."

"And when the Russians come marching over Henley Bridge," said Dad. "Tiddlywinks at dawn?"

"Dad, we can't spend our lives worrying about what some warped megalomaniac might or might not do. We must focus on building a better country with a more egalitarian and inclusive society. Other nations will admire our example and follow suit."

"A luxury we didn't have," said Dad. "If we had refused to serve our country in 1939, we'd be speaking German and living in fear of being shot for speaking our mind."

"Those were unique circumstances to which your generation responded magnificently," I said. "But if the previous lot hadn't castrated Germany at the Treaty of Versailles, there wouldn't have been a Hitler."

"Fair enough," said Dad. "In those days, power was invested in too few people."

"It still is, Dad. The wealthy still own almost everything funded by what their forefathers profited by or stole from the colonies. They control Parliament, not the voters."

"Britannia ruled the waves," said dad. "We had the largest Empire the world had ever seen."

"And you were proud of it, whereas we are ashamed by the brutal behaviour used to make them comply with our will. We must change things."

"You'll need the vote first," said mum.

"You watch us," I said. "In the next year or so, the voting age will be reduced from twenty-one to eighteen. Finally, the youth of this country who want change can have a voice."

"I didn't know you were interested in politics," said mum.

"As an observer," I said.

"Can't you see the Trade Unions are throttling Britain," said Dad.

"They too want change, Dad, and to be paid a fair wage. We are fed up with being controlled by rich white people determined to hang onto their wealth by paying peanuts, cutting costs, and never doing anything properly. It's why most British cars are crap. It's about time they shared power and wealth with all of us, not the few. Without our labour, they would have nothing. We should work as a team, not them versus us."

"Wouldn't that make us Communists?" said mum.

"Nonsense," I said. "Communism forbids freedom to follow your passion, and we need passionate independent people in positions to make appropriate decisions, not those supporting a dictated inflexible dogma. Our leaders should represent all of us, not those chosen for local constituencies because it's their turn or they went to the right school."

"With such enthusiasm for change, you should switch from Art to Politics," said Mum.

"Sorry, as I mentioned earlier, none of the

traditional professions excite me. And who would want to be a politician? The media shoots them down in flames whatever they do."

"What would get you up in the morning?" asked Dad.

"I like the idea of the police, preferably a detective."

"I'm surprised after what you've been saying," said Mum. "I can't see such a staid, plodding career turning you on."

"I enjoy unravelling real puzzles."

"It takes a while to climb the police ladder," said Dad.

"Yes, but at least I will be learning on the way up."

"True," said Dad.

"Have you made any inquiries about how to join or what qualifications you need?" asked Mum.

"No, but I could inquire at the local station."

"Good," said Dad.

"Sorry to disappoint you, but I don't want you to waste your money on educating me for a career I would be unhappy with."

"Does this mean you want to quit college?"

"I thought I'd persevere until the end of summer term. Would half a degree be acceptable?"

They looked at each other and sighed.

"Fine," said Mum. "But keep us posted about what the police have to offer."

"And try and keep up your rowing," said Dad. "After your success at smashing your personal best, you've let it go. Any reason?"

"I'm a bit young for a midlife crisis, but ever since Inge Lise vanished, I need to replace her huge hole in my life with something new. I'm experimenting."

"Dad was the same when he was demobbed," said

Mum.

"Demobbed?" I asked.

"A polite way of letting soldiers go because they were no longer needed as cannon fodder," said Dad. "We were given a suit, a few quid, and had to take any job. We had neither money, choice, nor escape routes. It was do something, anything to earn money or starve. Thankfully, I took to sales like a duck to water. Promise me this, son. Don't get involved with these new-fangled drugs. You don't know what is in them or how they may damage your mind."

"I can assure you, Dad, I have never touched them or been interested in doing so. It is dumb to play with unknown poisons."

"Alcohol is a poison," said mum.

"Yes, but it is socially acceptable, and I almost know how to handle it."

"And you'll get back to your rowing?" said Dad.

"I'll try."

"I can only note that the past is beautiful because one never realises an emotion at the time. It expands later, and thus we don't have complete emotions about the present, only about the past."

Virginia Woolf

CHAPTER 18

2023

It was Christmas Eve, and I almost missed the packed Twyford train from Paddington with standing-room only. I was beginning to regret accepting Anita's invitation. Thankfully, a young man restored my faith in human kindness by offering me his seat and helped me heave my case up onto the narrow shelf where it teetered dangerously. Hopefully, it wouldn't fall on my head.

What had Anita said about Christmas? Prime time nostalgia. Nightmare was more appropriate as I ticked off the list of things to hate about the season of Goodwill.

Exaggerated weather forecasts promising freezing temperatures and the elusive White Christmas. Santa's sleighs and red-nose reindeer dominated British airwaves, plugging the latest chocolate, drink, or perfume, without which Christmas would be a disaster. Repetitive Christmassy songs with jolly Radio DJs digging up Noddy Holder fifty times daily. Over ten non-stop feasting days, overindulging in mince pies, presents, and agony as dysfunctional families reunited for their annual battle for the remote in front of the TV.

If it was only for a day or two, fine. But all this comes after the retail build-up, which kicks off as soon as summer holiday suitcases are returned to the attic. Three months of running around packed high streets scouring for Grandma's sickly-sweet sherry, stinky socks for Auntie Doris, and too many inappropriate toys for ungrateful grandchildren. Why do so many run themselves ragged to celebrate a religious event from over two thousand years ago, believed by less than seven per cent of the population? Was it nostalgia for happy childhoods, ritual, tradition, or the combined power of all three? Is this what appeals to Anita?

I stopped celebrating when my parents passed over twenty years ago. My mother had been the driving force behind it. Like Anita, she adored everything about Christmas. My dad and I went along with it to give her pleasure. I had failed in the grandchildren's department, which meant I was her target. I received so many presents it was embarrassing. Rubbish went to the charity shop, and I donated the remainder to the Police Christmas Draw.

However, after shaky beginnings with yukky sandwiches, she had developed into an excellent chef. I often recalled her succulent meal while chasing dry turkey and lumpy gravy around a plate in the Police canteen or at the Golf Club staff lunch.

At least Anita can cook, I thought as I boarded the Henley train at Twyford.

Good King Wenceslas was blaring out over the tinny loudspeakers. People of all ages were wearing ridiculous reindeer or snotty snowmen pullovers. They were even smiling and chatting with each other instead of their usual silent scowling into phone screens.

When the train pulled out of the station, I texted Anita to tell her I was on my way.

We are all here, she had replied, even Norman. I'll pick you up.

Excellent, I thought as the train gathered pace. Norman Shannon and the rest of the gang together again. All because my memory after a few beers was pathetic. I wondered what the next few days would reveal. Since my last trip here a few weeks ago, no further developments have been added to my trip down memory lane. Nothing from Inge Lise or Chris, and absolute silence from John Harker. Perhaps he had a more pressing case but was probably enjoying the rest while crooks hung up their swag bags for a Christmas break.

The atmosphere on the train was infectious, and I found my usual grumpy self, almost chuckling along with the carefree banter spiked with a degree of healthy cynicism Brits do so well.

We disembarked at Henley as a jolly group of chums united by everyone wishing each other a Merry Christmas as we headed off to indulge our celebrations. Strangers were hugging and shaking hands, declaring eternal friendship. I shook my head, mystified by the difference a holiday makes. In ten days, they will be back to their usual tedious routine. Misery on the eight-ten to Paddington would once again prevail. By the end of January, they would start planning for the next one.

Anita was waiting at the end of the platform with another woman of similar age and appearance. I had no idea who she was, but as she gazed mischievously into my eyes, her younger face flashed before me. It was Virginia, Anita's older sister. The chubby cheeks and sensual grin had gone, but the brown eyes still sparkled, and her inherent warmth exuded around her like a halo.

We hugged.

Virginia wept.

I sobbed.

Anita joined us.

This was going to be the reunion of a lifetime.

Anita passed the tissues around as we walked to her car.

"Here," she said, giving me the rest of the packet. "You're going to need these."

We giggled like children.

As Anita drove her small electric car the short distance to her house, I sat in the back and looked at the two of them in the front. I had another flashback; we had done this before.

"Didn't we use to take weekend breaks together?" I asked.

"Eight of our gang travelled all over," said Virginia.

"We borrowed our mother's car for five of us, and three crammed into Andy's Sunbeam Alpine sports car," said Anita. "There was only room for one to squeeze in the back seat."

"Usually Sonia," said Virginia. "She was the smallest."

"Why didn't we take the Daimler?" I asked.

"We did occasionally, but it was too heavy on petrol and unreliable," said Anita. "We broke down in the middle of Dartmoor. Paul had to walk miles to find a phone box to summon the AA and didn't get back until the next morning with a mechanic. We slept in the car, all huddled up against the cold with no food and water."

"It was fun," said Virginia.

"Except when we needed the toilet," said Anita.

"I trust I behaved."

"You were always the perfect gentleman," said Virginia.

"Oblivious to our charms," said Anita.

"But then Inge Lise came along," said Virginia as we pulled into Anita's driveway. "And you were smitten."

"None of us stood a chance after that," said Anita. "Come, Ollie, let's introduce you to some of your oldest and dearest."

I was shocked by Norman.

He was waiting in the hallway in a wheelchair as Anita opened the front door and ushered me in. He was skinny and frail, but his eyes blazed with rage.

"Ollie," he croaked.

"He's almost blind," whispered Anita.

"And deaf," said Virginia. "And easily confused."

I approached the chair, bent down, and grasped his hands.

"Yes, Norm, it's me."

He smacked me on the side of the head.

My ear rang momentarily, but it wasn't a decisive blow.

"Norman," said Virginia. "You promised."

"I've been saving that for fifty-six fucking years," said Norman grinning like a Cheshire cat.

"Language, Norman," said Virginia.

"It was worth the risk," said Norman, cackling and rubbing his palms together.

By now, the other old friends had gathered at the rear of Norman's chair. I looked at them one by one with a pleading expression.

"What did I do?" I said.

"It's what you didn't do," said the medium-height bald man behind Norman's chair. His stature had changed, but the face with round, chubby cheeks was unmistakable.

"Paul?" I said.

He nodded.

"And Sonia," said a slender woman, popping her head behind him. She looked worn and weary, but I could detect the young girl between the wrinkles. "Poor Norm has been smouldering with rage ever since you vanished without so much of a goodbye."

I went around the chair and hugged them both.

"Don't forget," croaked Norman. "How he treated the gorgeous German girl, what was her name?"

"Christiane," said Anita.

"I bet he can't remember her," said Norman. "Useless when drunk. Inconsiderate and rude. I had to console her for weeks after you dumped her like a sack of trash and ran off with that slut of a barmaid. Gentlemen don't behave like that. Anyway, old friend, it's off my chest so we can relax and enjoy Christmas. Hug me."

So, I did.

He gripped me hard and sobbed.

"Feel better now?" I whispered in his ear.

"What?" he said. "Speak up, man."

"Good to see you," I shouted. "You look well."

"Bollocks," he croaked. "Three months, they've given me."

"They said that four years ago," said Anita.

"What's wrong with him?" I asked.

"Nothing," shouted Sonia into Norman's ear. "He's

a cantankerous old bastard squeezing as much sympathy as possible from his few remaining mates."

"Why don't you get a hearing aid?" I asked, using Sonia's more efficient communication method.

"Nothing wrong with my hearing," said Norman.

"He's tight-fisted," said Paul. "He made a fortune with Bitcoin but refused to spend any of it on his welfare."

"Where does he live?" I asked.

"Still in the same house at the top end of Norman Avenue," said Virginia. "He installed a lift so he can continue there as long as he can but refuses to splash out on a hearing aid. He's adamant they are for old people."

"He lives on his own?"

"No, I am his live-in carer," said Virginia.

"And wife," said Anita.

"I thought you were hung up on some actor guy?" I said.

"He died several years back," said Virginia. "We had no kids, so Norman and I made an arrangement."

"All I'm good for nowadays," added Norman. "Arranging."

"He never married," said Virginia. "Well, except me."

"Too busy making money," said Paul.

"Got to leave it to someone," said Norm, grasping Virginia's hand. "It won't be long now."

"How old is he?"

"Don't you dare," said Norm.

"He's eighty-seven," said Virginia. "I took a sneak peek at his birth certificate."

"At last, we have the truth," I said. "Talking of money. What happened to the Daimler?"

"Norm gave it back to me," said Paul with a wistful sigh. He looked well except for trembling hands. "Bit rusty, though."

"Keeps promising to do it up," said Sonia. "But no matter how much I nag, we still have to park our main car on the street because we can't move the damn Daimler out of the garage."

"You fell in love with me because of my beautiful jalopy," said Paul. "I can't get rid of it now."

"And now he never will," said Sonia, indicating his shaking hands.

"Lunch is ready," shouted Ginny from the dining room.

Anita led the way into a spacious room overlooking a charming back garden surrounded by tall fir trees, flower beds, and a terrace furnished with a timber table and chairs. A huge Christmas tree dominated the dining room corner next to an enormous fireplace with a pile of logs and kindling waiting to be lit. The mantelpiece was covered in cards, and several strings of cards hung from the walls, decorated with yet more fairy lights. My mother would have adored it.

The table was laid exquisitely with cloth napkins, crystal glasses, and gold-rimmed white porcelain crockery.

"The grandchildren made the place cards," said Ginny as I picked up a beautiful pen-and-ink sketch of an oarsman in front of Leander. It had my name on it, and the likeness to a younger me was incredible.

"Where are they?" I asked.

"They will be back for supper this evening," said Ginny. "We should make the most of the peace while we can."

"What about John and your husband?" I asked.

"They have gone to pick up Mike's mother," said Ginny. "She lives in a care home in Bristol."

"Another stubborn fool who won't move," said Virginia. "What is it about old people?"

"Stuck in our ways," said Norman. "We resist change because we've run out of energy to learn new things. It's why I no longer bother with my computer. They keep changing the operating system, and I can't keep up."

"Do you have kids?" I asked, looking at Paul and Sonia.

"Three," said Sonia. "Two boys and a girl but not a grandchild between them."

"Too busy," said Paul.

"Do they live nearby?"

"The elder son, Nigel, is in South Africa with my brother, Pete," said Paul. "He runs the family winery in Stellenbosch. He's gay."

"Nothing wrong with gay," said Norman. "I've swung both ways all my life."

"What?" I said, shocked to the core. "I never suspected a thing."

"My generation was used to hiding it," said Norm. "Don't forget, it was only legalised in 1967, before you vamoosed. What about your other children, Sonia."

"Our youngest son, Ray, works for the UN in Geneva," said Sonia. "He married a Swiss girl from a tiny village near Lausanne called St. Prex overlooking the French Alps. They sail on the lake every free moment."

"Our daughter, Barbara, has MS," said Paul. "She is in a hospice in Caversham. They don't expect her to last much longer."

"I'm so sorry," I said.

"It will be a relief for us all," said Paul. "We've nursed her ourselves for thirty years."

"And it was a real privilege," said Sonia, a tear in her eye.

"We've all got to go sometime," said Norman. "Let's try and enjoy what we have, and although he doesn't deserve it, welcome Ollie back into our fold. Ginny, my dear, can you pour some drinks? It's just the one for Ollie, though. We don't want him disappearing again."

Now I recall why I loved this man so much. He always could say the right thing at the right time to defuse the moment.

It was a light lunch of vegetable soup, farmhouse bread, cheese, and pickles. We drank water and exchanged anecdotes about the past before Sonia and Paul returned home. Virginia wheeled Norm back to Norman Avenue, and I adjourned to an armchair in the lounge and turned on the TV. Thirty seconds of the latest doom and gloom around the planet, well on its way to Armageddon, was all I needed to drop off.

When I surfaced around twenty minutes later, I paced around the charming room, looking at old framed black-and-white photos of Anita's parents with the girls at various ages. There were birthday parties with cake everywhere, school plays and trips to museums, or playing in the park on swings, slides, and seesaws. I was in many of them, grinning like a Cheshire cat. I was blessed to have enjoyed a happy childhood with such adorable people. Where had it all gone wrong?

Yet, had my life been that bad? I considered Norman's revelations about his sexuality. Now, he must have had a difficult life. All those hurdles to overcome, explaining to his parents why he had no children, having to lie about who he was and hiding in the shadows even from his dearest friends. But at such a grand age, he seemed happy and fulfilled; he'd enjoyed a life well-lived and could depart to his maker, content.

Could I say the same? I couldn't bring myself to declare my life had been terrible because it hadn't. It may not have been the life I envisaged because I hadn't married the love of my life. That was something I will forever regret, but by way of compensation, I relished my job. Married police officers do not make the best of partners; the conflict between work and family life is often cause for divorce. As a single cop, I didn't have to worry about what time I finished, and when I got home, I could reflect on a case without demands for my attention. In that respect, I'd been better suited to the career than many. If I pass tomorrow, could I also say I had a life well-lived?

I shook my head. I concluded it is a work in progress; more effort is required.

Anita brought tea and chocolate digestives around five and lit the fire.

"Did you ever see Sara again?" I asked.

"No, which was sad because we had been close from our first day at infant's school. I missed her and you. To have close friends disappear at the same time affected us all. You don't remember anything?"

"As Norm said, alcohol and I had a tempestuous relationship; it's why I've hardly ever touched it since."

"And women?"

"The day I left, I promised myself to remain celibate for the rest of my life."

"Bit extreme. Why?"

"I'm sure it's to do with the shame I experienced the following day."

"What caused it."

"I've been battling with it since. Finally, I plucked up the courage to come and find out."

"Have you had relationships since?"

"There have been a few close calls, but I backed out if they wanted more than friendship."

"Didn't you trust yourself?"

"I didn't want to risk falling in love and being hurt again, so no."

"You loved all three of them?"

"Inge Lise should have been my wife and the mother of our children, but when I heard nothing from her, it damaged me. I was so sure she was the one. I couldn't understand why she never replied to my letters, so I blamed myself. I must have said or done something to turn her off me. Perhaps something terrible happened to her, and she couldn't face telling me. Sara and Jenny never replaced the intensity of emotional bonding I had with Inge Lise, but in their different ways, they loved me and dragged me out of my downward spiral. After I left, I vowed never to put myself through a similar emotional storm again and so far, touch wood, have avoided doing so."

We watched the flames roaring up the chimney. Anita went over and closed the grate, and we sat, enjoying the silence and cosiness of the moment. Here, it was homely. Was it the flickering fire, the company, or because I was back where I belonged? It gave my home in Harborough a new perspective—a mere clinical and soulless box to see out my days.

"Would you say you've had a happy life?" said Anita, sipping her tea.

"I'm not miserable, but I sometimes feel lonely and unfulfilled. I guess this quest is to try and fill the gap. I find revisiting memories of the past therapeutic. Hopefully, when I die, I can go with no outstanding issues."

"We all do. As I said on your last visit, my life is how I want it. My kids are in enduring loving relationships, my grandkids are delightful, and I can see their potential even though they are teenagers. While I enjoy a giggle with old friends, I have dedicated myself to helping my family through this adversarial and complicated life. Baby boomers need to give something back. Our selfishness has contributed to the mess we are in today. We may have smashed down old values and formed a more creative egalitarian society, but we damaged family harmony in the process. People marry for the wrong reasons because they have grown up with ignorant parents too focussed on status, appearance, and success rather than putting family first."

"I can't disagree with your logic. Why did you and John divorce?"

"John and I were always good friends long before he started dating Sonia. When Paul returned from South Africa, Sonia returned to him, and John was in a dark place. I've always been a sucker for people in pain, and I did my best to console him. Our relationship developed into something sweet and tender, so we married. Despite us both knowing it was a convenient arrangement rather than a marriage made in heaven."

"He'd loved Sonia since school."

"He still does, and it chipped away at our domestic harmony. When my parents passed, I inherited their house. As it's around the corner, I moved out, but only for sleeping purposes. It improved our relationship, and the kids barely noticed. It has remained thus until this day."

"I was shocked about Norman's sexuality admissions," I said. "I had no idea. Did you?"

"Most of us girls knew Norman preferred boys."

"How?"

"His outrageous behaviour was to disguise his preferences, but he only wanted males. As he said, he lived in a time when it was illegal, and like many gay people, pretended to like women."

"But he'd often have two girls at a time? How did he manage?"

"Most were boys posing as girls. It's how he avoided attracting police interest or being denounced by nosy neighbours. They were usually from Reading or London, never from our gang, so we never knew them beyond rudimentary conversation. Virginia says he paid them, which I can believe."

"How about Virginia?"

"She never recovered from Stephen."

"The actor?"

"Yes, he also swung, but not with her. His whole life was spent travelling around, appearing in theatres. Plays ran for about six weeks, and without fail, he would have an affair with one of the cast members. He has five children scattered about with different women but refused to perform at home."

"Why didn't they divorce?"

"Virginia is religious and would not break her wedding vows."

"Why marry Norman?"

"It was a civil ceremony at the Registry Office, so it doesn't impact her beliefs. Norm insisted they marry because he wanted to leave her everything. As his wife, she won't have to pay so much inheritance tax on his not inconsiderable fortune."

"Is she happy with the arrangement?"

"It's another mutually beneficial relationship. She has a lovely room and bath to herself. Norm is exceedingly generous, and they have a hell of a laugh. She gives him the peace of mind that everything he has accumulated will be shared among his oldest and dearest friends."

"What about the launch?"

"It's moored near Henley Bridge. We haven't used it for years, but he keeps it well-maintained. Why don't you come to next year's regatta? We could take it for a spin."

"Sounds fun."

Anita's granddaughters Megan and Melissa were the first to arrive for the evening's traditional entertainment. They were excited and pretty teenagers with more angst about what people thought of their looks than I remembered from my youth. Ginny followed with John and Mike pushing his mother Doris in a fancy electric chair. We had a fun Christmas Eve singing carols and finishing off freshly baked mince pies.

Everybody returned mid-morning on Christmas Day. Doris didn't say much at first, but after half a glass of sherry, she more than made up for it. She and Norm began the battle of the wheelchairs, racing up and down the hallway cackling like children, with Doris the clear winner. Megan and Melissa distributed presents, which were eagerly opened. I added yet another pair of hand-knitted socks to my growing collection.

After destroying the delicious turkey and al dente

sprouts with chestnuts, we sang; *We All Liked Figgy Pudding* as Anita paraded the flaming platter around the table. To digest our overindulgence, we settled in the lounge to watch the usual repeats of comedy programs. The Morecambe and Wise Christmas shows from the seventies had us in hysterics. We agreed they don't make comedy like they used to. After a discordant chorus of gentle snores, we changed to one of the most excellent Christmas Classics of all time, *It's a Wonderful Life,* with Jimmy Stewart as George Bailey and Donna Reed as his wife, Mary Hatch. When George's youngest daughter, Zuzu, closed the film with the epic line, *every time a bell rings, an angel gets his wings;* we had to pass the tissues.

"Enough," said Ginny's daughters as the credits rolled. "It's dancing time." While Megan loaded her playlist into somebody called Alexa, Melissa went around each chair and pulled us up. Beatles, Stones, and Ed Sheeran pulsed around the lounge as we jived and twitched in time with the music while Norm and Doris rolled back and forth. The teenagers knew all the words, whereas we had forgotten many. We went our separate ways before midnight, and I slept better than I had for years.

This Christmas experience was one of the most enjoyable of my life. Three generations of old and dear friends spending time reliving their youth was rewarding. I found rebuilding the long-lost camaraderie an exciting experience. With the benefit of a long life and hindsight, it was softer, less confrontational than our youth, and somehow more enduring. Now we accepted each other as we were rather than taking the piss out of different opinions, career choices, outrageous hairstyles, clothing options, and music preferences.

By lunchtime on Boxing Day, I was done. The excellent but nonstop wining, dining, and joviality were too much for a man accustomed to solitude and tiny portions. I had to let my belt out a couple of notches. We'd flogged all the anecdotes to death and were now repeating ourselves in more ways than one. It was time to go.

A text from John Harker saved the day.

I have some news, it said. Can we meet?

CHAPTER 19

1968

Jenny's flat was on the first floor of a mid-nineteenth-century, terraced house on Station Road above a solicitor's office. It was a black timber Tudor-style building with white cladding. The last thing on my mind as I let myself in the front door and climbed the steep stairs was rowing or a career in the police.

I was curious about my new lover. Apart from knowing her physically, she remained an enigma. What were her origins, and did she have a family?

I wandered about the quaint one-bedroom space, looking for something to provide answers, but found not a single photo or personal item anywhere. It was decorated traditionally, and the timber furniture was old-fashioned, but it was spotless, and the sizeable brass-framed bed with floral print eiderdown was tidily made.

I helped myself to a beer from the enormous fridge, turned on the TV, and sat in a comfortable armchair. The next thing I knew, Jenny plopped herself on my lap.

"Wake up, sleepyhead," she said. "Pay attention to me."

"What time is it?"

"After midnight."

"Hard day running a knocking shop?"

"Two girls didn't show up; I had to renegotiate with the boys and the other girls."

"Was pimping included in your job description?"

"Whatever Uncle Sam demands, I supply. Now pour me a large bourbon and a hot bath."

"Yes, ma'am," I said.

It needed two drinks, a scalding hot tub, and a back massage to unwind the tightness in her shoulders before we went to bed and made love. There was no stopping her once she warmed up. Afterwards, all I wanted was to sleep, but she needed to unburden herself from the stress of her day. Despite the tough girl image she portrayed, it was impossible to disguise her nervousness. From later on today, she would be responsible for one of the most admired women in the world.

"Do you get to meet her?" I said.

"Of course, but most of my conversations will be with her assistant. She presents me with a list of requests, and it's my job to make them happen. I liaise with the security team to research any new venues or people she meets who haven't been validated."

"She can't go shopping wherever she fancies?"

"She shouldn't but does, which is when conflicts arise. Security advises against it, but she insists on going. Meanwhile, I am in the middle, attempting to maintain harmony on both sides."

"Sounds like fun."

"Not for the pittance they pay me."

"Is this her first visit?"

"Her fourth."

"They keep them ultra-quiet. There's nothing in the press. Why haven't I noticed the security team in the hotel before?"

"They stayed at Turville Grange, but it caused too many problems. Our testosterone-fuelled macho-men had to share rooms in converted stables. During free time, they had to stay out of sight in a draughty attic without TV, drinks, or girls. Boys, being boys, they went out on the town or tried it on with female staff. Two pregnancies later, Jackie's sister said enough and banned the security team from the premises. It fell on me to source alternative accommodation, and the Red Lion was perfect."

"At the expense of the American taxpayer?"

"In the scale of things, it's a scratch compared with the Vietnam War. But don't you think after losing a husband to a crazy assassin, she deserves it?"

"Fair enough."

"And what about you, Ollie? Where do you see yourself going?"

"I have no grand master plan," I said. "I'm groping around trying to figure out what I find appealing."

"What are you studying?"

"Art, but I'm not enjoying the course, and even if I did pass with flying colours, the jobs it would qualify me for would involve sitting in a studio or office all day. My preference is for something more out and about."

"Any ideas? Or are you just going to drift through life?"

"I was chatting with my parents about this earlier. My mother more or less accused me of the same, but I don't see the point of studying crap I don't enjoy to get a job I don't like."

"Does this mean you'll be happy loading supermarket shelves until you retire?"

"Of course not, but that's exactly what I mean. Some coworkers are happy with such menial work; others like me do it to earn money."

"So, you can drink more beer?"

"To save enough for a visit to Inge Lise."

"Now, that was a good cause. Why didn't you?"

"I never heard from her."

"That wouldn't stop me."

"That's where we are different, Jenny. I wouldn't dream of imposing myself on anyone who didn't return my letters. If she wanted to see me, she would have written."

"Fair enough, so what will you do with your savings?"

"I've applied for a passport. I will put what's left in a high-interest account."

"Mister conservative."

"I'm not the gambling sort, and money does not motivate me. Your professional ladies, for example, work only for money. I will not prostitute myself for any reason. It's debasing. Your women are either desperate or greedy, and I am neither."

"But you have to do something."

"There was a guy at school who impressed me. He enjoyed learning academically and quietly studied hard. From an early age, he knew he wanted to become a doctor. He's now at Edinburgh University and halfway to achieving his dream."

"Then why don't you do the same?"

"I will, but in my way and without the academic

bit."

"What could you possibly do without studying?"

"I want to do something that I like and suits my talents."

"Play golf or row a boat?"

"No, I like observing what makes people tick and solving puzzles."

"People watching and crosswords?"

"I'm going to the police station tomorrow to learn about joining."

"Not well paid."

"No, but good pensions and retire at sixty."

"You're a bright, handsome young man; you ought to be more ambitious."

"Well, I'm not. Can we sleep now?"

"No, I need some more loving."

"Are you always this demanding?"

"No, but I've catching up to do. You're my first since I've been in the UK."

"How long have you been here?"

"One year of a two-year assignment."

"A year with er no fun?"

"My boss frowns on fraternisation with the natives. He wants to avoid a repeat of the wartime over-sexed and over here accusations."

"So, you're breaking the rules?"

"Nobody else has been inspiring enough."

"Will I get into trouble?"

"Not if we keep this between us."

"Ok, by me. How about meeting my parents."

"I'd prefer not, later perhaps when we are sure of each other."

"Who is your boss?"

"I'm not allowed to say."

"Fair enough, I'm not prying but trying to learn more about you. Where are you from?"

"Washington DC. My parents work at the Pentagon, and I hail from generations of military."

"Did those connections help with this job?"

"The family name is well respected, but I still needed the right qualifications."

"Such as?"

"Fluency in French and German, top of my class for weapons training and unarmed combat. Plus, a master's degree in politics from Harvard, and," she said with her perfect English pronunciation while thrusting her naked torso at me. "I'm real pretty. Don't you agree, kind Sir?"

I looked her curves up and down, trying to keep a straight face.

"Yooawl looks good to me," I said.

"No, mate," she said in perfect Cockney. "Your accent needs more work."

CHAPTER 20

1968

I had no idea that managing the logistics of a Secret Service protection team could be so demanding. Every night, Jenny returned home exhausted. Every night, I helped her unwind and dump all the pent-up frustration accumulated while catering to the former first lady's often impractical requests.

Catering to the whims of a dozen Secret Service men accustomed to living and playing hard was also challenging. She became a mother, counsellor, sympathetic ear for their frustrations, and finder of solutions for their high-octane sex drive. Being based in town instead of Turville Grange may have improved their leisure time, but local girls were not interested in short-term affairs, and as soon as they detected an American drawl, they made their excuses.

As the nearest professional women were in Oxford, Reading, or London, Jenny had her work cut out finding enough willing to travel to Henley. As a result, many refused or didn't turn up even though top dollars were being offered.

As Easter approached, this relentless routine continued, and despite my ministrations, I could see Jenny wilting from the stress. There was nothing more either of us could do, and she wasn't a quitter. The consequences were inevitable.

Her temper deteriorated, becoming shorter with each passing day. She flew off the handle for no reason, and there was nothing I could do to help other than listen to her meaningless rants and raves. Many included me as the root cause of her problems. I knew she was blowing off steam, but some of her words cut me up, especially about my lack of ambition.

I'd popped into the local police station to research what qualifications I needed to be accepted as a recruit. A jovial desk sergeant confirmed I had passed enough A Level exams and gave me an application form. I took it home, filled it in, and posted it off. Even if accepted, I could withdraw my application. Although the job appealed, I remained doubtful it was the right career move.

Irrespective of my career choices swinging between Art and Police, both meant leaving Henley to work. The prospect of commuting didn't concern me; most Henley residents worked out of town. While there were jobs available locally, none appealed to me. I'd always anticipated working elsewhere, but leaving Henley permanently never crossed my mind. If I followed an art career, there would be graphic design jobs in Reading or advertising in London, and I could carry on living at home. If I chose the police, I would have to leave Henley for two months for my basic training in one of several colleges around the West London area and, on completion, could be posted anywhere. It would mean a significant life change.

Half of me was excited to explore new territory, and the other reluctant to leave my friends and everything familiar.

Jenny and I had been an item for a few weeks, and while I loved her, it became apparent that she wasn't the easiest of partners. When I considered the clarity of thought I had with Inge Lise about a future together and compared this to Jenny, there was no contest. No matter how hard I tried, I couldn't envisage life with Jenny.

Easter should have been a fun weekend, but not for her and, therefore, not for me. I guessed she must have sensed this because she came home early the following Wednesday, and we spent a beautiful evening in bed, which reinvigorated both of us.

The next night, though, she was back with a vengeance.

"How did it go at the police station?" she asked.

"I have applied and am likely to be accepted. I'd have to attend training for six weeks but, after, would start at the bottom of the rung as a beat policeman somewhere in the country."

"How much do they pay?"

"Not much, but enough for a single man to live in a bedsit, save a bit, have a few beers and the occasional round of golf."

"Would you be happy with that?"

"I think so; we'll have to see."

"I need a man who wants to be rich and successful. Why can't you try harder?"

"Sorry?"

"Is that all you have to say?"

"Well, yes."

"Your plans don't consider my wishes at all.

Doesn't that bother you?"

I looked at her in astonishment.

She was glaring at me with pure hatred.

"If at some point we marry, I would certainly consider your wishes," I said. "However, that has to work two ways, and we must compromise."

She punched me hard in the ribs and screamed, "I never compromise."

I was shocked.

Nobody had hit me before, ever. Through my pain and squinted eyes, I watched her face as the realisation of what she'd done took hold.

Seeing the horror on her face, I forgave her, and we made love with a renewed passion. When she left for work early the following day, I sensed everything was fine. How wrong I was.

She arrived home in a foul mood around ten and declined a drink or massage. Her eyes were blazing with rage, and her body was shaking. This was not the girl I fell for."

"What is wrong?" I asked.

"I can't say," she said, glaring at me as if I was the cause of her agony.

"Why not?"

Tears streamed down her face. I'd never seen her so upset.

"Is it so bad?" I said, reaching out to comfort her.

"It's terrifying," she sniffed, pushing me away.

"A hint, at least."

"I overheard a colleague say something unexpected. Ollie, I don't know what to do about it."

"What did he say?"

"If I tell you, I'm dead."

"Inform your boss."

She shook her head.

"My god, it's him."

She nodded.

"Do you have physical evidence?"

"Yes," she whispered.

"Write everything down, store it in a safe place, and don't mention anything to anyone until you are certain, especially me. You could be placing me in danger."

"You're worried about your precious self?"

I glared at her. I sensed nothing, not even anger.

"I'm done. Goodbye, Jenny," I said, turning away from her. I let myself out of the apartment and headed downstairs.

I'd reached the front door when I heard her thundering after me.

"Ollie," she said, trying to wrap her arms around me and kiss my cheek. "Please don't go."

I placed my hands on her shoulders and gently pushed her away, holding her at arm's length. She twisted out of my grip and stood before me, panting, her face contorted with anger.

I gazed into her eyes.

All I could see was hate and pain. The damage was too much. I had done nothing to cause or deserve such malevolence. "Once again, Jenny, goodbye," I said, turned, opened the door, and went home, not looking back.

My parents were already in bed asleep.

I changed into my pyjamas, lay down, and stared at the ceiling, my mind in turmoil. Had I been fair, was leaving Jenny the right thing?

When Mum brought me a cup of tea shortly after dawn, I was still trying to answer the question.

My mum sat on the bed while I sipped tea.

"Troubles?" she said.

"Funny how you always know."

"I'm your mother. It comes with the territory."

"I ended it with Jenny last night."

"Why?"

"Unreasonable behaviour."

"Yours?"

"No, hers. With Jackie Kennedy here, Jenny is under incredible stress. I've been trying to calm her down, but now she's taking it out on me."

"Your father and I are no angels. We also have differences of opinion."

"Does he hit you?"

"Of course not; we keep our distance, calm down, and talk it out. Was she violent?"

"Yes, and as a trained agent, she knows what she is doing."

"You did not attempt to restrain her or return the favour?"

"None."

"You've done the best thing, son. If she is this unstable after a few weeks, she will become worse. Any decisions on your career?"

"Not definite, but I'm leaning toward the police."

"Good," said Mum. "Whatever your decision, we will be happy for you."

"Thanks, Mum."

I dressed and went to college with a heavy heart.

CHAPTER 21

1968

The victory over the Bull was more than a rare win for the Red Lion football team. It lifted us off the bottom of the league table where we had been wallowing all season.

The beer flowed amid jeers and cheers as fans and team members relished the euphoria of victory and pride in our achievement. Richard Elsdon, the owner, made a rare appearance and bought a round for the team—only half a pint each, though.

Halfway through the evening, with Cliff Richard belting out *Congratulations* on the jukebox, Ivan, one of our heroic goal scorers, tapped me on the shoulder and said, "Sara wants a word."

I glanced toward the bar and caught her eye as she poured another pint. She reinforced Ivan's message with an urgent head movement. I squeezed through the crowd and stood before her.

"What is it?"

"Jenny needs to see you in the usual room."

"But I thought our American friends were using it."

"They've gone."

"Including Dwight?"

"Bastard didn't even say goodbye."

"Surely, they wouldn't leave Jackie unprotected; she's not due to leave until Wednesday."

"I don't know. Go and see Jenny. She will explain, and Ollie."

"What?"

"Please let me know. I don't even have Dwight's address."

"I'll be back. Look after this."

I left my half-finished beer on the bar, had a pee in the gents, and made my way upstairs. What could Jenny possibly want with me? Even though my head was buzzing with the alcohol, I couldn't imagine any reason for getting back together with her. If what Sara said was true, perhaps Jenny was leaving and wanted to say farewell. When entering the corridor leading to Room 118, I spotted the back of a man disappearing around the far corner wearing a long light-coloured mackintosh. Was he anything to do with Jenny? I tapped on the door.

"I told you to fuck off," shouted a female voice from within.

"Jenny, it's me, Ollie. Sara said you wanted to see me."

"Shit," said Jenny opening the door, pulling me inside and locking up behind us. She was dressed in her usual loose clothing with her blond hair in a ponytail and seemed troubled.

"Sorry, I thought it was a colleague," she said, looking sheepish.

"Sara is worried about Dwight," I said. "What's going on? Where are the others? Who is protecting the former first lady?"

"I can't tell you," said Jenny. "Shall we say that her visit has been cut short due to unforeseen circumstances, and the boys are no longer required?"

"Why are you still here?"

"I wanted to say goodbye and sorry," she said, looking remorseful. "You cannot believe how much stress I've been under. Thankfully, it's almost over."

"Then what?"

"I'll go home."

"To Washington?"

"Yes, to await my next assignment."

"At least you can see your family."

"I'd rather quit the service and stay in Britain."

"Why?"

"I've had enough. Your life isn't your own."

"For Queen and country, we say."

"For Queen and country," she mimicked. "Or Uncle Sam, it still means the same nonsense. Long hours, poorly paid for risking your life, and surrounded by an environment of lies and deceptions. It's doing me in."

"Without a job at the Embassy, you'll have to leave the country. I have experience of this."

"With Inge Lise?"

"Correct."

She moved toward me, put her arms around me, and cuddled into my chest. I was sorry for her and hugged her back. Perhaps she reminded me of the final moments with Inge Lise, or maybe too much beer confused me.

"We could get married?" she said, grinding herself against me.

"I pushed her away to look her in the eye."

"Sorry, Jenny. You're a beautiful woman but too complicated for me."

Her face clouded over for a second before contorting into the furious bitch I had seen a few nights ago.

"How dare you reject me? I'm the best thing that ever happened to you."

"Whoa, Jenny. Hold on. We've had an affair for three weeks; we fell out, and you hit me. Those are hardly grounds for a long and happy marriage."

"There you go again with your traditional values," she screamed. "Everything must be how men want it. When are you going to wake up to the modern world? Women are now equal."

"Equality doesn't justify punching people or bullying them into an unwanted marriage."

"Don't be a sissy?" she screamed, regarding me with hate as her face contorted. How could beauty and love morph into rage so quickly and, as far as I was concerned, for no reason? I was right to have left her. She was more than problematic.

"I'm wasting my time here," I said, turning to go. "It's impossible to discuss anything with you."

She spun me around and began punching me in the ribs with her fists. Fast and furious, as if I were a punching bag. It hurt.

Through the pain, I reacted instinctively to defend myself. I smashed her as hard as I could in the face with my fist.

I stared at her, frozen with shock. What had I done?

She stopped and shook her head, blood running out of her nose. With a cold expression, she glared at me before grabbing me around the neck.

Everything went blank.

CHAPTER 22

2023

I was happy to escape Anita's Christmas holiday camp. But as we gathered in the hall to exchange farewells, half of me remained confused. Having these old friends back in my life had been uplifting, and we agreed to reconvene regularly, which was most satisfying. However, meeting them again was to uncover my past, not to build a new and probably limited future.

I sighed with relief when a large black BMW pulled into Anita's crowded drive, and John Harker climbed out. He was burly but solid and fit-looking with cropped hair. He shivered in the cold December air, wearing a light pullover and chinos. He stood by the car door and waited. We had one final hug each, and I carried my bag over the frost-covered gravel. John put it in the boot while I climbed in the front passenger seat.

John started the engine, reversed out, and drove off. I waved but didn't look back.

"Whew," I said.

"Hard work?" he asked.

"Emotional," I said. "These were my closest friends over fifty years ago, and this was our first reunion. It went well, but I'm unaccustomed to spending so much time near humans, friends or not."

"Did they have anything to add?"

"No, but I have remembered some of what happened on my final night in Henley."

"Good or bad?"

"I hit a woman, John."

"That's a hell of an admission, Ollie. You're the calmest person I've known. Were you provoked?"

"To be fair, Jenny was a trained CIA agent. She attacked me, so I fought back, but she still overwhelmed me, and I blacked out. I have no recollection about how I got home, only that the next morning, I had bruised ribs, a sore neck, and a sense of shame so great I couldn't face my friends."

"At least you can stop beating yourself up about it."

"More information is required before I can completely let go. Since when have we been using fancy German cars?"

"Since the British stopped making them. They are more economical per mile than the wrecks we used to buy and are fast and reliable."

"Good point; I forget how often a crook outpaced us on the way to a crime scene."

"The Austin 1100 was a tinny heap of junk; the Ford Anglia resembled a box on wheels, but there was something about the leather smell in those old Jaguars, and the tone of their valve radios was incredible."

"Great to listen to when broken down, which was often. You mentioned news."

"I'll tell you later at my office."

"Fair enough. Did you find something?"

"I've been researching the Henley stalker. There isn't anything on the computer other than a reference to a file pending digitisation. I've tracked it down to Oxford, where it was sent when they closed the Henley Station. They are photocopying the content and will send it to me in the next day or two. As for the girls, there is a comprehensive file on Sara and her ex-husband, Colin."

"Is Sara alive?"

"Yes, we're going to see her first. She's in a hospice in Caversham."

"Oh dear. I fear it's the same place as the daughter of two of my friends. She has MS and is near death."

"So is Sara. She has level four pancreatic cancer, but her mind is still fine and feisty, according to the matron."

"She's expecting us?"

"The doctor, Sara, is not. How did you part company?"

"I think it was amicable. How long has she been divorced?"

"Over thirty years. I must warn you Sara and her ex have criminal records."

"For what?"

"He was a minor drug dealer. Sara was charged with dealing in small quantities of marijuana and sentenced to prison. However, when arrested, she came clean about her prior activities."

"Go on," I said, drumming my fingers on the door handle.

"While working in the Red Lion, she used to sell birth control pills to those not registered on the NHS."

"Such as au pair girls?"

"Correct, the problem was, the pills were fakes."

"Inge Lise said she bought some from a friend. Perhaps it was Sara?"

"It's one possibility that may be relevant to your conversations with Chris in Aarhus."

"Sara was always looking for ways to make money, and I suspected some were dubious. However, she had a sick mother who needed a live-in nurse who cost a fortune, so never challenged her about it."

"Her lawyer explained these mitigating circumstances to the court, which is why she received a mild sentence."

"So, she's not a bad person. Any further arrests?"

"None; after parole, she never darkened our doors again."

"Did she reveal the name of her pill supplier?"

"There's nothing in the record."

The hospice was a grand old eighteenth-century house on the fringes of Caversham converted into a National Health Service facility thanks to the state taking it over from its bankrupt owner. We drove through the open, white-painted entry gates onto a gravel drive and parked next to several other vehicles on a lot in front of the imposing red brick building. It had been extended left and right by two floors of more modern wards built in a similar style.

"Tell them your name," said John. "They will take you straight up to Sara's room."

I rang the bell and was buzzed into a spacious lobby acting as the reception. A puny Christmas tree blinked in a corner. Immediately, I noticed the cabbage odours. It was typical of the awful catering offered by state-owned establishments and reminded me of police canteens. Perhaps it was a deliberate policy to disguise the smell of death. Because this place was the final step to your maker, I had seen my parents suffer in a similar establishment during their final years, which spurred me to make a living will. I wanted control of how I departed this earth and not leave it to the whim of some doctor experimenting with my feeble body.

"Oliver Matthews," I announced to the mature lady sitting behind a counter in a white coat and tortoiseshell spectacles.

She pressed a button on a console in front of her.

Moments later, an internal door opened, and a buxom nurse around fifty in a blue uniform walked toward me with a severe expression.

"I'm sorry, Mr Matthews," she said. "Sara has taken a turn for the worse. I recommend we leave her in peace."

"Normally, I would agree," I said. "But we haven't seen each other for over fifty years. I am convinced our meeting will bring her joy to her final moments."

She looked at me with a doubtful expression and, after due consideration, said,

"Follow me."

We headed toward a grand staircase with portraits hanging on the wall of distinguished ladies and gentlemen dressed in fine clothing and posing with a cute dog or cat. We ignored the stairs and proceeded halfway along a corridor to a lift.

On the second floor, we walked to the end of the building and into a bright and pleasant room with buttermilk walls and white woodwork. The view was of the extension rooftop and fir trees marking the eastern perimeter of the estate. The heating must have been on full. It forced me to remove my hat and overcoat and park them on a cupboard by the window.

There was one hospital bed facing a flat-screen TV showing an all-day news program with the volume on low. Several pillows propped up a tiny, skeletal woman with no hair. She was dressed in a white stained gown and attached to a monitor with several drips feeding her nutrients and drugs.

"She's on morphine," said the nurse. "But her mind remains active. It might take a while to register, though. I'll leave you to it."

I approached Sara with some trepidation. I'd never been comfortable with illness and considered hospitals dangerous places; people die there. Her skin was wrinkled, pockmarked, and pale. Her hands were skeletal and covered in liver spots. Her eyes were closed, and she struggled to inhale. There was no resemblance to the woman I had known and loved, but my heart went to her. Tears filled my eyes as happy memories of our time as friends and lovers flashed before me. She bent over in her tight miniskirt and unashamed nudity as she pranced around the room after making love. Such a beautiful girl reduced to this withered old hag.

I pulled up a chair, sat down, and grasped her hand.

She squeezed mine back, opened her bloodshot eyes, and regarded me.

"Ollie," she croaked.

"Yes, Sara. Did they tell you I was coming?"

"No, I had a feeling you would."

"Why?"

"Call it women's intuition. Darling Ollie," she said, raising a gnarled hand and stroking my cheek. "Turn up the TV and lie on the bed."

"I'm not sure you are strong enough."

"I want to say goodbye."

After turning up the TV, I removed my shoes and jacket and lay next to her.

The smell wasn't too disgusting, and, in the police, I had become accustomed to humans in their degrading conditions. I turned on my side, put my arm over her chest, and hugged her. She hugged me back with surprising strength, and we wept together.

"Look at the back of my neck," she said after a few moments, her breathing more tortuous. I sat up, turned my head, and had the shock of my life.

She had a heart-shaped birthmark right under where her hairline used to end.

"What the?"

"Don't say my name. Can you forgive me, Ollie?"

I didn't know what to say, but my emotions instantly turned cold. This was Jenny, not Sara.

"Put your ear next to my mouth," she croaked. "It's easier for me to whisper."

I leaned over and did as asked.

"Now you know I am not Sara," she said. "Speak quietly; the room might be bugged. Whatever you do, never tell anyone who I am; it could lead to serious trouble for you. I'm sorry for my behaviour, but the circumstances were horrendous. My boss abused me, but I couldn't say anything because nobody would believe me. The plot I mentioned became a reality. That's why we evacuated Jackie Kennedy and the team immediately. Even a hint about it would have placed you in grave danger. If you want to know the whole sad tale, read my diaries. It's all there, and Ollie, it's huge."

"Where are the diaries?"

I looked at her as she fought for air. She looked at me with imploring eyes. "Can you forgive me?"

I studied her face, unsure how to respond, but her expression was so desperate that I'd have said anything to bring relief to such a tortured soul. "I forgive you," I said, stroking her cheek.

Her expression of relief demonstrated how much my words meant to her, but for me, it was just a kind thing to do for a dying person.

"The diaries?" I asked.

"Inge Lise," she whispered.

Her body went tense, and she held my hand with a vicelike grip.

She grinned at me, cackled, sighed, and her eyes glazed over.

I climbed off the bed and stood beside her. She was six years older than me, putting her at over eighty. According to what she had just told me, she had spent the last fifty-odd years hiding from former employers. They must not have considered her much of a risk because the CIA's tenacity in finding those they wanted was relentless, or perhaps she had been talented enough to outwit them. Regardless of the answer, I was no nearer to tracking down Sara.

However, her diaries were an exciting prospect. Not just for the content, they gave me a perfect excuse to seek out Inge Lise, regardless of whether she wanted to see me. I made a mental note to keep the existence of the diaries to myself. Until I had read them and could judge if they were a threat to anyone, they were best kept a secret, especially from John Harker.

I thought back to my last violent encounter with Jenny in Room 118, thankful for whatever reason she hadn't killed me. She looked at peace and, for the first time in years, no longer had to look over her shoulder.

One of the three loves of my life had departed. She

reminded me of my approaching mortality, but other than that brief moment of sadness, I felt nothing.

I closed her eyelids and went to find the nurse.

CHAPTER 23

2023

After the extreme heat of Jenny's room, stepping outside the hospice front door into the freezing December weather shocked my ageing bones. As I approached John's car, he put down his phone, reached over, and opened the passenger door.

"Longer than anticipated," said John as I fastened the safety belt.

"She died in my arms."

"I am sorry, but it was expected."

"Having seen her condition, it was for the best. A hospice was no place for such a vibrant person, whoever she was."

"Sorry?"

"It wasn't Sara."

"Did you recognise who?"

"Jenny."

"Positive?"

"Her birthmark."

"It was genuine?"

"Exactly as I recall."

"If it was Sara," said John, sighing. "I would have been worried."

"Wait. You knew it wasn't Sara?"

"According to the file, it should have been Jenny, but I had to know for sure before telling you the rest."

"Hence the deception. What are you going to show me in your office?"

"The file confirming it was Jenny."

"Explain," I said.

"During Easter, 1968 Jenny approached Military Intelligence with a proposal. She wanted to leave the American Secret Service."

"Why?"

"She was having a problem with a senior colleague pestering her for sexual favours and wanted out but was terrified of reporting him."

"Why couldn't she hand in her notice?"

"In those days, you couldn't quit without laborious third-degree inquisitions to satisfy Uncle Sam. They had to be confident former agents wouldn't compromise state secrets. If she had succumbed to such questioning, she would have to reveal what her colleague had been up to, which could have been dangerous. He was jealous of anyone coming near her and threatened her with violence if she looked at other men. She insisted on disappearing permanently and immediately."

"Did she provide evidence?"

"An incriminating tape recording of the senior colleague threatening her. If they needed ammunition to keep the Americans in line at some point in the future, they could use it. However, the tape wasn't why MI5 accepted her proposal."

"What was?"

"The Northern Ireland situation was worsening. Their offer to Jenny was that if she helped them and was successful, they would arrange a safe house and British citizenship."

John started the car, and we headed to his office in Central Reading.

"Why did Jenny approach MI5 and not Scotland Yard or the local Special Branch?"

"On the first of April 1968, Buckinghamshire Constabulary, Oxfordshire Constabulary, Berkshire Constabulary, Reading Borough Police and Oxford City Police amalgamated to become the Thames Valley Constabulary. The name was changed to Thames Valley Police in 1971. You can imagine the chaos Jenny faced. Who would she talk to locally? She wanted to keep her proposals secret from her colleagues in Jackie Kennedy's protection team. The last thing she needed was some blundering plod knocking on the American Embassy door and discussing her case with the Ambassador. So, she contacted an agent in Thames House. She had liaised with him before Jackie Kennedy's visit.

"What did MI5 want from her?"

"The IRA were threatening to use violence in Northern Ireland to speed up a united Ireland. MI5's scheme was to infiltrate criminal elements in the Irish Republican Army. Many were married to, or partners of, the gangsters using violence to control neighbourhoods. Some had been sentenced to drugs or burglary charges. MI5 decided someone inside jail befriending these women might yield names and hints of intentions. Behind bars, she would be safe from former colleagues who wouldn't dream of looking for her in an English jail. Jenny agreed to be charged with minor drug offences and was committed to Holloway, where for three years she uncovered a host of excellent intelligence."

"Didn't her American accent give her away?"

"What accent did she use earlier?"

"Now you mention it, Estuary English."

"Not a hint of American?"

"Nothing. Why didn't I notice?"

"You assumed she was Sara, but Jenny could mimic Estuary English perfectly."

"And Cockney. You're right; I'd forgotten. Where did Colin Marshall come in?"

"MI5 decided a man in Belmarsh might prove as revealing. They used the name of a long-dead crook from Newcastle and brought him back to life. In reality, it was an MI5 agent with a genuine Geordie accent. He started visiting Jenny in Holloway, built up his street cred in the London drug scene, was caught and sentenced."

"Was he married to Jenny?"

"They were officially married after Jenny had completed her sentence. The idea was to add more plausibility to Colin's background. Being married to a convicted drug offender worked well, enabling Colin to return to different prisons for years. And it gave Jenny a new name to hide behind."

"On our way here, you said Colin and Jenny divorced. Was that true?"

"Officially, yes."

"How did Jenny become Sara?"

"Jenny proposed the name, even provided a genuine driver's licence, passport, and birth certificate."

"What happened to the real Sara?"

"There's nothing in the file or public records."

We pulled into the underground parking entrance at Reading Police Station. John pressed a remote, and the metal door rolled upwards. We parked and headed to his office, stopping to pick up beverages from the vending machine en route.

"Here is the file," he said, clicking his mouse as we sat behind his desk, sipping the scalding hot liquid vaguely resembling tea. The Police logo disappeared, revealing an open document on the screen. I flicked through it. It confirmed everything John had told me except for one thing.

"What was the name of her boss?"

"Look," he said, scrolling back to the front page. "See the black mark at the top; the name has been redacted."

"How come you were able to access such a confidential file?"

"It's fifty-six years old and now accessible by authorised senior personnel. In another four years, it will go public."

"One more thing. The receptionist at the Hospice inquired about burial arrangements. I told her to proceed as usual."

"Meaning?"

"Jenny, under the name of Sara, will be cremated at state expense, and her ashes scattered in the Hospice grounds."

"Will you go?"

"Probably. They will email me the timings next week."

"They are obliged to announce Sara's death in the local paper. It might flush out someone who knew her."

"In which case I should go."
"I'll take you if you like."
"Thanks, John. One more thing."
"Tell me."
"If this was a secret service operation, how did my old friends in Henley know Sara married a Colin Marshall?"

"People, not places, create memories."

Ama Ata Aidoo

CHAPTER 24

2023

John dropped me off at Reading station, and I headed home to Market Harborough. The overcrowded carriage was noisy. A rowdy group of drunken Welsh people had started their New Year celebrations early. They sang *Land of My Fathers* surprisingly harmoniously as I considered what to do next. Should I contact Inge Lise or wait for Chris?

As the train departed, I wondered if Inge Lise had received Jenny's diaries. How long had she had them, how did she come by them, what did she make of them? Would they lead me to the real Sara and solve the final piece of my jigsaw? What secrets might they contain exposing me to danger? Seeing Inge Lise again had now become paramount. How could I rest with these unanswered questions dancing around my brain? I was more apprehensive now than when starting my quest.

Despite my desperation for more information, my instinct was to wait until Inge Lise declared her wishes.

While vital details were still missing from the big picture of my past, my trip down memory lane had yielded results. I had learned why I suffered a deep sense of shame, had to leave Henley, and declared a life of celibacy. Finally, I knew I had made the right decision.

Hitting a woman was an unspeakable act. I'd lost count of how many men I'd put away for violent offences against women. It never failed to give me a sense of righteousness to take these callous bastards out of circulation for a while.

One victim had been so grateful that when I'd visited her house to inform her about her husband's incarceration, she had thrown herself at me. She was attractive, and most males would have taken advantage of her, but my determination to avoid close relationships with women won through, and I let her down gently, which she respected.

There was no way I could allow another relationship to sour into the one I now knew I had with Jenny. It must have been why I had stuck to my guns for decades and kept women at arm's length. Now, I knew my decision had been right despite the many attacks of deep regret.

When seeing a happy family with delightful children, I often wondered how I would have been as a father. But now I knew I had a tipping point; I was thankful I wasn't. Alcohol and unreasonable behaviour toward me made me lash out with my fist. While it had only happened once, if I hadn't adopted celibacy and limited my intake in a relationship, I could have been violent more frequently.

I heaved a sigh of relief. My choices had worked out, but I wondered how the typical male would have handled the situation. Were we still wild animals resorting to violence as a matter of course? Or had we evolved into gentle, kind, and civilised beings? As a police officer, I was disproportionately exposed to the dysfunctional of society, so my view was distorted. If one believes in the fear-driven media reports of ever-increasing bad people, one's view of society would hold little hope for future generations. But who has faith in anything we see or hear nowadays when increased profit is the only agenda at the expense of the truth? I suspect the real world is not like that, away from the limelight. Most of us plod on through life and struggle to make ends meet. Our inherent goodness shines through with acts of kindness as and when possible.

As my train sped by green fields, then dense housing and industrial estates abutting the edge of the track, I tried to envisage what the real Sara would have done after she had been fired.

Finding a job in Henley would have been impossible. In such a small town, the negative connotations attached to her name and reputation would fly around within hours, yet she had a sick mother and was desperate for money. She had to work somewhere but needed papers. Perhaps she exchanged identities with Jenny? It was unlikely because the Americans would have found her. Had Jenny helped her with new papers?

Was it Sara selling fake pills or Jenny? Those poor women relying on them for contraception would have discovered they didn't work and been seriously aggrieved at their suppliers. Had Sara vanished because one of them sought revenge? Did she sell other types of pills? Had she and Jenny been partners? Had Inge

Lise been a client?

Sara's family would be an excellent place to start asking questions. They had been Henley people for generations, so should be easy to locate. The father had vanished when they were young, and the sick mother was probably long gone, but she had a younger sister. I could visualise her in school uniform, but the name escaped me. I made a mental note to ask Anita.

I was walking through my front door when my phone buzzed. It was Anita.

"Thank you so much," I said. "It was wonderful to see you."

"Ollie, it's not why I'm calling. Norman died last night."

"Oh no. I'm so sorry. I should have stayed."

"No, Ollie, don't go blaming yourself. It was inevitable and only a question of when. He was so happy to see you and deliver his slap. He must have had his closure and decided to let go. He passed in his sleep."

"It's how I would like to go. Any idea for the funeral?"

"You know Norman, big and loud. It will take a while to arrange it with the church and undertakers. I'll inform you as soon as it's organised. You can stay with me. There will be others, but I'll give you the upstairs room again so they don't get on top of you."

"You're an angel, thanks, Anita."

"Are you making progress?"

"I am. Sara also died yesterday."

"Oh no."

"Does she have family?"

"Her mother died about a week after you left."

"Do you recall her sister?"

"Yes, her name is Jill. She's married and has three kids and now grandchildren. She still lives in Henley."

"Do you know where?"

"Sure."

"When I know the date of the funeral, could you call her with the details?"

"Of course."

"One more question."

"Go on."

"How did you learn about Sara marrying Colin Marshall?"

"From Lee Somerville at the Catherine Wheel. It was before Christmas, 1969. We had ceased frequenting the back bar, but several popped into the front restaurant for a steak and caught up. Lee, now the manager, insisted on serving us. She showed us an advert from the Henley Standard announcing the engagement of Sara Cowan from Henley and Colin Marshall from Newcastle, both residing in Sonning. The wedding date was to be confirmed; friends were welcome. I checked the paper weekly for months, but no wedding date was publicised. Then Lee said something even more disturbing."

"What?"

"She offered Sara a job running the back bar starting Monday, the twenty-second of April 1968, which she accepted but never turned up for work. Is this useful?"

"Extremely. Listen, you must have calls to make; I'll see you at Norman's funeral."

CHAPTER 25

2024

I didn't bother with New Year. One disadvantage of living adjacent to the town centre is that when fellow Harborians decide to celebrate, they do so in large numbers in the square a few hundred metres from my abode. Thankfully, I didn't hear the scheduled rock band or fireworks. For once, the wind was in the right direction.

The following day, after a brief walk around the town centre, avoiding the mass of celebratory detritus and pavement pizzas, I stopped at the Three Swans. I joined my old golfing chums for our customary New Year's Day lunch.

"Nostalgia Man," said Ted, the provocative one. A retired solicitor and former president of the golf club. He used to be a tall, striking man with a prominent nose and full head of silver hair, but lately, he was turning frail, shrinking rapidly, and sprouting blood vessels in his chin. "How is the trip down memory lane?"

"You'd be bored with my explanation," I said.

"What, no tales of reconquering old girlfriends?" said Ted.

"Too saucy for old men like you," I said. "I wouldn't want to overexcite you. Your frail tickers might grind to a halt."

"In other words, a waste of time," said Joe, the ex-captain of the club. Retired owner of a kitchen goods shop in Adam and Eve Street and involved with the Rotary Club. He was mid-height and wiry with close-cropped grey hair.

"Not at all," I said. "Most fruitful."

"Why not regale us with your discoveries?" said Jonathan, the former club treasurer, retired accountant, and pedant. Everything had to be perfect, including his immaculate cut of white hair, moustache, and eccentric clothing. Burgundy trousers and sky-blue anorak. "Bugger, all else to talk about."

"Nonsense," I said. "You still have to debate your morning tablet consumption or compete for the dodgy knee of the day."

"Sad cases, aren't we?" said Ted.

"Whereas Ollie here has a purpose," said Joe. "His pet project gets him up in the morning."

"I have my potting shed," said Jonathan. "It keeps my mind inspired."

"I find the threat of a few weeds invading your winter beans astonishing," said Ted. "Is that enough to tempt you from a cosy bed?"

"Seriously, gents," I said. "For retired folks, keeping the brain engaged with purpose is crucial to mental and physical health. If you don't have a reason to get up in the morning, neither will your metabolism. Jonathan, it would be best if you wrote a book about the secrets of nurturing winter beans. Ted and Joe, you could collaborate on the history of Market Harborough Golf Club. For example, I had the longest drive up the first. It still leads by miles in the record book."

"It was blowing a gale, and the ball bounced off a sprinkler head," said Ted.

"One needs a bit of luck in life," I said. "Which jogs my memory, remember Speedy Sebastian?"

"Fastest eighteen holes in the club's history," said Jonathan. "What about him?"

"When I was dithering about my decision to go for assisted living or a live-in carer, I made a point of watching others who had already taken the carer route. You must have seen the older men and women trailing around the square on a forced march prodded by an ex-Bulgarian weightlifter or enticed by a tasty young Polish lass. Anyway, I spotted Sebastian with his choice of carer."

"Weightlifter or lass?" said Ted.

"Neither; she was an attractive, athletic-looking woman in her mid-forties. For a while, I was confused about my selection of the assisted living route."

"Get to the point?" said Joe. "Honestly, Ollie, your waffling is getting worse."

"Thanks for the kind remarks, Joe. Usually, carers have difficulties keeping their charges going long enough for their walk to be considered exercise. With Sebastian, it was different."

"For heaven's sake, tell us, Ollie," they all demanded.

"Sebastian was way out front; she couldn't keep up."

"Excellent, excellent," said Ted. "But seriously, Ollie, how is it going in Henley?"

"I am making progress," I said. "I've met several old

friends, but sadly, one died in my arms, and another passed almost immediately after my visit. I have to go back again for a brace of funerals."

"It's all I seem to do nowadays," said Jonathan. "As I am sure you recall, I was shipped off to a military boarding school and am an active member of their Old Boys Association. I have to dig out the school tie once a month nowadays as the old soldiers fade away."

"Sadly, it goes with the territory at our age," I said.

"I'm likely to go first," said Ted. "I'm getting to the point where I can't be bothered. Everything is becoming too much effort. I hope you can all come and see me off. It would be nice to think that as I lie in my coffin awaiting the flames of hell, a few of you will remember the fun we've had."

"Have you left instructions?" asked Jonathan.

"Crematorium, cheap coffin and no memorial plaques," said Ted. "I don't want eulogies either, but it would be nice if those inclined would stand up and say a few words. Hopefully, it will not be too insulting or vomit-inducing. I'm just an ordinary man who lived a simple life. Anything else would be embarrassing. What about you, Ollie? You have two funerals to attend. Have you thought about what you might say?"

"Good point, but not yet. I'll wait for something to inspire me, but I agree, Ted. Understated works best. The last one I attended for a former colleague had flowers saying *dad*, or, *gin and tonic*. Nothing could be so tacky."

"Shame," said Joe. "I was wondering what colour flowers to choose for my final farewell."

"And what words of wisdom did you have in mind?" asked Ted. "*Half a pint?*"

"Fuck you."

And so, the same old banter repeated itself. After a light tuna salad, I retired for a nap.

CHAPTER 26

2024

I was beginning to sense I'd re-joined the ranks of commuters as I once again caught the Henley train from Twyford. This time, I'd brought my larger suitcase because I'd be staying for a week with Anita, attending two funerals and studying the Henley stalker file with John Harker.

The first ceremony was for Jenny.

Anita had spoken to Sara's sister Jill and passed on the timing details, but she hadn't confirmed.

Anita met me at the station.

"You'll have to move back to Henley," she said as we hugged at the platform end. "I haven't provided such regular taxi services since my granddaughters declared independence."

"Once the funeral season ends, I'll visit occasionally," I said. "I only downsized recently to an assisted living complex and vowed never to repeat the relocation experience."

"I could come to you," said Anita as we exited the car park.

"I only have one bedroom," I said.

"I'd be happy with the sofa."

"Can we resolve this another day? I need to bring you up to date on my quest."

"You've heard from Inge Lise?"

"Sadly not. This is about the infamous last night."

"You've fathomed what transpired?"

"More or less, and must warn you, it paints another picture of me."

"Not the saintly figure I envisaged?"

"More monster."

"I'll brace myself."

"As John said, we were hitting the Sherbert with full gas in the Riverside Bar. Sara told me that Jenny requested my presence in Room 118. Did you know about the room?"

"Everyone did, Ollie."

"Did, er, you ever have cause to use it?"

"Certainly not."

"Anyway, I went up with some trepidation, bearing in mind I had ended my relationship with Jenny a few days before."

"Why did you end it?"

"Her unreasonable behaviour. She demanded I be more ambitious and turned violent when I didn't share her enthusiasm and mentioned joining the police."

"She hit you?"

"Hard. Did you know she was a trained Secret Service agent?"

"No."

"When I entered the room, Jenny threw herself at me, wanting to make love. But when I rejected her, she exploded and punched me in the ribs."

"How did you respond?"

"Somehow, I had to stop her, so I punched her in the face as hard as I could. She was shocked but jumped at me. Afterwards, I don't remember anything. Somehow, I found my way home and woke up in bed the next morning with a sore neck and bruised ribs, feeling ashamed but not knowing why. I don't know if she knocked me out or if my usual inadequate capacity for alcohol wiped my memory clean. But what I do know is that for the first time in my life, I became enraged enough to hit another person. In this case, a woman. Anita, I can't tell you how awful this is for me. All my professional life, I have defended women against violent partners. It gave me pleasure to lock them up. Now, it turns out, I'm as bad as the rest of them."

"Ollie, no," said Anita as we pulled into her driveway. "We'll continue this over tea in the kitchen when you've unpacked. You are not to beat yourself up over this. Jenny was a wild animal. All you did was defend yourself. You handled her perfectly."

I hefted my suitcase up two flights of stairs and into the bedroom under the eaves. I unpacked and then gazed out of the window overlooking the rear garden.

Anita had struck the right nerve.

I'd never met anyone resembling Jenny before or since, including all the evil and disturbed characters I had locked up.

I went downstairs feeling a tad chirpier, which improved even more when I confronted one of my most significant weaknesses on the kitchen island: a plate of chocolate digestives.

"You know how to push the right button," I said between munching. "You never said what you did for a living."

"Forensic psychologist," said Anita.

"You worked with the police?"

"As a freelance consultant to law firms but only part-time when they had a difficult case."

"Which makes your comments about Jenny even more therapeutic. Thank you."

"Ollie, although I counted Jenny as a friend, I wasn't impressed. She was bosom buddies with Sara, but I could never understand what Sara saw in her."

"Why?"

"Jenny used to hit Sara as well. Always in the ribs, never where any damage might show."

"She hit Sara?"

"Sara told me. They had some business. I never knew what, but I suspected it was bordering on illegal. When things went wrong, Sara wanted out but still needed money. Her mother was sick. Thanks to underfunded NHS services, there were no hospice spaces available, and while they had some attendance at home, she had to pay for a nurse for the rest. Jill was away at University in France, so all the responsibility fell to Sara, hence her moneymaking schemes such as Room 118."

"Sara also sold fake birth control pills and other illegal substances such as speed and marijuana."

"I'd heard it was steroids for athletes, particularly for elite oarsmen. Did you indulge?"

"Never, but it could explain how poor performers magically raised their standards. If Leander even heard a whisper some were artificially boosting their stamina, they would ban them from club and sport."

"Sara must have dealt directly with the athletes."

"Logical, they used to drink in the Red Lion. If Jenny also hit Sara, does that imply she was unstable?"

"Yes, especially under stress."

"She had a high-pressure job and was having problems with a male colleague who fancied her and bullied her if she looked at other men. No wonder she was desperate to escape."

"It would tip her over the edge."

"I recently discovered it drove her to an unexpected course of action."

"What?"

"She stole Sara's identity and did a deal with MI5. She's been in the UK ever since."

"Sorry, I'm confused. Whose funeral are you attending tomorrow?"

"Jenny's."

"Wait, Jenny, is Sara?"

"I saw the heart-shaped birthmark on the back of her neck."

"Did you check her toes?"

"Yes, no fusion of the second and third on the left foot."

"You knew about them?"

"Of course, Sara and I were lovers. I thought they were cute and kissed them regularly. How did you know?"

"Girls changing rooms."

"Nobody let on."

"We were loyal to our mates in those days."

"Do you know what happened to Sara?"

"Nobody has seen or heard of her since your infamous night."

"Surely, she would have taken another identity."

"You'll have to ask Jill."

CHAPTER 27

2024

The day of Jenny's funeral was sunny but cold and crisp with no wind. John Harker picked me up from Anita's, and we headed for the hospice in Caversham. As we drove through the gates, the expansive lawns were covered in slowly thawing frost, and clusters of snowdrops littered the flowerbeds. The tiny stand-alone chapel was located to the extreme left of the main building. John parked outside, and we went in. It was empty, but a few minutes remained before the service commenced at eleven am.

We took seats at the back, keeping our coats on to counter the lack of heating. With a few seconds to spare, a woman in her early seventies with short grey hair entered wearing an elegant black full-length coat with a fur collar. She bowed her head at the altar and sat next to me.

"I recognise you, Ollie," she said. "I'm Jill."

"Hi, Jill," I said. We hugged briefly. "This is John Harker, a former colleague. We're trying to unravel what happened to Sara. It's becoming more mysterious by the day."

"Perhaps I can throw some light on that," said Jill. "Can we go for a coffee after the service?"

"We can use the canteen here," said John. "It's not too disgusting."

On the dot, the double doors were pushed open. Four porters in dark suits carried a cheap coffin on their shoulders and placed it reverently on the stand at the front of the chapel.

A lady in her mid-fifties wearing casual dark clothing followed the coffin and stood by it.

"My name is Stella Jones," she said after clearing her throat and regarding us. "I'm a lay preacher at St. Paul's, the nearest church. It's my turn to accompany today's deceased to the chapel here and onto Reading crematorium. When Sara's ashes are returned sometime tomorrow, my colleague Brenda will scatter them around the hospice gardens. Are any relatives present?"

"I'm Jill, Sara's sister," said Jill. "She doesn't have anybody else; these gentlemen are friends from many years ago."

"How lovely. Sadly, many hospice patrons depart this world alone. I regret I never met Sara. Was she religious?"

"No," said Jill.

"Then I won't bother with the traditional service, but would you care to say a few words?"

"I haven't seen my sister since the night of the twenty-first of April 1968," said Jill, moving next to the coffin. "I have no idea where she has been living or what she was doing with her life. All I can say is our long-dead mother was eternally thankful for Sara's efforts to pay for her care. She passed shortly after

Sara's disappearance. So, my dear sister, I accept I will never learn about your life. All I can do today is wish you well for your next journey."

Jill kissed her hand, tapped the coffin, and returned to her seat. She was remarkably calm, and I was impressed. I wondered how she would react when I told her the truth.

"Thank you, Jill," said Stella.

The four pallbearers returned, and we watched as Jenny began her final journey.

We made our way to the canteen.

I stuck with the tea.

"Can you tell us about Sara's last night?" I asked as we took a window seat overlooking the rear garden and sipped our drinks.

"I'll never forget," said Jill. "And Ollie, you might find it illuminating. I had recently returned from University in Paris for the Easter break. I was studying French. And ultimately became a technical translator for legal documents. I was asleep when the phone rang. Sara begged me to come to the Red Lion to help solve an urgent problem. I hated leaving Mum alone, but she sounded desperate. I ran down and found her in her room. Her case was open on the bed, and she was packing."

"She said that she had been fired but not to worry because she was starting at the Catherine Wheel the next day. They had been after her for months."

"Why was she fired?" I asked.

"She'd been illegally renting out one of the hotel rooms to raise money for Mum, and the owners found out. They told her to tidy the room before she went, or they would inform the police she had been stealing from the hotel. It meant the Catherine Wheel would cancel her job offer. If she did tidy up and leave that night, they would pay her outstanding wages and say nothing about the theft. When I asked her why this couldn't wait until she came home, she told me the tidying up involved removing you, which is why she needed my help. We went up to the room to find you prostrate on the floor. I assumed you were drunk again, but Sara told me Jenny had beaten you up and looked like she was about to strangle you. She had you in a neck hold, cutting the blood flow to your brain. Sara wrenched her away from you; Jenny ran out and left Sara to it. Someone had reported the racket, and Richard Elsdon came up to investigate and demanded you were taken home. We heaved you into the bathroom and splashed cold water over you, which stirred some semblance of consciousness. You threw up in the sink but then could stand without falling over. We half-led, half-carried you home, opened your front door, and shoved you indoors. The last we saw was you crawling toward the stairs. I went straight home to check on Mum. Sara returned to the hotel to finish packing. I never saw or heard from her again."

"Thanks," I said. "I always wondered how the evening ended. What did you do when Sara never came home?"

"I went to the hotel the next morning to talk to her, but she wasn't there. Her room was exactly as we left it. I went to see the Elsdons to suggest I make a missing person's report to the police. They were insistent I shouldn't waste police time. They offered to give me Sara's wages on the basis I left making the report for a few days and assured me Sara was bound to turn up."

"I took the money. I was due back in Paris but had to stay with my mum and care for her because we had nothing to pay the nurse. Mum died a week later. After the funeral, I made a missing person's report about Sara to the police in Henley and returned to my studies. When I came home in the summer to sell the house, the police had made no progress, and the file had been put at the bottom of the pile. Anita calling me the other day was the first thing to happen in the long-unsolved case of my missing sister. It surprised me. I had assumed Sara was long dead."

"Why?" said John.

"I assumed she died on the way back to the hotel. Either by suicide or the stupid stalker took her. Either way, I sensed she'd gone."

"Hardly grounds for an investigation?" said John.

"I know, which is why I left it alone. If Sara were alive, she would find me or send a message, but there has been nothing until now."

"How would you react if it wasn't Sara in the coffin?"

"Unsurprised. I sensed no connection. Who was it?"

"Jenny."

"At last, the crazy cow met her maker. Sara tolerated her because we needed the money, but it confirms my suspicions Sara died on that night."

"Could Jenny have killed her?" said John.

"As you experienced, she was more than capable, and if their business arrangements had been in jeopardy, it could have been sufficient motivation. Her temper was wicked."

"Tell me about it," I said.

We headed out to our respective vehicles, where I hugged Jill and said thanks.

As John and I walked toward his car, my mind was

spinning.

Finally, I had third-party evidence confirming I had hit a woman because I was fighting for my life. I felt a massive sense of relief. I wasn't a monster, except for one tiny outstanding issue. Around that time in my life, there had been many nights involving too much beer when I couldn't remember anything. Did this mean I could have been the Henley stalker?

CHAPTER 28

2024

"Impressive lady," said John as we sat in his car outside the hospice chapel and watched Jill drive away.

"I agree," I said.

"And finally, you have closure for your night of fame."

"Yes, but two of my three loves remain unaccounted for. Inge Lise is still unresolved, but I know where she is. Was there a missing person's case registered for Sara?"

"There was, and as Jill said, they found nothing, so it slipped to the bottom of the pile."

"I find it difficult to understand why they failed to trace her," I said. "Jenny was using her identity; on paper, Sara still existed."

"We can only speculate," said John. "But I expect MI5 sanitised all traces of her in case the Americans suspected Jenny had taken Sara's identity."

"Did you receive the stalker file and evidence from Oxford?"

"Still tracking down the semen sample, but the file

arrived last night, but I only glanced through. It's quite thick."

"Did you see if the dates of the stalking incidents coincided with the Jackie Kennedy visits?"

"I did, but none matched, which is a shame because the stalker was turning nasty."

"In what respect?"

"He'd moved on progressively with each reported case. Touching and groping and about a month before your last night in Henley, severe wounding and rape. After which, he stopped completely."

"Any explanation why?"

"For the early incidents, he didn't need anything other than good timing and luck because it only took a minute. For rape, he needed more planning, and it took longer, which exposed him to greater risk. Perhaps the experience frightened him enough to stop."

"Or he moved away. Perhaps you could check other forces. See if they had any unresolved stalking or rape cases from a similar perpetrator after 1968."

"Good idea."

"Who was the victim?" I asked.

"Margot Hedenblad was a young blond Swedish girl around nineteen walking alone after midnight up Norman Avenue. She admitted to being a bit drunk on her way home to where she was an au pair off Greys Hill. He stepped out from behind a tree on Norman Avenue and hit her over the head with a log. There was a fragment of wool from black gloves stuck on the log along with her blood. He carried her over his shoulder into the graveyard at the back of the Holy Trinity Church, where he stripped off her clothing and raped her on the thick grass. She recovered consciousness a few hours later and screamed bloody murder. The neighbours called the police, and a local detective found a running shoe print and collected a semen sample but no culprit."

"So, his modus operandi was always at night and on foot. He must have had thorough local knowledge to avoid the night-time foot patrols."

"They still had them?"

"The evenin' all Bobbies were certainly active when I left Henley. John, this man had to be local. Someone connected to Leander, tall, strong, and probably living in the town centre."

"You've described yourself. Ollie, sorry, but we need to eliminate you from this inquiry before we reopen the case. I can't tie up valuable resources when I might have the culprit in front of me. Can you recall any alibis you might have had for the dates?"

"I'm not familiar with the dates, but I agree. I don't know if I was the stalker or not. Can you email me the incident dates and locations? I'll chat with the gang to try and build a picture of my movements. A list of the victims and their descriptions might also help. Perhaps there was a relationship between them beyond being au pairs, or they fit a profile. Could he have stopped because he was arrested for something else?"

"Good point, we'll check the records from Henley and the surrounding towns. Moving back to Jenny. Could she have killed Sara?"

"She was capable, but her main driving force was to escape the Americans, but she may have known Sara was dead."

"How?"

"Anita implied Jenny and Sara were in a drug dealing business. Perhaps the supplier killed Sara because she wouldn't or couldn't pay the extra? Jenny either witnessed the crime or found out and stole Sara's papers."

"It could explain why Jenny used Sara's identity without fear of recrimination," said John. "Look, Ollie, we are wasting our time trying to solve what happened to Sara from this perspective. There are too many imponderables, loose ends, and a lack of hard evidence. MI5, or whatever we call them nowadays, will have deliberately obfuscated any lines of inquiry. Even if they know and have a file on the case, it will never see the light of day for the likes of us."

"I understand, but it would be nice to know why the Americans vanished overnight?"

"Nice to know is no grounds for an inquiry? We've proved the Henley stalker wasn't American, so they have no case to answer."

"What are you saying, John?"

"The only way forward is to investigate a criminal case where we have jurisdiction and control. We already have evidence and crime reports for the Henley stalker. The culprit may even be linked to Sara's disappearance. However, before I agree to let my dogs loose, I need your alibi."

"The gang is reconvening for a funeral in a few days. It will give us something to talk about. Can you send me a list of the stalking details?"

"Of course. Let me know how it goes. Meanwhile, I'll check the arrest records for someone who fits the suspect's profile."

John dropped me at Anita's. I entered tentatively, but nobody responded to my *anybody home* inquiries. I made a pot of tea and raided the chocolate biscuit tin. As I munched in ecstasy at the kitchen table, I reviewed the latest revelations about my last night and asked myself a few questions.

Was I happy to call an end to my quest?

Although some pieces of the jigsaw were falling into place, the current puzzle was much bigger than my initial objective. Until I had more answers, I could only define where I was as a work in progress.

CHAPTER 29

2024

Virginia offered me the position of usher at Norman's funeral, which I accepted. It would allow me to reunite with old friends as they arrived at the church and build a list of people to question at the wake being held at the Red Lion.

Once again, I donned my dark grey suit. Out of respect for Norman's flamboyancy, I knotted a pink tie around my neck, which was the theme for his day.

It was a cold, grey January morning as I entered the light and spacious St. Mary's church to pay respects to my grandparents at their memorial plaque on the eastern wall. As I stood before their names engraved into the marble, a wave of shame and guilt washed over me. In my mind, I apologised for my lack of attention. This was my first visit, and I vowed to attend more regularly.

I bowed and moved to the church door to greet the first arrivals. The talented organist played a medley of haunting Moody Blues, which echoed around the interior. Pink carnations were everywhere, including my coat lapel. Nobody was allowed to be sad. We were here to celebrate Norman's life, not to wallow in misery at his demise.

Notwithstanding, there were damp eyes and forced smiles as I escorted his still-living friends to their seats. Virginia and Anita were my co-ushers, and we knew most mourners. Some fellow drinkers from the Riverside bar days were instantly recognisable despite the aged features and sagging fronts. Others bore no resemblance to the youngsters they once were.

I didn't know several men; by their disposition, they had been among Norman's boyfriends. They insisted on sitting together at the back of the church, sniffing into their pink handkerchiefs.

When the hearse arrived, all forty-odd of us stood silently, including Anita's children and grandchildren. Four uniformed pallbearers in black tails and crisp white shirts heaved out the pretentious pink coffin with pink handles. They carried it slowly onto the pavement and into the church, swaying in unison as they moved up the aisle, accompanied by a musical version of *I Am Who I Am*.

The vicar, a tall, jolly, bald fellow and surprisingly young for such a traditional church in a wealthy middle-class town, watched them slide Norman onto a stand before the altar. He moved to the coffin's side and indicated we should sit down.

"We receive many different requests nowadays," he said in a booming upper-class voice, pronouncing r as w. "For a different style of thanksgiving service tailored to suit the deceased. I never met Norman but heard from his dear friends Anita and Virginia that he was an eccentric buffoon with more money than sense but with a loving heart and generous spirit. He has indeed made a huge donation to our church roof fund so we may continue to keep you dry for your grandchildren's hatching, matching, and despatching, which is all we seem to be needed for nowadays. But no matter, my instructions are to keep this brief so you may proceed to the Red Lion and celebrate in the style more suited to your memories of our dear departed. Norman requested that should anyone feel inclined to say a few words, they should do so. However, he reminds you he is watching and won't take kindly to any disparaging remarks. Please stand and read with me the script on the card in front of you."

He glared at us while we picked up the order of service, coughed, and shuffled into silence before reading an alternative version of the poem *The Gypsy, by Clare Harner.*

Do not stand at my grave and weep,
I am not there; I do not sleep.
I am a thousand winds that blow,
I am the diamond glints on the snow.
I am the sunlight on ripened grain,
I am the gentle autumn's rain.
When you awaken in the morning's hush,
I am the swift, uplifting rush,
Of quiet birds in circled flight.
I am the soft star that shines at night.
Do not stand at my grave and cry.
I am not there; I did not die.

As Norman intended, there wasn't a dry eye in the house.

I exchanged tear-stained glances with my fellow mourners in the pew at the front where his oldest and dearest friends were gathered. They indicated I should proceed, so I stood, smoothed the front of my coat and walked to the coffin.

I looked at it fondly, seeking inspiration for what I should say. The absence of words had plagued me for the last couple of days, but as I expected, Norman's spirit moved in mysterious ways, and a theme immediately struck me.

"Good morning, dear friends of Norman Brownlow Shannon. Excuse my first disparaging remark, for which I will no doubt have to suffer Norman's wrath on some unknown date and venue. He hated his second name and vowed to eradicate anyone who promulgated it, along with his age. He was eighty-seven. Now I've done it.

"For the uninitiated, Norman's father was an avid reader of Charles Dickens. Mr Brownlow is a character from his 1838 novel *Oliver Twist*. He was a bookish and kindly middle-aged bachelor who helped Oliver escape the evil clutches of Fagin. By the end of the novel, he had adopted Oliver. It's an appropriate story to tell because my name is also Oliver.

"Norman, whose bachelorhood was the only similarity to Brownlow, was my mentor and an elder brother to me. If you can't face standing up here and relating any Norman anecdotes, don't worry; there will be plenty of opportunities to do so later in the Red Lion, and I look forward to hearing them. They don't have to be about Norman. If you recall anything unusual about our youth in the late 1960s, particularly the Red Lion football team or the mystery of the unsolved Henley stalker case, I would be delighted to listen. I recognise most of you, but there are a few I haven't met yet or have changed so much that I have forgotten who you are. Thank you."

I tapped the coffin and returned to my seat.

Virginia stepped forward and replaced me.

"Norman was the first openly gay man I ever had the pleasure of meeting," said Virginia. "I was and still am a deeply religious woman, and when Norman first came out back in 1967, I was shocked. Suddenly, a person I had known since I was a young girl and had assumed was unmarried by choice fell into a category of person ostracised by the teachings of my Christian church. Only recently, some half a century later, is it beginning to accept homosexuality isn't a crime. It's the way some people are or prefer to be. They still need love, kindness, and support like all of us. In the 1960s, society, particularly the church, wasn't as tolerant, flexible, and forward-thinking as it is today, and neither was I. Initially, I was confused. Norman was still the same person I had always admired, and he continued to treat me like a princess. Should I now not like him?

"I spent years ignoring him, attempting to resolve whether he was a friend or foe. What a waste of valuable time. I didn't have much luck in the relationship department. My first husband wasn't gay, but he was a serial adulterer. Again, my beliefs stood in the way, and I couldn't bring myself to divorce him. After my first husband passed, I was at last free from this lengthy conflict zone. I returned to Henley to be near my loving sister and her darling family. Still included in her circle of friends was dear Norman. We rekindled our long-lapsed friendship, and what a pleasure it has been. When it became apparent that he was struggling to live alone, it was inevitable that as a former nurse, I would offer to help, and what a brilliant decision it was.

"Mentally, Norman hadn't changed a bit. He was still as bent as a nine-bob-note but no longer physically capable of following through. He used to say these were the best years of his life; finally, his brain has relocated somewhere between his ears instead of wallowing around in the smut between his legs.

"Despite our differences, we evolved into loving companions and shared many laughs and tender moments. My only regret is our brief lives together have come to an end. However, our bond will survive. His final request is I should use his fortune to help those who show potential and are determined to succeed using their talent but lack the means to do so. If we all let such humanity shine through, perhaps the world could live productive lives in peace and harmony. That's what I want, as did my dear husband, Norman. Therefore, let us recall his favourite poem's final lines again.

"*Do not stand at my grave and cry.*
"*I am not there; I did not die.*

"And so, dear friends, please join me to celebrate Norman's amazing life. Now, we will gather around the grave outside to ensure his remains don't escape, after which The Red Lion awaits."

The pallbearers returned and collected Norman. We filed out after the coffin and gathered around the freshly dug grave adjacent to a large fir tree, which gave us a fine view of the front of Chantry House, which, in a perfect world, would have been painted pink, not lemon.

The vicar commended his body to the ground with the usual ashes-to-ashes blessing, and we adjourned to the Red Lion. Virginia and I rushed ahead.

I shook hands with everyone as they filtered past me into the function room. It was a finger buffet, and you could help yourself with drinks so we could mingle freely. Regretfully, the conversations added nothing to my knowledge of the 1960s or the Henley stalker. Most of us had filtered our memories of Norman and those times through rose-tinted glasses. We had wiped clean the bad and accentuated the good. From the amount of goodness I heard about Norman, it would be safe to assume he had lived in a monastery.

After a few hours, I thought I had conversed with most, but a man in an electric wheelchair approached me. He was in his early seventies and seemed healthy enough and well-dressed in a tweed suit. His legs were withered and twisted. His glass eye matched the colour of his real one perfectly but never seemed to stop staring at me. I hadn't seen him at the church or welcomed him earlier at the door.

"I'm Mike Garnet," he said. "Norman's neighbour. Sorry, I'm late, but I forgot to charge the battery on the damn chair. I'm here now, and Virginia pointed you out to me. I need a word. Could we find somewhere quiet?"

The buffet table had been decimated and cleared by now, so we moved over. I pulled up a chair and sat next to him.

He looked around furtively. Happy no one could overhear us, he said, "It's about the Henley stalker."

"Go on," I said.

"I've been in this chair since a motorbike accident when I was seventeen," he said. "We were at school together, but I was a couple of years behind you, so you probably don't remember me."

"Sorry, I don't."

"I understand. I used to row, and you were my role model. Sadly, I was injured before reaching my potential. My coach was also Rick Phipps. My best friend was his son Mervyn."

"Rick must be long gone, but is Mervyn still with us?"

"No, he was killed in the same accident as mine."

Mike paused and took a deep breath. I reached out and patted his shoulder.

"May I ask when your accident was?"

"April twenty-first, 1968, but still feels like yesterday. I wanted to tell you that, late one evening, about a month before the accident, I was looking out my bedroom window as I still often do. It faces out onto Norman Avenue. I like watching the trees and people who use it as a cut-through to Trinity Church and Greys Road. Anyway, on the night the girl was raped, I saw a tall, athletic man wearing a light-coloured top with the hood up and a dark scarf wrapped around the lower part of his face. He was loitering behind a tree and kicking logs around."

"What colour was the scarf?" I asked.

"In the gloom of the dull streetlight, it could have been black or dark blue. The thing is, I had seen this man heading up or down Norman Avenue dressed the same on several occasions. Sometimes, he was sprinting like a madman."

"Did you tell the police?"

"I did. I also told them I thought his stature and how he moved resembled you."

"Take care of all your memories."

Bob Dylan

CHAPTER 30

2024

Once again, the vision of a girl walking in front of me flashed before my eyes. Was this another massive memory gap from the 1960s? Was I the stalker? I shook my head. Indeed, I would have been aware of such a significant incident. In all my police cases, I had never come across a guilty rapist or murderer who couldn't recall committing the crime. They might swear until they were blue in the face that it wasn't them, but when presented with irrefutable evidence, they usually relented, even if it was years later during their parole hearing.

I could understand my memory being blanked by alcohol, but stalking and raping needed clinical preparation, quick wits, and a clear head for escaping the clutches of any police night patrols. A culprit confounded by too many pints of Brakspear's would make mistakes and risk arrest. There had to be another reason for this man presuming he saw me in Norman Avenue.

"Did Mervyn have a Leander top?" I asked.

"Of course. He wore it all the time," said Mike. "As did I. I attended every event to watch Mervyn, you, and the others compete at home and away. I have copies of all the race sheets from 1967 until my interest faded in the 1990s. I marked up the results."

"You probably know more about my rowing than I do, but I stopped in 1968. I have a list of the stalker incident dates and want to ascertain if I was in Henley on any of them. Could I come to your house and go through them together?"

"Can I be frank?" said Mike.

"Of course," I said, puzzled.

"What if you are the stalker? I'd be a fool to go somewhere with you alone."

"You live on your own?"

"No, but my carer won't return until this evening."

"What if I ask Virginia to accompany us?"

"I'd feel better."

"I'll go and ask."

"Fine, let me know."

Many of the mourners were heading home. I noticed the wine had hardly been touched, and the spirits remained unopened. I guess I wasn't the only one to have substantially cut down on alcohol intake. It didn't combine well with blood pressure and cholesterol tablets.

"Can I walk back home with you?" I said when I found Virginia chatting with Anita.

"Abandoned me already?" said Anita.

"Never again," I said. "No, Mike has old race programs from our 1967/8 Leander competitions. He's agreed to compare them with stalker incidents to ascertain if I was in Henley or elsewhere. However, he's nervous about going home alone with me."

"Ridiculous," said Virginia. "

"Hopefully, you're right," I said, grateful she was confident about my innocence. "However, I'm happy to give him peace of mind if you are."

It was drizzling as we left the hotel and headed towards Mike's house. Virginia pulled a telescopic umbrella from her handbag and held it over herself and Mike.

"This was the tree," said Mike as we stopped outside Norman's house. "My bedroom is on the first floor. You can see I have a clear view."

"I never doubted you, Mike," I said.

"Fine," he said but couldn't look at me.

Virginia regarded both of us with one of her duh expressions.

Mike unlocked his door, rolled his chair up the ramp, and led us into the front lounge. The spacious room with a high ceiling was painted white and traditionally furnished with a floral three-piece suite and mahogany sideboard. A magnificent fireplace with a moulded plaster surround of interwoven vine leaves and bunches of grapes dominated one wall. An electric imitation log fire flickered away in the grate. Art Deco wall lamps switched on automatically as we entered.

Mike wheeled over to the sideboard, extracted a large cardboard box, and removed a thick wad of clear plastic folders. The atmosphere was tense; Mike appeared as nervous as I was. I brought the stalker incidents up on my phone, and we compared them with the race sheets.

It wasn't good news.

None of the attacks coincided with rowing events.

"Do you have any other helpful documents?" I asked.

"Sorry," said Mike.

"Are you positive it was me?" I asked.

"I said I thought it was you, but I couldn't swear in court, which I told the police."

"Ok, thanks, Mike."

We said our goodbyes and left.

"My last chance," I said.

"In what respect," said Virginia as we paused outside what was now her property.

"I must prove to the police I wasn't the stalker. Otherwise, they won't reopen the case."

"Why?"

"Sara disappeared on my final night in Henley. Nobody knows why. There has been no trace of her since. Perhaps she was a victim of the stalker. Reopening the case might substantiate the truth."

Virginia looked at me perplexed.

"What?" I said.

"I might be able to help."

"How?"

"Two of those weekends you mentioned with stalker incidents. I vaguely recall we went on a camping expedition to Snowdonia on one and visited your uncle in his pub near Bristol on the other."

"Her words immediately conjured up images of both trips."

"We went to Snowdonia in Paul Best's Daimler."

"There were seven of us. Four girls and three boys."

"Ye Olde Inne, in Westerleigh near Chipping Sodbury, was my uncle John and Auntie Ed's pub."

"She hated it."

"Whereas he revelled in it. Amazing steak and kidney pies."

"We slept on the floor of the upstairs bar. Come

in," said Virginia, unlocking the back door. "I have photos somewhere."

"You can remember the exact date of each trip?"

"Don't worry, you'll see."

We descended into the cellar to hunt for Virginia's old photo albums. Eventually, we discovered them in a wooden tea chest. There were hundreds of albums, but she knew exactly what she was looking for and dug out two for 1967 and two more for 1968.

We went to the kitchen, and while she put the kettle on, I sat at the red and white checked vinyl-covered round table and flicked through the first album. I was amazed by how many photos there were. We had travelled around more than I had thought. Trips to see various bands performing live. Camping holidays at Lyme Regis and the Norfolk Broads. A bank holiday weekend in Brighton with thousands of mods on their scooters. At one stage, we had been herded into a corner by police and searched for drugs, but they found nothing.

"You must have taken millions of photos."

"My dad was a keen amateur; he generally handed me down his old cameras when he bought a new one. He had a darkroom in the basement, so we developed everything into negatives and made prints of the better images. If you look carefully in the bottom right-hand corner of each photo, you'll find the date."

I took out my reading glasses and inspected each photo closely. I spotted the date in faint orange numbers on the bottom right-hand corner of each picture. I resisted the temptation to dwell on every page and moved quickly to the Snowdonia weekend. I stared myopically at every image. I was picnicking from the boot of the Daimler and riding the train up to the top of the mountain. Virginia was right; the dates confirmed that for the fourth stalker incident, I was not in Henley. I heaved a sigh of relief as Virginia poured the tea and perched on the adjacent stool.

I looked at her and grinned as I showed her the photos.

Not only was the visit to my uncle's pub dated on a later stalker incident, but we were in Norfolk when the girl was raped.

I heaved a sigh of relief and sipped my tea.

"Can I take one of each?" I asked. "I'll bring them straight back."

"Of course, but I will unstick them. I don't want any damage."

"Am I so clumsy?"

"No offence, but just in case. Why don't you wander around? Try the lift, but before you go, remove your shoes."

I padded around the familiar surroundings. I had been drunk in this house more than anywhere else but still recalled every inch of it except the lift.

Virginia's suite was at the top. It used to be four rooms but was now a bedroom, dressing room, and spacious bathroom with a huge corner tub with water jets. The first floor was as it used to be. Norman's bedroom was still papered with album covers from the sixties. The same bubble lights were on the same bedside cabinets.

The downstairs rooms no longer contained sofas everywhere but were now the dining room, study, and man cave. In the man cave, his vinyl albums, cassettes, CDs and DVDs, and books were tidily arranged on floor-to-ceiling shelves. I glanced at some of the novels.

Kill a Mockingbird by Harper Lee
I Know Why the Caged Bird Sings by Maya Angelou
In Cold Blood by Truman Capote
Dune by Frank Herbert
The Autobiography of Malcolm X by Malcolm X with Alex Haley
Catch-22 by Joseph Heller
James and the Giant Peach by Roald Dahl
Clockwork Orange by Anthony Burgess.

Nothing from today, I thought. It must have been the advent of the Internet. I moved to the study and sat in his Charles Eames Softpad leather chair, standing behind his antique desk. He was so proud when he bought the classic, timeless chair designed in 1953 but still used today in TV studios and the Mastermind Quiz Show. He never allowed any of us to sit in it. I did that and ran my fingers over the latest Apple iMac keyboard. I pictured him spending many happy hours here tweaking his investments.

I returned to the kitchen.

The three photos were on the table, protected by clear plastic envelopes.

I went over and put my arms around Virginia.

"Thank you," I said, pocketing the pictures. "You have saved my liberty. One more thing, why don't I recall Mike Garnet?"

"As he said, he was two years below you. We looked up to the years ahead and ignored the grunts coming up behind."

"Yes, but as an oarsman and member of Leander, I would have trained with him, and he would have travelled with us to away matches. What did Norman say about Mike?"

"Their relationship only developed during the last

thirty-odd years. Mike took years to recover from his accident, not physically but mentally. Norman saw him sitting in his front garden one day and went to talk with him. They discovered a mutual love for computers, so Norman visited him regularly. He proffered investment advice and generally made sure he was ok."

"What about this live-in carer?"

"As I heard, Mike's parents lived in Spain but returned to help him through the initial stages of his recovery. They advertised a live-in carer, and this tall woman applied. She's been there ever since, and as soon as Mike was well enough, the parents returned to Spain. Menorca, I believe."

"What's her name?"

"Natalie."

"Have you talked with her?"

"Yes, but only to say hi. I used to bump into her in the supermarket, but now they have home delivery, and I rarely see her. Mike told me she also has mobility problems and joked his carer needs a carer. In reality, they both do."

"What was your impression of her?"

"Extremely tall and sturdy for a woman but a shy and retiring person who spoke softly. She was always impeccably dressed but used too much make-up for my liking. It must have taken her hours to plaster on every morning."

"I notice they have a well-maintained garden."

"Mike was a keen gardener. Natalie used to grow their vegetables and make pickled onions in their shed. Norman raved about them. Nowadays, a man comes once a week to tidy up."

"So now you have this gigantic place to rattle around in on your own and a huge garden to look after;

what will you do with it?"

"Anita asked me the same question. I'm not a great one for living on my own. I spent decades alone while my first husband was galivanting around the theatre circuit, and I enjoyed sharing this place with Norman. I'll probably move in with Anita. We can be two elderly spinsters, seeing through our years, and we could even play bridge. I could give you the first refusal on this place if you like."

"I'm accustomed to living alone, but this place is too large and way above my budget. If your garage is for sale, I could probably afford it."

"It will take at least a year to unravel Norman's estate. Meanwhile, what do you want to do with his launch."

"Pardon?"

"The day he heard you were coming for Christmas, he instructed his solicitor to change his will and bequeath his launch to you."

"Why?"

"He remembered how much pleasure you derived from steering it."

"I'd forgotten. But what am I going to do with an old boat?"

"Ollie, it's a vintage Taylor Bates gentleman's launch. It's immaculate and a much sought-after collector's item worth over a hundred thousand pounds."

"What?"

"A hundred thousand pounds."

"I don't know what to say."

"Take your time and let me know. It's stored in a boathouse by Henley Bridge. The estate will continue to pay the annual fees, but they will become your responsibility after you accept the inheritance. Selling is the best option. If you like, I can handle the disposal on your behalf."

"As you suggested, I'll mull it over."

"There is also another bequest."

"Stop, Virginia, please. I can't deal with this."

"Ollie, you will love this, come."

We wrapped ourselves in ponchos, put our shoes on, and headed outside into the pouring rain toward the garage. She unlocked the rear door, and we entered the musty but dry interior. Under a grey dustsheet was a vehicle of some sort, but I knew instantly what it was. I lifted the cover, and there was Norman's red E-type Jaguar."

I gasped for air as tears streamed down my face.

CHAPTER 31

2024

"Did you know that Enzio Ferrari declared this car the most beautiful in the world?" I sputtered as I stroked the gleaming paintwork of the E-type. "Norman purchased it from new. It's a 1964 three-point, eight-cylinder convertible roadster. There can't be many right-hand drive versions left in the world. Most were left-hand drives exported to America.

"It's also in immaculate condition," said Virginia. "With only forty-three thousand miles on the clock. The last valuation was a quarter million pounds because it's completely original. It is still taxed and insured, but the only trips over the last twenty years have been to the mechanic and back, who took it for its MOT."

"Sadly, I haven't renewed my driving license since I stopped playing golf over three years ago, so what should I do with it? Where would I keep it?"

"My father always said gentlemen don't drive red cars. I suggest the money would be more useful," said Virginia. "Do you want me to sell it?"

"I have no idea. I could always renew my license, but I'm too old for the aggravation. Virginia, I'm trying to offload my responsibilities, not take on new ones."

"There's plenty of time to reconsider. It can stay here until I sell the house, which won't be for a while."

"Fair enough," I said, checking my watch. "Anita will wonder what we are doing, so I should return. Thanks for well, everything. For the first time since I decided to take this trip down memory lane, I'm beginning to conclude it has been more than worthwhile."

"Except, you still want to find out what happened to Sara and Inge Lise?"

"And if I am a parent or not. At least we've proven I'm not the stalker, but despite that, I feel connected. The pink Leander top, the stalker's physique, his local knowledge, fondness for au pair girls, and Mike's statement add to someone resembling me. For my peace of mind, I need to identify the stalker or at least help the police find him. My dearest Virginia, thanks again; you've been amazing. I'll be in touch."

We hugged, and I left her to lock the garage.

The rain had eased as I headed to Anita's house. I stopped under a vacant bus stop shelter on Greys Road and called John Harker.

"Ollie, how is it going?"

"Making some progress. I have found evidence proving my absence from Henley on three of the stalker incidents, including the rape. A friend has photographs of me elsewhere on the dates in question."

"Just as well; I've read the file, which includes a witness statement implicating you."

"From Mike Garnet?"

"How did you know?"

"I met him after the funeral. We compared stalker dates with Leander away fixtures involving me."

"And?"

"Nothing coincided, but Norman's wife has photos proving I was out of Henley."

"How?"

"Her camera marked the date onto the negatives. I have a copy of each, but we can confirm the camera was accurate if you prefer."

"It was before Photoshop so that the images will be good enough."

"You'll reopen the case?"

"I will."

"Did you find any suspects on the arrest list?"

"No names I recognise or tie in with people matching your profile."

"I have another name for you."

"Go on."

"Mervyn Phipps. He and Mike Garnet are a couple of years younger than me but are physically similar. They had Leander tops and long hair. Garnet lives on Norman Avenue in the same house as the sixties. Both Garnet and Phipps were involved in a motorcycle accident on April twenty-first, 1968. Garnet was mobility impaired, but Phipps was killed."

"That date is proving crucial in a growing number of incidents," said John. "Your battle with Jenny, Sara's disappearance, Jackie Kennedy and all her protection team departing and now this accident. But nothing connects them."

"Or the stalker. It would be interesting to read the file about their accident. Can we trace the hospital where Garnet was admitted? Garnet also has a live-in carer called Natalie. I don't have more details, but she is tall and around my age. She has lived with Garnet since his return from hospital."

"Good stuff, Ollie."

I wound my way up Deanfield Avenue and let myself into Anita's. I found her in the kitchen cooking.

"Chicken risotto, okay with you?" she asked, stirring rice into creamy stock.

"Perfect. I'm eating much better than at home, but my waist is complaining."

"We are in holiday mode," said Anita, sipping a glass of white wine. "Your arrival back on the scene has put us on celebration street. Can I pour you one?"

"A dribble will be excellent. I am enjoying myself but will be glad to get home, out of your hair and away from your irresistible temptations."

"Back to a slice of cucumber and a lettuce leaf?"

"Exactly, it's all I need nowadays."

"Me too. How did you enjoy your inheritance?"

"Two minds. Half of me is incredibly grateful, the other irritated by the extra responsibilities. I don't need the boat, car, or the money they may generate."

"You could go on a world cruise."

"I could afford to take you and Virginia, but consider the stress involved. Packing, airports, currency, vaccinations and insurance, it's all too much. Popping down the pub is so much easier."

"I respect your lack of ambition, Ollie. You always preferred the simple life, even in college, but I'm sure Norman would have wanted you to do something with it."

"I've been kicking the idea around to produce a book about the history of rowing in Henley and my family involvement in the sport. Now, I can afford to pay an author, have it professionally printed, and donate it to Leander. It will give me more purpose than swanning about the globe on a luxury cruise ship."

"That is so you. How did it go with Mike?"

"None of the stalker dates coincided, but your darling sister found some photos of our trips to Snowdonia, my uncle's pub, and Norfolk. The photos had the dates on them, proving my absence from Henley at the key moments. John Harker is reopening the case. What do you recall about Mervyn Phipps?"

"He was creepy."

"In what respect?"

"Mervyn was always on the fringe of our group. Too young and dorky to be of any interest to us girls, yet constantly trying it on. I had to slap him once when he took too many liberties. Several other girls did, too, including Sara and Virginia."

"What about Mike Garnet?"

"Similar. He and Mervyn used to hang out all the time. Especially when Mervyn's dad bought him a motorbike. Mike was reserved. He was interested, but it was never a problem."

"Could either of them have been the stalker?"

"It wouldn't surprise me. Did Mike mention Mervyn was killed?"

"Yes, but he found it difficult to relate the details."

"Mervyn was speeding down Remenham Hill coming back from Chez Skinners with Mike on the back. They swerved to avoid a head-on collision with a car approaching from the opposite direction. It was overtaking a bus, forcing them to crash into a wall. There was an explosion and a terrible fire. Mervyn was burned beyond recognition. Mike was thrown clear but into the middle of a hedge. I can't recall the full story, but it was described in the Henley Standard. What I do recall was after the accident, there were no further reported stalking incidents."

"When was the accident?"

"The same day you vanished. At Mervyn's funeral, we mourned the loss of him and you. Other than my parents, it was the most emotional funeral I attended."

CHAPTER 32

2024

What a quandary, I thought as I opened the door of my apartment back in Market Harborough. It has taken seventy-six years and a self-indulgent trip down memory lane to own the car of my dreams.

Now, I didn't want it.

I dumped the week's dirty laundry into the basket for Maria, my Spanish cleaning angel, and went for a walk to clear my head and replenish the empty fridge.

The High Street was quiet as I meandered, holding my hat in the gusty breeze. As usual, it was impossible to wander far without bumping into old friends, so the intended exercise was quickly forgotten and replaced by a half pint in the Three Swans bar with Ted. He surprisingly offered to pay. Things were looking up.

"How was funeral week," asked Ted as we settled into a table by the window.

"Cheers.," I said, raising my tankard for a sip of Everard's Old Original Ruby Ale. "It was a confusion of emotions. Sadness at the dear departed, relief from finding answers to outstanding questions, and joy from an unexpected inheritance, followed by irritation."

"Care to share?"

"Still a way to go with two girlfriends, but I discovered what happened on my final night in Henley."

"Caught with your pants down?"

"No, a lot worse. I punched a woman in the face."

"You what?"

"There was a fair amount of provocation, and I was acting in self-defence, but when combined with too much alcohol, I clearly could not control my temper."

"Does knowing make you feel better?"

"Actually, yes. It confirms I made the right decision to remain single. The thought of me being an abusive husband fills me with dread. I've witnessed so many cases where alcohol inflamed a minor disagreement into severe injury, even death. Now I can face my maker with a clear conscience."

"Which was the main point of your nostalgic journey."

"Yes. There are remaining issues, but out of my hands."

"What about the inheritance?" asked Ted.

"What would you do with a vintage luxury launch and E-type Jaguar?"

"I get seasick on the lake at Wicksteed Park in Kettering, but a vintage car with no garage, I'd weep."

"How about a vintage car with no driving licence?"

"Drowning myself in said lake would be too good an end."

"It's the added responsibility, administration, insurance, and worry that some crook might relieve me of. I find it irritating," I said.

"Totally with you, old boy. I would sell both and

use the money for my grandchildren or some good cause. Pass the responsibility and give pleasure to others who aren't bothered by the extra hassle."

"My thoughts precisely," I said. "Providing I can escape the money scammers, but there is no rush. I will take my time to make a well-informed decision because there is another option to consider."

"Tell me."

"I have rediscovered endearment with my place of birth and renewed old friendships. I grew up with these people, and despite not seeing them for half a century, we carried on where we left off, which was magic. I can buy a property there and reduce my substantial investment in train services."

"May I remind you of your vow never to have anything to do with estate agents, solicitors, and removal vans? Have you quickly forgotten the adverse experiences with utilities, carpet fitters, and hanging pictures or curtains?"

"You're right, of course, but if the motivation is powerful enough and the result worthwhile, I'll happily wrestle with the challenge."

"Ollie, I admire your determination to keep moving forward, but you are seventy-six years old. Isn't it time to sling your exhausting project list into the trash, put your slippers on, and relish your final moments? Otherwise, I fear the stress will drive you into the hands of the Grim Reaper sooner than you wish."

"Sorry, Ted. I hear what you say. But I won't be done until I stop learning and experiencing new things."

"You are lucky you don't have a wife."

"Why?"

"You never have anybody else to share or disagree

with your plans."

"True, but there are moments of loneliness, and frankly, disagreements are healthy; they make for better thought-through decision-making. When I argue with myself, I generally only consider half the story."

"When we were younger, I would agree, but after fifty-odd years of marriage, there are no secrets. I know exactly how her brain functions, and she mine."

"You should try learning something new; it might add a spark to your repetitive conversations."

"Such as what?"

"Don't you have any mutual interests?"

"Ollie, when I retired from my legal practice, there were two things I had been relishing for years. One was to improve my golf handicap, and the other was to lick the garden into shape, including revamping the potting shed. Once I had achieved those and had time to watch more Rugby, I was promoted to handy person. My wife worked most of her life but always managed the house and family. I was told where to be, when, and which wardrobe items were appropriate for the occasion. Nowadays, nothing I enjoy is deemed too important to interrupt. I am no longer a husband, father, and grandfather but a janitor, errand boy, and taxi driver. The role may not be intellectually demanding. But I happily fulfil my tasks in exchange for marital harmony. Now it's too late, and I don't have time to learn anything new."

"Ted, your brain is working perfectly, but you have fallen into the trap of so many retired people. I don't recall how often I've said this, but you've stopped exercising it despite it being the most important part of your body. If you can keep it fed with new and exciting challenges, it will reward you with a longer and healthier life. Having a purpose in getting up in the morning is best. Join a walking club, play Bridge, learn the piano, photograph or paint or write your biography. Anything to engage those dwindling neurons."

"In theory, you are right, but I find new things too much effort at eighty. It's easier to go along with what her indoors decrees."

"I fear for you, Ted."

"It's already happening. She treats me more like a child every day. I am doomed to being a blithering idiot for the rest of my days, incapable of making sensible decisions on my own or heading to the butchers without comprehensive directions and a dreaded list."

"Only because she worries about you."

"I know her motivations are driven by love, but when I dare to comment on her memory lapses and constant repetitions of the same instructions, she hits the roof."

"Surely, there is something positive you can share?"

"She can play the piano. It's something we could do together, and I've always dreamed of bashing out something half decent of my invention on a keyboard, which might distract her from her latest obsession."

"Which is?"

"My health. Life is a constant round of medical appointments. Even though I'm perfectly fit. Plus, I object to being shoved out of the house in all weathers for daily exercise dressed like her grandfather."

"Hence, the tweed jackets and checked shirts."

"Yes, but I drew the line at the cloth cap."

"At least you have company."

"On the contrary, I'm glad to escape to the pub to avoid the constant stream of children and grandchildren coming to say goodbye in case I pass at night."

"Don't forget the stimulating TV."

"We watch what she wants. Usually mindless rubbish. Why do you imagine I played golf all those years?"

"I hear you, which is precisely why I must keep going. The thought of yet another repeat of Eastenders fills me with dread."

"I agree."

"Are you looking to leave her?"

"Heavens, no, I couldn't live without her. Her tolerance of me and our companionship stirs me out of bed most mornings."

"No doubt accompanied by a scalding hot cup of tea."

"What else?"

"Talk it through with her and agree to buy a piano or an electronic keyboard. Imagine a Darby and Joan musical at the Harborough Theatre."

"Good idea, Ollie. Tell me, why are you contemplating moving to Henley? What is there you don't have here?"

"Old friends."

"Here, too."

"A beautiful town surrounded by glorious countryside."

"Here also, although I admit your fancy launch won't travel far on the narrow river Welland. Ollie, if you don't mind me saying, what excites you about Henley is that it is an unfinished business from your youth. Let me tell you about Rosemary Cumberland."

"Never heard of her."

"She was the first girl I kissed. We were about

fourteen, and I can recall her soft lips as if they were five minutes ago. It was the most exciting thing in my life, and I loved her with unbridled passion."

"I've never seen you so animated; she must have broken your heart."

"Not at all; I was kissing Gina Riley the following week. My point is those early experiences of love and friendship are imprinted in your memory with far more intensity than the fifth or sixth girlfriends, whose names and descriptions are long forgotten. Returning to Henley is doing this to you. It's taking you back to those first teenage experiences still deeply embedded in your psyche. You yearn for those years and intense emotions back again. You assume moving there, swanning around in your launch or antique car, will somehow be rewarded with youth. Ollie, the novelty will soon wear off. In three months, you'll be wondering how everybody is in Market Harborough and be catching the train back up here. Such effort, stress, and expense for what? Nothing. I understand you want to visit more regularly, and the train journey is long and tedious, so instead of buying a property, why not hire a car and chauffeur as and when you need it? You can afford it, and the drive to Henley is eighty-odd miles. A couple hours through some of England's prettiest villages and green rolling hills."

"You should have been an agony aunt," I said, impressed by Ted's wisdom. That's good advice."

"Heed it, old friend."

"I'll give it some thought, thanks," I said, finishing my beer. "And talk to your better half about a piano. Sorry, but my empty fridge is awaiting a fresh salad delivery. I ought to be off."

"Me, too," said Ted, checking his watch. "Her

indoors will be wondering where I am."

"Keep me posted."

I wandered around the supermarket and bought far more than I needed. Sadly, lettuce doesn't come in individual leaves; the most miniature cucumber was half a whole one. If another trip cropped up in the next day or two, I'd have to throw most of it away.

I headed home and, after a light snack, settled into my armchair. I was reaching for my current reading material just as the phone pinged.

I checked the screen and saw it was an email from Chris Jepsen.

I opened it up with shaking hands.

My heart was pumping at an extreme danger level.

Sorry to have taken so long. I read. There have been developments. When can you come?

CHAPTER 33

2024

Positive developments or not? Whatever Chris was trying to convey, this was not a conversation for texts or telephone. It had to be done face-to-face, but where should I go? I assume home meant Aarhus or Grenaa? I sent an email with the question and received an immediate reply. Chris would pick me up from Aarhus airport any time I cared to arrive. A week should be enough, he wrote.

I booked a flight for the coming Saturday but left my return open. It was pointless to speculate where this was going.

I texted John Harker to inform him of my plans. He replied that he had made no progress tracing the accident report or hospital files on Phipps and Garnet and would let me know.

I caught the train to Stanstead, still unsure what to do about the launch or car, and informed Virginia I would decide upon my return from Denmark.

No hurry, she replied, and good luck.

Over the North Sea, I gazed out the plane window

and reflected on Ted's advice. Should I relocate to Henley or not? By the time we landed, my head was spinning. It proved impossible to decide while the elephant in the room loomed large. Was I a parent or not? Once resolved, perhaps clarity might return. My only concrete conclusion was that whatever transpired, I wanted to see Inge Lise and learn why she hadn't contacted me. Anything else with Jenny's diaries would be purely a bonus.

There was a separate queue at passport control just for British passengers. The European nationalities in the other fast-moving line regarded us as inferior citizens. We had to wait twice as long, bear more scrutiny, and have our passports stamped.

Chris was waiting for me at the arrivals gate wearing a heavy coat and a hat with fur earmuffs.

He smiled warmly as soon as we made eye contact. We hugged.

I pushed him away, still holding his shoulders, and looked him in the eye.

He returned my inquiring gaze with a steady eye.

"How do we do this?" said Chris.

"You're the one with developments," I said. "We're in your hands."

"You'll have to cut me some slack. Not everybody meets their birth father for the first time at fifty-six years old."

"Are you sure?"

"Without being too dramatic, this is a potentially life-changing event with implications for all of us. Sorry it took so long, but I had to be sure you and Inge Lise were my parents. We were waiting for the DNA test results, which came out early this week."

"Did you test mine?"

"Of course, Inge Lise had your note from her office. The lab was able to take a sample."

"You've seen her?"

"It's a long story which she insists on telling you herself. We'll put you on the train to Grenaa tomorrow so you can spend a few days reacquainting. If all goes well, we can arrange something for the weekend. Now, we are going to meet your daughter-in-law and grandsons. Ok, er, dad?"

We hugged again, he grabbed my case, and we headed out into the bitterly cold wind.

"How does it feel?" said Chris as we drove out of the airport.

"It hasn't sunk in yet, but the initial reactions are favourable but scary."

"You're afraid of me?"

"Of you, no, but our new situation is surreal, and I feel completely inadequate about how to deal with it. After years of being alone, I have no clue how to behave around young people or be a parent. Forgive me if I'm a little discombobulated."

"That's quite understandable. I've had a few days to adjust, but now that you are here, I am beginning my life again."

"Your parents will always remain your parents."

"They will, but they should have shared this with me."

"I agree. Did you have a good relationship?"

"They were cold and reserved, but apart from mentioning Inge Lise and you, they did all the right things and were particularly supportive when I thrived at rowing. They played a significant role in my training and keeping up my motivation. Still, on reflection, I threw myself into the sport, seeking compensation for their lack of affection. For example, I have hugged you more than my father."

"I've always been a hugger. Instinctively, it seems the right thing to do."

"Me too."

"I appreciate Inge Lise wanting to tell me herself, but who started the ball rolling?"

"She did. After returning from Copenhagen, she read your note and called me immediately. I drove up there the next day and met at her house."

"How did it go?"

"Like you said, surreal. We stood at her doorstep and appraised each other. I went in, and within seconds, we hugged and cried despite not having exchanged a word, but I knew she was my mother instantly. It was as if half a century of bottled-up emotions came bubbling to the surface in a giant explosion. It took us half an hour or so before we could talk. We sat on her sofa, the same one you will sit on tomorrow, where she told me her story and told me all about you. She loved you and adored your parents, but I will leave the rest for her to relate to."

"I can't wait to see her."

"She feels the same."

"Has she met your family?"

"Not yet. We wanted to come to terms with the two of us first."

"Have you?"

"After three meetings, we feel comfortable with each other, but it's impossible to unwind fifty-six years in a few weeks. It will feel strange for a while."

"I understand. How will you proceed from here?"

"It depends on what you two decide."

"What do you mean?"

"I don't fancy driving to Grenaa once a week to see my mum. Flying to England for a brief, superficial conversation with my dad in an airport lounge is not how I see this progressing. In an ideal world, I want my parents in my life daily, which means having you both close, especially as neither of you is getting any younger. How would you feel about living in Denmark?"

"I have no idea, but I'm open to anything provided everyone agrees. Can we put it on the back burner until after your mother and I have worked things out?"

"There's no pressure, Dad. I'm trying to express what a significant change this is to all our lives. It's opened a whole new world I am eager to explore."

"How do Carolyn and the boys feel about it?"

"Apprehensive but excited about discovering our new set of roots. The boys have been avidly reading up on your father, but whatever they find concerns his career on the water. There's nothing about him as a person or your mother. It's why we need you."

"I hadn't considered any of this."

"Why should you? You've only ever had yourself to worry about. Now you are a parent and grandparent; a bomb has exploded on whatever future you had envisaged. You can embrace it, dabble with it to fit your routine, or run like hell."

"When it comes to decision-making, I'm a plodder. Right now, I feel ill-equipped to consider it."

"I understand."

"Have you had this conversation with Inge Lise?"

"Yes, but her reaction was different."

"Why?"

"She's always known of my existence, exactly where I was and what I was doing?"

"How?"

"She employed a detective to monitor my development and came to watch me at major events. School plays, rowing tournaments, and even flew to Barcelona in 1992 to see me win my silver medal. It makes me shiver to know she was so close but so far."

"What was your opinion of her explanation?"

"I understood but couldn't accept her reasoning and still don't, but you can judge for yourself tomorrow. It is a heart-wrenching story, so be prepared with plenty of tissues. Meanwhile, let us concentrate on getting to know each other."

"How do you feel?"

"I'm over the moon. Overnight, I've gone from four to six in my family. Unless you have more tucked away in Henley?"

"I hope not, but until I began this journey, I didn't know you existed."

"You mentioned unanswered questions that initiated your return to Henley. Would you care to share?"

"I've answered the main one, but there are still outstanding issues that various people are helping me with. Hopefully, when they report back, I can finally bury my demons. I'll tell you about it when I understand the complete picture."

"Fair enough. Closure is a funny thing. When my parents passed away, I assumed it was the beginning of my end. I counted my blessings. I could enjoy the remaining years, hopefully with good health, the joy of my family, and helping others discover the thrills of rowing. I expected nothing more, wasn't even looking, and was happy with my lot. But instead of sitting on your backside and waiting for your maker, you went to

Henley on a wild goose mission and found us. It's an incredible story."

"One needs to be careful what one wishes for. You never know what surprises are around the corner. Where do you live?" I asked as we approached Aarhus Centre.

"We have a huge old townhouse in the Latin Quarter," said Chris. "Everything we need is within three hundred metres, and I can walk to work in under twenty minutes."

"Sounds perfect," I said as we turned into a narrow, cobbled street lined with red brick houses and ancient timber-frame buildings. One had a fascinating giant mural of green trees painted onto a white gable end.

"Here we are," said Chris as we stopped outside a red brick three-floor house.

"Looks nice."

"We like it, and my sons don't need a taxi service. It was my parents' house, so I've lived here most of my life. Underground parking is moments away, and we have great neighbours, most of whom I grew up with. It's a happy and social way of life."

"Sounds idyllic. No wonder your sons still live there."

"We love having them with us," said Chris as we clambered out of the car. "Come and say hi to your new family."

"It's such a pleasure to meet you," said Carolyn as we entered the front door into a spacious lobby and hugged. She was in her early fifties with a highly athletic and shapely figure, a cute button nose, and an elfin face. Her short blond hair and blue eyes reminded me of Inge Lise. My grandsons, Lars, twenty-five, and Rikard, twenty-seven, were strapping lads with long blond hair and intense blue eyes. They brushed aside my proffered hand and hugged me tightly, slapping me on the back.

They spoke English with no trace of an accent, so much so I was beginning to imagine I was in Henley.

"My mother remembers your mother," said Carolyn, leading us into the bright, airy living room. "They were in the choir together at St. Mary's during the 1960s."

"Gosh, she must be," I said, making myself comfortable on a beige sofa before a roaring fire.

"Ancient, yes, she is eighty-four and still going strong. She reckons it's incredible you are my father-in-law and can't wait to meet you."

"What is her name?"

"Susan Harcourt nee Burton."

"Does she have a sister?"

"Yes, Sally, but much younger."

"Amazing, I had a brief encounter with Sally."

"So, mum said."

"How is Sally?"

"No idea. She immigrated to Australia in the early seventies, never to be heard of since, but don't worry, she wasn't pregnant."

"Phew."

"Enough surprises for one year, eh dad?" said Chris, and we laughed at my expense.

"Was your father Sidney Harcourt?"

"Well remembered, we used to live on Albert Road."

"Wasn't he a GP?"

"Correct."

"He was our family doctor."

"Probably for most of Henley in those days. After

Gillot's, I studied Physical Education at Henley College and worked at Leander, where I gained my certification as a physiotherapist. It's where I met Chris."

"I had a thigh strain," said Chris.

"I touched the right nerve," said Carolyn.

I am beginning to enjoy this, I thought, as we shared another good laugh.

"Tell me, Oliver," said Lars. "Don't get me wrong, I'm delighted to have a new grandfather, but it would have been so much better for all of us if we had met sooner. What prompted you to start this trip down memory lane so late in life?"

"Good question, Lars. Your dad asked the same thing. Let me put it in words you can relate to. You're what, twenty-seven? At your age, I had met and lost your grandmother, had been recently promoted, and was the proud owner of a vast mortgage costing me a fortune in interest payments. Like most cops, I was underpaid and overworked but loved what I did. The fond memories of Henley and the wonderful people I was proud to call friends have never failed to bring joy to my solitary existence. However, as the years passed, my memories clouded, and I started viewing them through rose-tinted glasses. I wanted to remember only the good old days and forget the bad.

"But bad was always lurking in the background. I left Henley suddenly, driven by a sense of shame. My problem was I couldn't remember where the shame came from, but yearned to find out. It has taken me all these years to accumulate enough courage to go back and find answers. I still haven't resolved everything, but I am nearly there. No matter how good or bad the outcome," I said, wiping a tear from my eye before continuing with a shaky voice. "The incredible coincidence of discovering I have a family has pushed my initial motivations to the back burner. This is a whole new ball game, and frankly, it scares me."

They all rushed to me for a family hug. Tears streaming down our faces.

"Sorry," I said after a while as we separated. "I'm being pathetic."

"Dad," said Chris. "It's ok. Crying is good."

"I've been more emotional during the last couple of months than in my whole life," I said. "The boys back at the station would tell me to toughen up."

"Why can't you remember the shame?" asked Carolyn.

"I have a problem with alcohol," I said. "After a few beers, I still function normally on the outside, but my brain stops recording. We celebrated our football team's first victory on that final night in Henley. I overdid the beer, and various things happened, which caused me to be aggressive toward an ex-girlfriend. There are other outstanding issues related to this, so I can't explain everything, but I will do so when ready. Anyway, because of my behaviour, I took a vow of celibacy and have remained distant from women ever since. I also limit my alcohol consumption so I'm always in control."

"We used to have the same problem with the men in our house," said Carolyn, glaring at her husband and sons. "One bottle of our infamous Elephant Beer, and they behaved like wild animals."

"We agreed to be an alcohol-free house," said Rikard.

"Family harmony has been much improved," said Chris. His expression was painfully embarrassed.

"Indeed," said Carolyn shakily, placing a hand over

her cheek with a distant frown and the hint of another tear.

"To change the subject to a happier note," said Rikard sheepishly. "What shall we call you? Grandpa, grandad, grandpapa, or shall we use the Danish Bedstefar or Farfar?"

"The Matthews traditionally used grandpa, but whatever you feel comfortable with is fine with me."

"Grandpa, it is," said Lars.

The boys exchanged grins and said together, "Grandpa."

"Pleasure is the flower that passes.
Remembrance, the lasting perfume."

Jean de Boufflers

CHAPTER 34

2024

Inge Lise was waiting outside the exit door in the middle of the Grenaa train station platform. I could see her clearly among a small gathering of meeters and greeters. Dressed in a black full-length coat and fur hat, she stood out like an angel hovering among the masses. As I approached, our eyes locked. Visions of her as a young woman flashed before me, alternating with her face of today. Her short silver hair framed the still beautiful elfin face. To me, she hadn't aged one iota. I stopped in front of her and let go of my case. We fell into a tight embrace, tears streaming down our cheeks.

"Come, Ollie," she sniffed after what seemed an eternity. "We can do this in private at my house."

She grabbed my case with one hand, tucked her arm in mine, and snuggled her head into my shoulder, just as she used to.

Grenaa was still grey and freezing cold as we headed for her car—an all-electric Volvo.

"How did it go with Chris?" she asked as we drove toward the port.

"Emotional, draining, and incredible," I said. "We cried, laughed, and had amazing fun exchanging anecdotes about our backgrounds and parents."

"Tell me about the boys and Carolyn."

"I often fantasise about the life we could have had, should have had together. They are everything I wished for and more. Intelligent, caring, fun, and interested in learning all about the Matthews tribe, and Carolyn is a great cook. I've eaten so much; I'll need to diet."

"Lettuce and cucumber, ok? They are all I eat nowadays."

"Perfect, me too."

"Here we are," she said, pushing a remote-control button and pausing the car while large full-height metal gates opened inwards, revealing a large two-floor modern detached house roofed with photovoltaic tiles and walls rendered in white plaster. She drove into a double garage and parked beside an old black VW Beetle. "My first car," she said as we climbed out. She plugged in the car, and we headed through an internal door into a modern kitchen. Next to wall-mounted white cabinets, a sink and marble worksurfaces was a round island surrounded by bar stools. A small rectangular table in blond wood was set in a bay window. It was surrounded by moulded plywood butterfly chairs instantly recognisable as the Danish classic scattered throughout cafes and airports worldwide.

"Let me hang your coat," she said, slipping out of hers and revealing those gorgeous curves I had dreamed about for decades. They were not quite as tight as they used to be, but to my ageing eyes, were still attractive. She opened a built-in wardrobe by the garage door. After hanging our clothes, she said,

"Now, your shoes."

"Like my mother," I said, handing them over.

"Yes, but I have sensible coloured rugs, not white carpets," she said, opening another cupboard for footwear. "You'll enjoy the underfloor heating more in your socks. Tea or coffee?" she said, placing my case by the door into the hallway.

"Water is fine; I'm trying to decrease caffeine consumption."

"Through the hallway, you'll find the living room with a sofa overlooking the garden. Could you wait there while I use the facilities, and I'll bring your water."

How domesticated, I concluded as I meandered through to the rear of the house and stood by the panoramic window overlooking the garden. A terrace paved with a porous material led to pot plants and a greenhouse laid out on fine grey gravel. At the far end, fifty meters away, were rows of solar panels pointing south.

"Here's your water, Ollie," said Inge Lise.

"Doing your bit for global warming?"

"When my mother finally passed, I inherited the timber yard and decided to build the first carbon-neutral development in Jutland despite the rubbish climate. This house was where our family property stood for over two hundred years. I built twenty more properties in the yard using closed timber frame panels for superb insulation. Each house harvests its water supply, and the urbanisation has a mini recycling and composting plant. We use the latest smart switches, water boilers, heat recovery systems, and underfloor heating. This house earns money by selling excess solar energy back to the grid. I've become a bit of a green freak."

"Admiral stuff, hence joining the council?"

"Yes, I had a problem obtaining planning permission for what then was a revolutionary technology. The council was so impressed with my explanations they asked me to join and oversee new developments, but I retired last year."

"And your child psychology?"

"I still dabble, but I'm down to two days a month, aiming to stop entirely at Easter. Ollie, do you mind if we cover this later? I owe you an explanation; I sense you are waiting for it. Can you be patient with me? It won't be easy. As you can see," she said, bringing a box of tissues behind her back. I'm well prepared. Shall we sit?"

At first, we were a reasonable distance from each other on her incredibly comfortable floral sofa.

Our gazes locked.

She took a deep breath.

"After our farewell in Harwich, I cried on the ferry and then in the car from Esbjerg with my mother. I was inconsolable."

I reached out my hand, which she grasped tightly as tears filled her eyes.

"About halfway home, we stopped for lunch, and I noticed Mother was crying, too. I tried to joke about lovesick teenagers being a burden on their parents. When she shook her head, I realised my problems were not what was upsetting her."

Inge Lise wiped her eyes. I pulled her towards me, and we hitched up next to each other, thighs touching. I released her hand and put my arm around her shoulder. Once more, she snuggled in, which set me off. I put my hand out for a tissue. She giggled and passed over a handful.

"To put this in perspective," she continued. "I need to describe the relationship with my parents. My dad was desperate for a boy to carry on the family business. To say he was disappointed with my elder sister Angelika is putting it mildly. My mother, however, was delighted and doted on her. By the time I came along four years later, he had mellowed, and when I turned out to be a bit of a tomboy, I became his favourite. Both Mum and my sister resented this. I could do nothing to escape the relentless tension in the house. I had to wait until the opportunity arose in Henley, and off I went, relieved to be away."

"Why didn't you tell me this?" I said, caressing her neck.

"I was worried it might put you off me."

"Fair enough, but I loved you, not them."

"In Denmark, the entire family is involved in every relationship.

"Sounds idealistic."

"It works fine among most families, but ours was dysfunctional, and when a series of disasters happened simultaneously, we weren't unified enough to deal with it."

"What disasters?"

"My sister had a stillborn baby. Her husband went off the rails and was not able to cope with the grief."

"Was this why your mum was upset?"

"If that had been all, we could probably have coped, but Mum had been recently diagnosed with blood cancer. They'd given her about two years."

"What rotten luck."

"There's more. The dead child was a boy, so my father lost the plot, too. Having set his heart on a grandson taking over the firm, he turned into a raging bull. He was drinking a bottle of schnapps a day, hitting Mum regularly, all the staff were quitting, and the business was losing customers fast. To top off the drama, Angelika left her husband and moved back home. Ollie, I was the only person here with a degree of sanity. I had to do something."

"I understand. No wonder you had no time to write to me."

"This was before your first letter arrived; it was what I came home to."

"What about Erik?"

"He met a girl in university and remained in Hamburg. I've never seen or heard from him since."

"Where did you start unravelling the mess?"

"The business was my priority. Without its income, we were helpless. I had been working in the office and yard since I could walk. I knew the workers, the technical aspects, and the customers. I had the accountant analyse the books to see where we were, then confronted Dad with the outcome. If we carried on as we were, the business would last three to four months. He shook his head as if I was making it up. Then I screamed he would be responsible for bankrupting a successful two-hundred-year-old family business and make a mockery out of the Oleson name."

"How did he react?"

"He went out into the yard with his schnapps and hung himself in the sawmill."

"Can it get any worse?"

"Not until later. After the funeral, I visited the staff at their homes and persuaded them to return. I visited the customers, offered better deals, and started exporting. Within months, I had stopped the rot, and we were safe. I was so busy that I failed to notice my periods had stopped until I started vomiting every morning. I never dreamed I was pregnant. Mum's doctor visited her weekly. On his next visit, he confirmed my condition. I was delighted, but instead of celebrating, I had a huge row with my sister and mother. They still considered single mothers as shameful. Denmark was hugely conservative, so I agreed to keep quiet and out of the way to protect family harmony. I promoted a well-respected worker as manager for the yard, and while I made all the decisions, he fronted the business while I tried to relax and enjoy my pregnancy."

"I thought you were taking the pill?"

"I was, which confused me."

"You bought them from a friend. Was it Sara?"

"Yes. What happened to her?"

"She disappeared, but it was rumoured she was selling a whole range of drugs, many of them fake."

"But she was my friend. Why would she be so rotten?"

"Her mother was ill and needed a private nurse. She was desperate for money, hence her scheme with Room 118."

"Nothing we can do about it now."

Inge Lise sat up and looked at me, her eyes moist but tender.

"I'll never forget our room," she said. "I can still see you now. Ollie, I am so sorry I never wrote to you. I realise you must have been through hell wondering when my reply might arrive."

"I did, but so did you. Let's put it behind us and move on. We don't have much time left, so rather than agonising over what we've missed, shall we focus on our son and grandchildren?"

"I thought I was the psychologist, but you're right. Our love created Chris, and we should find a way together to treasure him and his family. But before we talk about how I must finish telling you what happened."

"You don't have to on my account."

"I've been dreaming of cleansing my soul for decades and never considered I might have the opportunity to do so. It will be therapeutic."

"I understand, but please stop if it's too painful."

"You're here now; hold me tight, please."

I pulled her to me.

She started weeping, her shoulders shuddering. I turned her toward me, kissed her cheek and forehead, and murmured comforting sweet nothings in her ear.

"My sister," she began in between sobs. "Angelika took it upon herself to care for me. She attended to my every need as if it were her pregnancy. As the bump grew bigger, she would stroke it, put her head to my navel, and converse with the baby. I knew it was a boy by now, and while I found her obsession with my foetus alarming, it was helping her recover from her loss. She'd been told she could never have more children, so this was her way of dealing with it. I'd never seen her so happy, so I tolerated it and even had her present at the birth. She cut the cord and was the first to hold him. She brought him to me for breastfeeding and even argued about what to call him. For me, there was never any doubt. He would be Chris after your second name, but I conceded on the second name using Karl, my father's name. Once she agreed, she insisted on registering the birth. She took control of maternal duties when I came home from the hospital. The only thing I was good for was as a milk cow. She chased after me with the breast pump and screamed bloody murder if I as much as looked at a gin and tonic."

She paused for an eye wipe and nose blow.

"My mother was failing fast. When she became bedbound, I employed a daytime nurse but did the night shifts myself. The yard was running well, but I gradually eased my way back into more involvement. One morning, I was in the cutting sheds chatting with the manager and spotted Angelika heading out for yet another walk with Chris in the pram. It struck me his father, you, should know about his son, and I should take him to see you in England. You could hear a pin drop when I announced my intentions at dinner. Over my dead body, announced my sister."

"When," said Inge Lise shuddering. "When I awoke the next morning, Angelika had taken Chris with all his stuff."

CHAPTER 35

2024

I hugged Inge Lise tightly as she wept uncontrollably. When she had recovered enough to continue her harrowing tale, she said, "I blame myself completely for never suspecting my dear sister had an agenda for Chris, which didn't include me. I had happily agreed to let her help me. I presumed it would lift her out of her depression after losing her baby. Meanwhile, I soldiered on looking after Mum and running the business. Foolishly, I had completely underestimated Angelika's determination until I discovered she had registered the birth with her as the mother and her estranged husband as the father."

"Where had she taken Chris?"

"I assumed she had returned to her marital home in Aarhus. I left numerous messages on her machine telling her as soon as I found a carer for Mum, I would come and collect Chris. It took a few days to find a suitable care home, but my mother refused to go; she insisted on dying at home. I was stuck between a rock and a hard place. I wanted desperately to collect my child but couldn't leave my mother without some form of assistance. My mother suggested I allow Angelika to keep Chris, and in return, she would change her will and leave everything to me. I understood her motivation to try and make her favourite daughter happy and had no worries about him being well looked after, but I was his mother. I couldn't let my disturbed sister steal him."

"Why didn't you involve the police or social services?"

"And open up a huge can of worms? I wanted to confront, reason and resolve this with my sister first. We are, after all, mature adults. Anyway, I eventually found a carer to live in for a few days, about a week after Angelika had left and set off for Aarhus. I stopped outside their house and was about to leave when Angelika and her husband came out the front door with Chris. They both looked so happy together, and Chris seemed content as they chatted with the neighbours, which left me wondering. I did not doubt that my sister would give Chris a loving and happy childhood with both a mother and father. What if I confronted them both and took Chris? What would happen? I hardly had time to cope with the business, let alone my mother; all three on my own would have been impossible to the extent that none of our lives would be happy. Angelika and her husband would try to take Chris back through the courts and accuse me of being a single and incapable mother. Angelika needed Chris for her mental stability and, without him, might well have a complete breakdown. The courts might decide Chris should be removed from such a toxic environment. In other words, my whole life would be dominated by adversaries, turning me into a bitter and twisted person hating myself, which was hardly the best motivation for good parenthood. Remember, I wasn't even twenty. So, with the heaviest of hearts, I restarted the car and returned to Grenaa. I had the lawyers draw the necessary papers and hired a detective to monitor his life. I often went to see him, even to Barcelona, when he won his medal, but do you know what the hardest thing was to deal with when I saw him?"

"Sorry, no."

"Every year, he looked more and more like you."

"I was easy to find."

"I know. My detective located your address in Nottingham. I booked and cancelled many flights to East Midlands airport; the travel agency must have thought me crazy."

"What stopped you from flying?"

"Fear of rejection. My confidence was at such a low ebb I couldn't handle the thought of you turning against me when you learned what I had done with our son."

"We could have fought for him together."

"I took the best advice, but all the lawyers were extremely negative. We weren't married. It would take years for you to obtain a visa to live and work in Denmark. What work could you do with no language skills? I wouldn't be granted permission to take him out of the country without a permit to live and work in the UK. It was all too complicated and expensive, and it would take years of more adversary and heartache, not knowing if there would be a positive outcome. It was like chasing rainbows. Ollie, I didn't want to disturb your life with all my shit."

"Inge Lise, my love. I hope you feel better getting

this off your chest. It explains clearly why you didn't write to me, but it is yet another example of the selfless angel you have always been. You put everybody before yourself despite your suffering. Whatever the rights and wrongs of your actions, Chris has turned out to be a fine man. We should concentrate on involving ourselves in his family life."

"I agree. Are you sure you still love me?"

"I've never stopped."

"Me neither. What did you do when it became obvious I was gone?"

"I went off the rails. After brief affairs with Sara and Jenny, I joined the police, but only after dramatic events in Henley forced my hand."

"Only Sara and Jenny?"

"My trip down memory lane revealed a few others, but you wouldn't have known them. What about you?"

"There have been a few affairs but nothing serious. Nobody compared with you. Eventually, I resigned myself to being single. Tell me about Sara and Jenny. I knew they fancied you."

"Sara was fun but easily distracted by her money problems. She moved on to an American guy, a colleague of Jenny's. Didn't you meet Dwight?"

"He was ok, but Jenny's boss, Chuck, was a creep. What happened to Sara and Jenny?"

"Sara, I don't know; she vanished in April 1968. Jenny also disappeared at the same time but died a few weeks ago. I found her in time to forgive her."

"Forgive her what?"

"Jenny started shy and reserved but quickly developed into a raging wildcat. She attacked me but justified it by saying she was under a lot of pressure because her boss was trying to get into her pants."

"She must have meant Chuck; it doesn't surprise me after my experiences with him."

"Well, you've cleared one thing up."

"What?"

"Chuck was Jenny's boss. I'll explain the significance in a minute."

"When did Jenny hit you?"

"Once at her apartment and again on that final night. We were celebrating our first football victory and were all buzzing. Sara told me Dwight had vanished, and Jenny wanted to see me in Room 118. I went up, and when I declined her advances, she attacked me, so I punched her in the face."

"You hit a woman?"

"Inge Lise, it was the worst moment of my life. I had never been aggressive with anyone. Thankfully, Sara arrived in time to stop Jenny from killing me. Sara and her sister Jill took me home. The next morning, I had no memory of what had transpired but was haunted by a great sense of shame. I left Henley the same day to begin my police training, and until I saw Chris last year, have never been back."

"A tad dramatic?"

"More logical. When I realised I couldn't trust myself with alcohol, control my temper, or risk more stormy relationships with women, I cut back drinking and have been celibate since."

"Perhaps we can address the celibacy later," she giggled and wiped her eyes. "So, you returned to Henley to find out what happened on your final night?"

"Correct."

"I have something to thank Jenny for. Without your burning resolve to solve the mysteries of the past, you would never have seen Chris and wouldn't be here now."

"I still find the whole experience incredible. Modern technology and coincidence have combined to unite us, but why hadn't we considered this years ago? After seeing Chris, I found you easily on the web?"

"It's frustrating, but it is how it is. So where do we go from here?"

"Nothing would pleasure me more than rekindling our love and sharing the little time left. But the shadow of my latent violence would be hanging over us like a pawl. It could gnaw away at our feelings and ruin our memories of each other."

"Bullshit. Jenny had it coming. She used to hit Sara, and you were acting in self-defence."

"There is no excuse for hitting a woman, ever."

"Admirable sentiments expected from a gentleman, but Jenny was a trained government agent, not your average weak female victim. She could have killed you in two seconds. Anyway, if you stay off the alcohol, there shouldn't be a problem."

"I hardly touch the stuff."

"Me neither, Chris also. He said he had a similar problem with his temper after too many beers. Our grandsons, too."

"Perhaps it's an inherited trait from the Matthews genes."

"We all have our faults; look at me, abandoning our son to a mentally challenged sister. Now that might gnaw away at us."

"It's good we can recognise and talk about our shortcomings."

"We always could. So, what shall we tell Chris?"

"His parents are reconciled and would like to find

ways to be a family."

"It still comes back to the visa problem, especially after Brexit, but I would like you to live with me here in Grenaa for as long as you are allowed."

"Ninety days at a time."

"Ridiculous."

"Isn't it? You can live with me in England for the next ninety days."

"Fine for now, but as we age, we won't want to be gadding about changing armchairs every three months, and our family is here in Denmark; they won't want to travel all the time to see us."

"I agree, but somewhere lurking among the complicities is a solution. The important thing is we want to find one and will stick at it until we have."

"I love your stubbornness."

"I adore your…"

"Shut up and kiss me."

CHAPTER 36

2024

"At least I won't be getting pregnant again," said Inge Lise as we lay in each other's arms in her massive bed.

"I doubt my pathetic contribution would raise a hair, let alone a child," I said.

"Charlie Chaplin became a father older than you."

"Yes, but with a vibrant young lass who did all the work. Imagine those sleepless nights and nappies at our age?"

"Terrifying, but it's nice we can still make love."

"It's surprisingly beautiful, but don't expect a rematch for a month or two."

"For me, it's the tenderness and being in your arms again."

"Me too; any chance of some food? I'm starving."

"Lettuce and cucumber?"

"Isn't there a decent restaurant nearby? I can count the number of occasions we dined out on one hand. Now we can afford it; wouldn't it be great to celebrate without washing up after?"

"Grenaa isn't much of a gastronomical centre; we'd

have to go to Aarhus or Randers, but there is Meineche's on Østergade in the town centre, which is good. Shall I book a table?"

"Please, but it is my treat. All I ever bought for you was a beer or sandwich."

"Fine, but I want to cook our first meal home."

"I have a few specialities I've picked up."

"Then we can enjoy fighting over chef of the day."

"I also love browsing food markets, especially for fresh fish."

"Me too. Shall we have a shower together and unpack your clothes?"

"Mmm, I didn't bring much."

"Enough for a few days?"

"More or less."

"Let's spend the week here getting reacquainted, and if we haven't killed each other by Friday, drive down to Aarhus to spend the weekend with the kids. We can buy more clothes there."

"Clothes shopping is not my thing and certainly not with anyone else."

"In which case, we are in for some new experiences."

"I'm flexible but refuse to buy anything involving checks or cloth hats."

"What a relief. I want my boyfriend to look young and vibrant."

"I haven't been called any of those for a while. I suppose you must be my girlfriend."

Inge Lise pulled me to her, and we kissed deeply.

"Should we marry?" she said, coming up for air.

"I would love to be your husband. At our age, it's more becoming than boyfriend. And you?"

"Likewise, but we shouldn't rush into anything. We

have the family to consider."

"It will take some getting used to."

"The family?"

"No, considering anything from another person's viewpoint. We'll have to help each other adjust to our new circumstances."

"It won't be easy," said Inge Lise as we walked hand in hand to her bathroom and into her walk-in shower. "But it is amazing we are in a position to try. How long can you stay?"

"Up to ninety days, but I ought to go back and resolve a few issues sooner rather than later."

"Can you tell me?"

"Of course. Do you remember Norman Shannon, the older gentleman with the garish tartan trews?"

"Vaguely."

"He died recently and left me some items in his will for which I need to sign papers before disposing of them."

"Anything worthwhile?"

"His vintage Jaguar and the launch he took us out on a few times."

"I loved them both?"

"Their estimated value is well over three hundred thousand pounds. Why don't you come with me? You could see my Harborough apartment and meet up with the remaining gang members?"

"I'd love to. Anything else you need to resolve?"

"What happened to Sara? A police officer friend, John, is investigating a few leads that might provide an answer. But what about you? Surely you have commitments?"

"I do, and when we're dressed, I'll show you."

"Intriguing," I said when we were ready and headed

downstairs.

"Listen, Ollie. I'm not your typical pensioner. I do not play Bridge, attend book clubs, or shop. I'm not a clubby type, and many call me antisocial because, other than walking, I rarely go out or meet people. I order everything online but spend most of my time doing this," she said as she opened a door off the downstairs lobby and invited me to go in.

It was a study overlooking the garden. The latest Apple desktop was sitting on a spacious blond pine table. A huge ergonomic chair faced the monitor. Behind was a floor-to-ceiling bookshelf. In front was a meeting table surrounded by four chairs and a sofa in the corner.

"Look at the books on the middle shelf," she said.

I spotted twenty books with the name Inge Lise Oleson on the spine. I pulled them out one by one and looked at the covers.

I couldn't understand the titles, but the cover images conveyed nonfiction books about eco-housing, child psychology, and hypnosis. The final three were fiction, with ominous images of a man in a pink hoody stalking a woman with a knife. To the right of the bookshelf were wall-mounted framed certificates. I browsed through them. Some were university qualifications, others were awards.

"Impressive," I said.

"They are only in Danish, I'm afraid. I started with child psychology and hypnotism before describing my experiences with eco-housing. When I ran out of ideas, I switched to writing fiction on a subject that has haunted me since I was in Henley."

"Me?"

"Hardly. I was stalked by a tall man wearing a pink

hoody and a blue scarf over his mouth."

"You never mentioned it."

"It happened before we met and wasn't scary."

"I wish you'd told me."

"Why?"

"He became known as the Henley stalker and went on to rape a Swedish girl. Thanks to my investigation into Sara's disappearance, my police officer friend John has reopened the case."

Inge Lise went pale, and her eyes watered.

I put my arms around her.

"What is it?"

"Rape, you said?"

"And she was severely wounded."

"I was lucky to be his first victim."

CHAPTER 37

2024

"How do you know you were the first? I asked.
"The police were sceptical when I reported it," said Inge Lise. "They told me."

"Where did it happen?"

"On Norman Avenue. I was walking home after a night out with my au pair girlfriends, and he jumped out from behind a tree and followed me right up close. He said nothing but breathed heavily down my neck. I ran toward the main road, and he pursued me but stopped as the streetlights grew brighter. As I passed the gas station, I saw him looking at me, holding his hands in front of his chest and wiggling his fingers."

"Can you remember what he was wearing?"

"A light-coloured hoody, dark jeans and some kind of scarf wrapped over his mouth and nose."

"What were your impressions of him?"

"He was about your size and build."

"Age?"

"Difficult to estimate but athletic looking. My strongest memory is he reeked of beer."

"How awful."

"Do the police have any suspects?"

"Me."

"What?"

"The night of the rape, a resident in Norman Avenue saw a man matching my description lurking under a tree. He'd seen him several times, sometimes sprinting. This resident knew me well from rowing and school and reported he moved like me."

"It could have been you. Was it?"

"The light-coloured hoody was a pink Leander Club training top, of which I have several—also, those of my father and grandfather. I still have flashbacks of following a girl that forced me to question whether I had it in me. Thankfully, I had perfect alibis for three of the cases, especially the night of the rape. The police have found the original file but have yet to locate a semen sample from the rape. If they find it, hopefully, a DNA test should reveal a culprit."

"My first stalker book was based on my own experience, but I fictionalised it and relocated it to Aarhus, where they were also having problems with a stalker."

"When was this?"

"Must be thirty-odd years ago."

"Did they find him?"

"No, but there were so many similarities to the Henley guy; it was as if he had relocated to Aarhus."

"What similarities?"

"Height, athleticism, not speaking, finger wiggling and stinking of beer."

"Creepy."

"Thankfully, he stopped."

"Did they have any clues?"

"Only what I described, but no suspects and no DNA."

"How many incidents?"

"Around five reported. It was all over the media, which is how I heard about it. It inspired me to write a mini-fictional series using imagined cases about stalkers, what motivates them and how their victims suffer. It sold extremely well because it helped many victims understand their experiences. I also had quite a few calls to my clinic from men who had stalking fantasies and were unsure if they had stalked anyone."

"Were you able to help them?"

"I hypnotised them to relive whatever was triggering their fantasies. It helped a few, but others were impervious to hypnosis. However, I did uncover two stalkers and was able to nip their potential careers in the bud. I also attracted some cranks and weirdos. After my third book, I became disenchanted with trying to save the world from stalkers and returned to helping children."

"Are you still writing?"

"Not at the moment, but I have a few ideas for cooking."

"I don't know if Chris mentioned, but I want to produce a family rowing history and donate it to Leander with our trophies, old tracksuit tops and photos. Chris has photos of my father participating in a regatta at Aarhus in 1959. I have no idea how to make a book or write it, but I have the content. Would you help me?"

"Of course, we can also do it in Danish. Many rowers here would be interested. Ollie, I love having projects."

"Me too, it's what keeps me alive. It's what drove

me here."

"And now we can work on them together."

"Perfect because I'm not particularly domesticated. Hate gardening and refuse to mention sickness and tablet consumption."

"We should make a perfect couple."

"We always did."

"Our first project can be unravelling a whole bunch of diaries."

CHAPTER 38

2024

"When did the diaries arrive?" I asked as we sat together behind Inge Lise's desk with a flask of coffee after a leisurely breakfast of fruit and tablets in the kitchen.

"Over a year ago," she said, opening a drawer, extracting a heavy brown cloth bag and placing it in front of me.

We looked at each other lovingly.

"It seems like five minutes," I said.

"Where did the time go?" she said. "Go on, open the bag and let's begin our first project."

I fumbled around inside and extracted over thirty diaries. They were all the same except for the year gold blocked onto the front. The covers were dark, blue-grained plastic wallets with open sleeves inside, into which the outer cardboard pages of the printed interior were inserted. The initial pages were standard diary content of sunrise and sunset hours, notes, calendars for previous, current, and coming years, notable dates, travel information, conversion tables and a wine vintage chart. The diary pages were a week to a double page, which didn't leave room for long-winded entries.

We sorted them into decades.

"Was there a cover letter?" I asked.

"Just a brief note saying, keep these in a secret place. Don't tell a soul; one day, he will come."

"What did you conclude?"

"My first instinct was to bin them, but then I wondered if he might mean you. On the off chance, I decided to keep them."

"How were they sent?"

"They arrived by registered post from Reading in Berkshire, England. I assumed because I signed for the packet, whoever had sent them would be informed they had arrived safely."

"Have you read them all?"

"Cover to cover. It's how I worked out who was the sender. My name was mentioned in 1967, and the early ones contained references to training at Langley. It had to be Jenny."

"Didn't you wonder why she sent them to you?"

"I was confused. Perhaps you can help resolve that?"

"Any revelations?"

"They are cryptic in places, but I believe, yes, and they certainly answer your questions about what happened to Sara."

"Go on."

"You ought to read it yourself to confirm I understood correctly, but on the night of the twenty-first of April 1968, Sara was on her way back to the hotel to collect her belongings after taking O.M., which I assumed to be you, home when Dwight, pulled alongside her in a car. He said the police were going to arrest her the next day for drug dealing and she should come with him to America. So, she did. Dwight, whose surname was Vinson, took her to St. Andrews Air Force base, where they married almost the next day, and she became Christine, her second name, Vinson. Because of Dwight's connections, she could fast-track a green card and citizenship, and they went on to have two children. There is a happy family photograph of the four of them ten years later. It's tucked into the back sleeve of the diary."

I rummaged through the sixties pile, picked out the diary from 1968 and peeked in the rear sleeve. Sure enough, there was a battered photo. I eased it out and was immediately shocked. Both Dwight and Sara were enormously obese, and the kids too. A boy and a girl were all grinning and appeared happy. Neither of the kids looked like me. I turned the photo over and saw it written in Sara's handwriting: Thanksgiving 1979, *In the garden of our new home in Annapolis*.

"Did you ascertain if Sara was still alive?"

"The diaries began in 1962 and stopped in 1968 until 1972 when they restarted until the mid-nineties. There are several references to letters from Sara; the last entry in 1985 announced Sara had the same disease as her mother and was unlikely to last the year."

"At least we have the answers about Sara. I'm sure her sister Jill will appreciate the news. Was there anything about a plot?"

"There were two more items worthy of consideration, both of which are potential nightmares for the CIA."

"Wow. Go on."

"The first contains condemning evidence about the death of Mervyn Phipps. Did you know him?"

"We went to the same school and used to row for Leander. He was like me in appearance but a bit of a creep with the ladies, according to my friend Anita."

"Jenny described him the same. He was their drug supplier."

"What did she imply by *their*?"

"If you pull out the interior for 1968, there are notes written on both sides of the front and back covers."

I fumbled again and slid out of the interior. The outer covers were filled with neat but tiny handwriting. I held the first page closer to my eyes and, with difficulty, began to read.

"Dearest O, two items in these notes are worthy of your attention. I am sending them to Inge Lise because I don't know where you are, and eventually, you two are bound to find each other again. I have recently been diagnosed with cancer and have been given about a year. Beyond learning about Sara's demise, you should know what we were up to in Henley and why my behaviour toward you was so despicable. By the way, Sara and I communicated through a PO Box, so she never knew where I was. Sara and I ran a drug resale business. Sara to raise money for her sick mother, me to supplement my pathetic income and assuage my greedy ambitions. We purchased marijuana, amphetamines, birth control pills and strength-boosting steroids from Mervyn Phipps. Sara sold them to a range of customers in the Riverside Bar. I used some of the dope myself and sold everything else to colleagues who used them when off duty and smuggled some back to the States on Air Force transport, where they resold them at various CIA offices. Trade was ticking along nicely when Mervyn Phipps upped the ante. He insisted we buy in bulk, pay up front and store the products in the Red Lion staff quarters. This forced us to change from a small, relatively risk-free business into a scale beyond anything we were comfortable with. So, we declined and searched elsewhere for a more amenable supplier. Phipps was furious and threatened violence unless we accepted his demands. I could handle Phipps, but Sara was terrified and informed Dwight. He was protective of Sara, and between the two of us, we cooked up a scheme to adjust the brakes on Phipps' motorcycle. His fatal accident solved our problem in two ways. It removed Phipps, and we ceased trading. Harmful as the drugs and elimination of Phipps sounded, it was the second item which forced me to approach MI5 and disappear—continued on the back cover.

I paused and looked at Inge Lise.

She topped up my coffee. I preferred tea, but coffee was the Danish way. Thankfully, the coffee was decaffeinated, or I would have bounced off the walls.

I turned to the inside back page and continued reading.

In the rear sleeve of the 1969 diary, you will find a photo of Chuck Wainwright. He was my boss, the one who bullied and sexually harassed me. You met him briefly in the bar after a soccer game. Although his treatment of me was the initial cause of my approaching MI5, it was a coded telephone conversation I overheard between Chuck and another unknown person in English. He said *before you go to LA. We have another friend we need you to meet in the UK. You will be picked up at Heathrow and taken to her house near Henley. Can you book the flight for this Friday?*

I discussed this with Dwight, and he reported it to Chuck's superiors, who initiated the withdrawal of JK and her protection team. If you recall, Robert F. Kennedy was assassinated on June 6, 1968. With the benefit of hindsight, responding to this telephone call was highly significant, and I believe we saved JK's life. Sadly, we were so busy moving her to safety that it distracted us from R.F.K., which may have been the plan. Last time I heard, Chuck was still in Leavenworth prison, but he never gave up his fellow conspirators or any hint about what was to happen to R.F.K.

What I hadn't considered was the consequences of my disappearance into the British prison system. Because I wasn't around to confirm Dwight's explanations or what I overheard from Chuck, the CIA might have suspected I was part of Chuck's team and may have been searching for me ever since. They haven't found me, and I have no idea if they are still looking. My objective here is purely to inform you what I was going through to attempt some justification for my awful behaviour. The stress I was under disturbed me mentally, and you were the one I took it out on. Sorry. I did leave several clues, such as the engagement advert in the Henley Standard, hoping you would one day look me up, knowing you would want an answer for our last night in Room 118. If we don't hook up, I hope you can find it in your heart to accept my apology and maybe forgive me. You were the only man I ever had strong feelings for, and when reflecting on the ruins of my life, I often wonder how it might have been between us if I had been in another line of work. Once you have satisfied yourself with the events of 1968, I suggest you burn the diaries and forget everything I've told you. Take care, and enjoy being back with Inge Lise. She deserves you; I never did. J

"This is dynamite," I said. "It turns all the

conspiracy theories about R. F. K.'s death upside down by proving his assassin wasn't working alone but on instructions from another power."

"With all the troubles in Ukraine and Gaza, does the world need to revisit this?" said Inge Lise. "It will throw more oil on troubled waters."

"I agree. We should burn them."

"Shame. The writer in me would love to exploit this, but you are right. Let's remove all the interiors and shred them. The covers can go into recycling."

A thought struck me as we fed the interiors into Inge Lise's shredding machine.

"Was there anything else of interest in the diaries?" I asked.

"Nothing concerning us."

"So, I'm not missing anything."

"Only her biography, which frankly, after the excitement of her CIA career, wasn't worth the read."

"Accept your past without regrets,
and face your future without fears."

Paulo Coelho

CHAPTER 39

2024

I tingled with satisfaction. Finally, I had answers to most of my burning questions. The identity of the Henley stalker was still outstanding but was out of my hands. Hopefully, I can move on, enjoy life, reacquaint myself with Inge Lise, and get to know my family.

I treasured the concept of *Family;* it was warm and comforting to be surrounded by loved ones instead of a solitary oddball. The change from me to us was equally fulfilling and a natural and instant transition. It had been amazing how quickly the intensity of our feelings had been reignited—almost as if there had never been a gap of fifty-six years.

Although I knew my decisions concerning celibacy and alcohol were suitable for the time and circumstances, they did not apply to Inge Lise. I could no more raise my hand to her than a tiny baby, but this didn't give me a new licence to consume more alcohol.

We decided not to enlighten John Harker about the content of Jenny's diaries. I knew he would have enjoyed the closure but could not avoid reporting the findings to his superiors and MI5. Which would open a can of worms and, if leaked, provide enticing fodder to conspiracy theorists. No, our secrets of the past should lie undisturbed.

By way of justification, our knowledge of them stemmed from resolving our situation. It had nothing to do with patriotism. We suspected Sara's husband and children, even Chuck languishing behind bars, would respect our silence on the matter. Notwithstanding, we could have made a fortune from the publishing rights.

For the remainder of the week, we explored each other physically and mentally, filling in the vast gaps in our relationship. Inge Lise introduced me to her town, places of interest and the surrounding countryside. I helped clear out her office at the clinic, renewing my brief relationship with Greta, her assistant, who couldn't stop beaming with happiness as we pottered about emptying cupboards and shelves. I claimed Inge Lise's comfortable office chair as my own so we could swing back and forth behind her home desk as we kicked around ideas for our next project, the rowing book.

On Friday, we caught the train to Aarhus, trembling with excitement. It would be our first family get-together.

The train stopped at Lystrup station, where a large advertising poster promoting something unpronounceable pictured a pair of outstretched hairy male arms striving to reach a decidedly unhappy little blond girl floating in a cloud.

The vision formed in my mind, and while preoccupied with it, I must have missed something Inge Lise said. She sat beside me and started shaking me when I failed to reply.

"Where are you, Ollie?" she asked concernedly.

"To be honest, I don't know."

"You were daydreaming about something."

"Guilty."

"Can you tell me?"

"Of course. It's this recurring daytime vision I've had since my twenties. The poster by the platform triggered it. Normally, when I see or read the word April, it takes over my brain. Have you any idea what it could mean?"

"Describe it."

"A girl with long blond hair is walking in front of me. At least, I assume it's me; I am following her, catching her up with my arms outstretched. As I am about to touch her, she vanishes. From your experience, have you ever heard of anything similar?"

"The mind is a labyrinth of complexity, my love. We are still unravelling its mysteries, but the mainstream views are that human memory is not inherited but acquired. Mentally ill patients such as people with schizophrenia often have visions; however, as you are firing on all cylinders in that department, I suspect its roots are something rudimentary. Without detailed counselling and maybe hypnosis, I can only suggest that somehow you have acquired this from your childhood."

"Could I have overheard my parents talking about it?"

"Or your grandparents. Either way, it could have shocked you, which made a deep impression on your psyche, which you repressed. The vision could be your mind fighting back, saying, *Oi, listen to me*. Have you ever had urges to put the vision into practice?"

"None, but why does April kick things off?"

"Perhaps it was April when you heard it?"

"Possibly, but I hit Jenny during April. With all my outstanding questions resolved, my mind should have put the vision to rest."

"It hasn't, which suggests something else is still lurking in your subconscious. We need to monitor this. Perhaps a pattern might emerge. Can you let me know when the vision returns and what triggered it? I'll track them. It might tell us something."

"Would hypnotising help?"

"Possibly, but I need to learn more about the vision first to determine what questions to ask while you are under. Since you only recently answered the questions about Jenny, perhaps your subconscious needs longer to let matters go. It's best to leave it for now but monitor how often and what triggers its return."

Chris met us at Aarhus station. We hugged tightly, and he regarded us both carefully. Happy with what he saw, we headed off arm in arm to his car.

"You appear happy and well-adjusted to each other," he said as he drove us home. "I know you've only had a short time together, but have you come to any conclusions about the future?"

"It's like the fifty-odd years have flashed by," said Inge Lise. "We carried on where we left off and have agreed to focus on the future rather than dwell on the agonies and errors of the past."

"Life is too short for procrastination," I said. "I have some issues I need to resolve in the UK, so we are travelling there together next week. Immigration laws determine the options for where we live. I can spend ninety days in Denmark at a time only twice a year, and your mother has similar restrictions on her time in the UK. Our goal, though, is to spend as much time as we can with you. I guess we'll develop a workable solution that suits everyone over time. However, there is one thing we can say for sure. We do not intend to move in with you. After years of living alone, we first need to adapt to cohabiting. Once we've overcome the many hurdles, we can make a better-informed decision about the future. Is that acceptable?"

"Sounds good to me, Dad and Mum."

I glanced at Inge Lise in the back seat. She was glowing with pleasure.

Carolyn and the boys welcomed us with big hugs, and we sat in the lounge, enjoying delicious home-baked Danish pastries and yet more coffee as we swapped anecdotes about our lives.

The following week whizzed by. Every day, we found various activities we could do together, most of which involved walking somewhere in the still chilly Aarhus. It wasn't Henley or Harborough, but I enjoyed its charms equally. However, I needed warm underwear, woollen socks, and thick plaid shirts to fend off the cold.

My favourite time was sitting around the dining table where we could regard each other face to face as we talked and sampled a range of Carolyn's delightful Danish food.

My favourite was *Aebleflæsk,* a traditional dish of cured pork belly fried with apples, sugar, and thyme. It can also be served on rye bread, but we skipped the usual accompaniment of schnapps or beer. Another delicious lunch was *Stegt flæsk med persillesovs og kartoffler,* often considered the national dish of Denmark. It is crispy pork with parsley sauce and potatoes. *Frikadeller* are meatballs made from pork or a mix of beef and pork or fish served with parsley sauce and potatoes, and it would be irreverent not to mention *Rød Pølse,* a red sausage served with bread, mustard, ketchup, and fried onion. Another favourite was *Smørrebrød,* an open-face sandwich with a variety of toppings. No wonder Denmark was considered one of the happiest countries in the world. Their language was another matter. It is a complicated language to understand because it is mumbled with potatoes stuck in the throat. Our funniest moments were me attempting the odd sentence or two. They were impressed by my memory of love and swear words but teased me with my attempts at place names such as *Rødovre* and *Hvidovre*. I was happy to be the cause of laughter, but I drew my line in the sand.

I was beginning to forget about stalkers and hadn't had a vision since we were on the train. However, the morning we were flying to Stanstead, my phone pinged. It was a text from John Harker. It said we needed to meet urgently, but beware of crossing borders.

What did his cryptic message imply?

The outstretched arms returned with a vengeance.

CHAPTER 40

2024

Chris and Carolyn dropped us off at Aarhus Airport. They insisted on parking and accompanying us to the check-in desk, where we hugged tightly. Having other people express emotion about my leaving was another first to which I could happily become accustomed. We dropped our bags and, holding hands, headed off to security.

The flight landed on time at Stanstead. We scanned our passports at the E-gates, walked through the barrier, and waited for our cases to be disgorged onto the belt. I found a large trolley, and when they eventually arrived, I loaded them on board and headed off to the customs hall. We approached the nothing-to-declare exit when two burly, serious men dressed in dark suits stepped forward.

"Mr. Matthews," said the eldest, who resembled a hard man from a gangster movie. I wasn't alarmed. I knew who they were; we had been expecting them after John's cryptic message.

"Yes."

"Could you accompany us, please?"

"Certainly."

They led us to a door deep in the customs hall, where we were separated from each other, our luggage, and our phones. Equally serious women led off Inge Lise.

It was a typical interview room, similar to those I had sat in thousands of times during my career. There were no windows, a small table with a closed beige folder sitting ominously on top, two chairs on each side, and a large mirror on one wall through which no doubt the boss of these men would be watching. I paused with my hands in the air, expecting them to search me.

"Not necessary," said the hard man. "Please take a seat."

"Can I see some ID?" I said, staying where I was.

They glared at me but extracted their badges inside their jackets and placed them on the table before me.

It was as I thought.

Graham Jones and Frederick Smith. These are probably not their real ones, with no titles, typed above Security Service MI5, Home Office, Thames House, London.

"How can I help?" I asked while they were taking their seats, hoping they would not notice my high levels of intimidation.

"We've received information you have been taking an unauthorised peek at top secret intelligence files," said Hard Man. "Under the Official Secrets Act, we are considering charges."

"I have never signed any agreement to comply with the act, so please, go ahead and charge me. Before I answer further questions, I demand my rights to phone my lawyer and have her attend this interrogation."

They looked down at the table, knowing their opening gambit had failed to concern me, although my knees were trembling.

The hard man opened the folder, slid a black-and-white photograph across the table, and asked, "Do you recognise this person?"

I reached out, turned it around and scrutinised the pretty young woman with long hair. I knew who it was but took my time before replying, "Yes."

"Can you tell me her name?" said the complicated man, irritated.

"I knew her as Jenny Leovich."

"How did you meet?"

"In the bar at the Red Lion Hotel in Henley-on-Thames. She was with my friend your colleagues are talking to."

"What was the nature of your relationship?"

"Friends and lovers."

"When?" perked up the brutal man's colleague in a public-school accent. With his clean-cut looks and baby face, he resembled a chorister.

"In 1967/8."

"When did you last see her?" said Baby Face.

They were testing my truthfulness as they knew I had read her file.

"On the twenty-sixth of December last year at approximately eleven am at her care home in Caversham," I replied.

"What did you talk about?"

"Not much; she died in my arms after about five minutes."

"She must have said something?" said Baby Face.

"She begged for my forgiveness, which I happily

granted."

"What was to forgive?" said the hard man.

"A personal matter which needn't concern you."

"We'll be the judge of that," said Baby Face.

"We will end this conversation now," I said, returning their glares.

"No need to be uncooperative," said Hardman.

"I've agreed to talk without my lawyer being present and am happy to say what I know about Jenny, but only regarding matters concerning her work. I consider what we had between us as private."

"When did you learn she was a foreign agent?"

"The same day she died."

"I don't believe you," said Hardman.

"Until DCS Harker showed me her file, I only knew she was a logistics attaché to the American Embassy organising the protection team for former first lady Jackie Kennedy's visits to her sister."

"She never mentioned her work?" said Baby Face.

"A few minor details."

"For example," said Hard Man.

"Trivial stuff, such as what a long hard day for little pay."

"Tell me about it," said Baby Face. "Anything else of substance?"

"Well, er, yes."

They sat forward, eyes bulging with curiosity.

"Go on," said Baby Face.

"Some of her responsibilities were to organise professional women to entertain her colleagues during their leisure time. Not all the women had turned up, and she had to persuade those who did to work overtime."

They looked disappointed.

"What was the relationship with her boss?" said the hard man.

"He was pressing to get into her pants, but she kept him at bay. Only when I read her file did I learn he was more aggressive than she described."

"Did she complain about her problems with the boss?" asked the hard man.

"If she reported him, it would end her career."

"Did you notice signs of drug use?" asked Baby Face.

"None, although she liked a whisky or two after a long day at the office."

"Don't we all," said Hard Man, grinning for the first time. "Did you meet her boss?"

"I might have done, but I never knew who he was, so I can't be certain."

"Can you recall any of her colleagues' names?" said Baby Face.

"Forgive me, it was a long time ago; one was maybe Dwight, and the other perhaps Chuck. Their surnames were not mentioned. I saw others in the team drinking in the Red Lion bar but never talked with any of them. They kept themselves to themselves."

"Is there anything else you can tell us about Jenny?"

"No, but perhaps you can answer a question."

They looked a little shocked.

"Depends," said baby face.

"Jenny used the name of Sara Fletcher nee Cowan after she married one of your colleagues. The real Sara Cowan used to be the bartender at the Red Lion. She was also a dear friend and former lover who disappeared on the twenty-first of April, 1968. I've been searching for her but without success, and her sister Jill has never heard from her. Can you throw any light on her whereabouts? I would love to say a final farewell."

The two men exchanged expressionless glances.

"Sorry," said Baby Face. We never suspected there was a real Sara, so didn't look."

"We're done," said Hard Man standing.

"Thank you for your time," said Baby Face. They led me back to the door leading to passport control and returned my suitcase.

I grabbed hold of it, opened the door and went through to find Inge Lise leaning against the wall opposite the passport gates. Her expression of relief was unmistakable.

She followed me through customs and into the arrivals hall, where we stopped and hugged.

"How did it go?" I whispered.

"As expected," she said.

"Don't say anything else until we are sure our luggage doesn't contain a GPS tracker or transmitter."

"Isn't this exciting?" she grinned and announced. "I need a coffee."

"Of course you do," I said. "You're Danish."

CHAPTER 41

2024

"Welcome back, Mr Matthews," said Leanne, the receptionist at the Red Lion in Henley. "Pleasure to have you with us again."

"Thank you, Leanne. Would Room 118 be available?"

"I've allocated it to you as a courtesy," said Leanne, swiping my card.

"Most kind. This is my friend Ms. Oleson. She is also fond of room 118."

"Happy memories," said Inge Lise, blushing.

"Can you find your way?"

"Of course."

"I'll have the porter deliver your luggage."

"Thanks again."

We went up in the lift and paused outside Room 118.

"How do you feel?" I asked.

"Not as nervous as our first time."

We opened the door, entered and stood by one of the windows. Squirrels were still scampering over the

Tudor house roof.

"This is surreal," said Inge Lise. "I never expected to be back here, especially with you."

"Happy?"

"Ecstatic but sad. It reminds me of how much we've missed, but this is an improvement," said Inge Lise, bouncing on the bed. "The mattress is perfect."

"Not a squeak to be heard. All the better for a perfect night's sleep."

"Not if I can help it," she said, hugging me and tucking her head into my shoulder.

"We'll have to see if anything pops up."

"I can't wait."

"Remembering?" I said as tears filled her eyes.

"Hmmm."

We stood in each other arms, swaying back and forth, lost in our thoughts, until the door knocked, and the porter delivered the cases. After placing them on folding racks, I gave him a gratuity, and we peered again from the window on the terrace below.

"Not a scooter in sight," she said. "I love what the new owners have done. It's modern, clean, and smells incredibly sweeter but retains its character. What's the food like?"

"Hungry already?" I asked, putting my arm around her.

"Yes, but first, we should unpack," she said, indicating the bags.

With all our things in their respective cupboards and drawers, we examined our cases inch by inch and found no trace of devices. To be safe, we shut them in the wardrobe and turned on the TV before speaking.

"Does this mean MI5 were satisfied with our answers?" whispered Inge Lise.

"It seems so, but we should remain mindful of what we say. The size of modern technology is miniscule, or they could be tracking our phones. Either way, we should remain alert. I have a monitoring device in my apartment in Harborough; we'll have another check then."

"How long did you say we were staying in Henley?"

"For three nights. It allows us to meet with John Harker and catch up with old friends."

"Do we have an agenda?"

"We're seeing John in the morning; he's joining us for breakfast. Tonight, we are meeting several of the gang at Norman's house for dinner, where I need to decide what to do with my inheritance. After which, we are free to explore as we wish."

"Which means," said Inge Lise hugging me. "We have time for a nap?"

After a week of abstention, while staying with Chris and the boys, we made love with abandon. The sense of euphoria afterwards was heavenly. We sighed with pleasure and fell asleep in each other's arms.

It was a gorgeous evening as we strolled along the riverbank and gazed down at the bench where we first kissed.

I read the brass sign screwed to the centre of the timber backrest.

In memory of the Right Honourable Valentine Fleming (1882 – 1917), MP for Henley (1910-1917), who died to defend this country in the Great War. Father of Ian Fleming.

"I never noticed the sign before," I said.

"Other matters on your mind," said Inge Lise, pulling me down onto the bench and kissing me.

"Shouldn't be snogging at your age," said some oik

as he cycled by.

We laughed out loud.

"And here we are in our own James Bond movie," I said.

We kissed again and headed off to Norman Avenue via the boat house by Henley Bridge to see Norman's launch.

It was immaculate, and having clambered all over it, I instinctively did not want to sell it. At least, not before having the pleasure of sailing it up and down the river a few times.

It was an emotional reunion in Norman Avenue as I watched Inge Lise hug old friends. She immediately recognised them: John Francis, Sonia and Paul, Ivan and Keith, wearing their best but jaded suits. Anita had pushed the boat out, and we enjoyed a delicious meal in the dining room overlooking the back garden, which used to house the making-out sofas in our youth. There were several embarrassing jokes about friends being discovered in various stages of undress. Thankfully, none about me.

After dining, Virginia showed Inge Lise about the house. When they returned half an hour later, my love seemed most pensive. Had she learned something unsavoury was my initial reaction.

We couldn't leave without seeing the Jaguar, so we trooped out to the garage. It was still red, shiny, and beautiful, and once again, it renewed my desire to drive it.

We said our goodbyes.

On our way back to the hotel, Inge Lise was quiet and clingy.

We undressed in silence, climbed into bed and turned out the light.

"Care to tell me?" I said, reaching out to touch her. She burst into tears.

I stroked her shoulder and waited.

"The house was everything I dreamed of where we would live should I have married you all those years ago," she exclaimed eventually. "The launch and car were icons of my time here with you. I guess I'm mourning our lost lives together. Maybe we would have had more children."

"Did Virginia mention the house is for sale? She doesn't want to live alone in such a massive space, so she is moving in with Anita."

"Yes. She did explain."

Inge Lise sat up and switched the bedside lamp.

"Ollie, I know managing this ninety-day nonsense will be difficult, but at least we should do it in style. What do you think if we bought Norman's house? It has a lift so we can grow old in it. We could keep the boat and car and be here with Chris and the boys for regatta week. Carolyn often brings them over to see her mother and family. They could stay with us rather than in a hotel. The boys would adore your new toys. Just think they could have the enjoyment we missed, and it would be amazing to watch their pleasure."

I was astonished. Here I was, thinking about how we could squeeze into my apartment, and she had the perfect solution figured out.

"One tiny problem?" I said.

"You can't afford it."

"Exactly."

"Ollie, I made so much money from my eco-houses that I could buy another one. I have plenty left over, and you wouldn't need to sell your inheritance."

"I'm not sure I could be comfortable spending your

money."

"Don't be ridiculous. If we had married, it would have been our money. Now that we are together, it is our money, which we should invest and protect for Chris and our grandsons."

"I could sell my apartment and contribute something?"

"No need, rent it out. It's another good investment."

"I hate all this moving and stuff."

"I will happily deal with it."

"You mean it?"

"I've never been so sincere about anything, and Ollie?"

"Yes, dear?"

"Could we be married in Henley church?"

CHAPTER 42

2024

The hotel restaurant at the Red Lion was busier than my visit before Christmas. As the same pretty, dark-haired young lady guided us to our table, I couldn't help but reflect on how much my life had changed since. The what-if game had indeed yielded a surprising outcome, mostly positive. All those unanswered questions nagging me for years had been wiped out almost completely.

As predicted, it had been a rollercoaster of emotions but well worthwhile. Five pairs of them, albeit with a somewhat larger shoe size, assuaged my yearning for the pattern of tiny feet. I had gained a daughter-in-law, and the love of my life had been found and, amazingly, still wanted to be with me. As we placed our hot food orders, I hoped the good fortune would continue with the following and hopefully final phase of my trip down memory lane.

John Harker joined us as our Eggs Benedict was served, and Inge Lise sipped her third cup of coffee.

"Sorry I'm late," he said, sitting opposite me and

looking at Inge Lise with raised eyebrows. "Parking in Henley is still impossible.

"No worry, John. As you can see, I've moved on somewhat since we last spoke. May I present Inge Lise Oleson from Grenaa in Denmark? You may also have discovered she was the first victim of the Henley stalker. She is as interested in hearing what you say as I do."

"Then I'll come straight to the point," said John after ordering a full English.

"We located the sperm sample from the rape of Margot Hedenblad, the Swedish girl. Did you know her by any chance, Inge Lise?"

"Sorry, no."

"Having now read up on all seven victims," said John. "Our man only attacked blond-haired au pair girls. Without exception, all had blue eyes and either blond or fair hair. Four were Scandinavian, two German and one from Seville in Spain."

"She must have been, Lola," said Inge Lise.

"Correct," said John.

"I knew her but not well," said Inge Lise. "Was she hurt?"

"No, her attack was like yours, except he touched her breasts. She was the last victim before the rape. We tested the sperm sample, and Ollie, it is not good news."

My pulse raced as I waited for John to elucidate.

"Go on," I said as Inge Lise grasped my hand.

"We compared the result with what we had on file for you, and the similarity was so close that I almost sent out an immediate arrest warrant, but the photographs you sent me saved the day. If they were correct and we had no reason to suspect they were, you were not in Henley on the day of the rape, so I asked the lab to double-check. Last week, they confirmed it wasn't you but a close relative."

"How close?" I said, my mind shooting in all directions, culminating in the vision flashing brightly in front of the remains of my eggs.

"The DNA is of a male four or five years older than you. He is a Matthews but combined with a non-related female."

"That implies my father had a child with another woman before he met my mother."

"Possible," said John. "But your grandfather could have also been the sperm donor. With these possibilities in mind, we searched the birth records of 1944 and 1945 and found a match.

Inge Lise and I exchanged nervous glances.

"Sixteen male children were born during those years in Henley without a registered father."

"So many?" said Inge Lise.

"It was during the war. Many women had relationships while their partners were fighting overseas or listed as missing in action. To avoid embarrassment, single mothers usually omitted the father's name. The married ones used their husband's names and prayed he didn't return from the war or would be forgiving."

"Have you located them?" I asked.

"Some have died, but others are still with us," said John. "We tested them or surviving relatives and were able to eliminate fifteen."

"You found him?" I asked.

"He's under arrest pending interview."

"What is his name?" I asked.

"Nathaniel Garnet. He lives with his half-brother

on Norman Avenue and Ollie. He will only speak to you."

"How odd?" I said. "I thought the person living with Mike Garnet was a woman called Natalie."

"I can confirm the person we arrested was dressed as a woman when our officers called at the house. He was asked to declare which gender he identified with before he was informed of his rights and was advised by his half-brother to be male. It would be less hassle with make-up and clothing. He agreed willingly to give a DNA sample, and it came back a perfect match to the rapist. He is in a single cell under my office, pending an interview. Could you come with me after breakfast?"

"Of course. What will you do, my love?"

"Don't worry about me. I have arrangements to confirm."

We left Inge Lise at the table, drinking another coffee and sending texts.

"I assume Inge Lise is your girlfriend from all those years ago?" said John as we headed to the station car park.

"And the mother of Chris," I said. "And grandmother to two strapping grandsons."

"And have you resolved what happened last night?"

"About as much as I ever will."

"Care to share?"

"It was as Jill described after the funeral, and I finally did recall punching Jenny. Irrespective of whether she was a highly trained agent, I was still wracked with guilt for hitting a woman while drunk. It was my cause of shame and why I decided to drink little and remain celibate. Thanks for the cryptic message. We were stopped by MI5 and interviewed on our return from Denmark, but I had nothing to add to what they knew about Jenny. Did they come and see you?"

"No, but I had a long telephone call. Sorry, but I had no option but to tell them everything."

"I have no problem with the truth, John. Hopefully, the matter is now closed."

"It is as far as I am concerned. There is no trace of Sara, so we can safely assume she must be deceased."

"I agree. It is pointless to investigate further, but at least you have closed another cold case because of me coming back into your life."

"Although, I reckon nothing will happen to the perpetrator. The Swedish girl who was raped refuses to bring charges preferring not to rake over something she put behind her decades ago. Nathaniel isn't in good health, as you will see shortly, so unless someone is prepared to bring charges, I fear the Crown Prosecution Service won't be prepared to take this to court."

"Would a full confession do?" I said as we climbed into his car.

"Even if he pleads guilty, his sentence would not be proportionate to the crime or the amount of work involved in bringing the case to court."

"How about his mental state?"

"I'm sure a good lawyer would be able to build a solid defence around his frailty and state of mind, but as he won't say anything, it's difficult to form an opinion."

"Did you discover anything about Mervyn Phipps or Mike Garnet?"

"No record of the accident or hospital treatment, but they usually dispose of medical records after ten years of death, and now we have our stalker, all other lines of inquiry have ceased. Here we are."

We pulled into Reading Police Station and parked.

John left me in an interview room while an officer was sent to collect Nathaniel.

When he came in a few minutes later and hobbled over to sit down opposite me, I had the shock of my life.

His resemblance to my grandfather was uncanny.

CHAPTER 43

2024

"Scary, isn't it," said Nathaniel Garnet as he leaned his elbows on the desk and regarded me through black-framed glasses. His face was petite compared to my grandfather, he was slender compared to me, and his mannerisms were distinctly feminine, but there was no doubt he carried the Matthews genes. The blue eyes and tall stature were instantly recognisable. His hair was cropped short, and he wore jeans with a button-down collar shirt and a V-neck sweater not too different from my attire. His voice was soft, and difficult to identify as male or female.

"Do you mean how similar you are to my grandfather?" I asked.

"That and finding family skeletons in the cupboard so late in life. I take it you don't remember me."

"We've met?"

"We used to play together regularly until you were nearly three. Did you know your father was married to my mother?"

"He never mentioned it."

"I'm not surprised. It's probably best if I tell you the details. They go some way to mitigating my behaviour as an adult."

"I'm listening."

"My mother was Christine Larkins. She came from a dysfunctional council estate home, which she survived, but it caused her problems as an adult and parent. She was beautiful, though not the brightest light on the tree. She attended Gillot's school two years below your father's, and they were childhood sweethearts. They married without consent from her parents, mainly so she could escape the tortuous family home and make her own life. Within weeks, your father had been called into the military and was posted to Africa, where he served with the Desert Rats in the campaign against Rommel. He was an explosives expert and was in demand, so he rarely came home on leave. During his extended absence, in steps your gallant grandfather. He helped practically and financially and ultimately wormed his way into her bedroom. This was unknown to your grandmother. Christine fell pregnant, and naturally, when your father did come home on leave to find a baby in the house, obviously not his, he sued for divorce and returned to the front.

"Your grandmother discovered what her husband had been up to but refused to divorce and insisted he provide properly for the now ex-daughter-in-law and child. Your grandfather used to bring you to visit, and as you grew old enough to walk, we played together. The problem was my mother wanted a girl and insisted on letting my blond hair grow long and, on weekends, would dress me up in girls' clothes. We used to run around the garden with you chasing me, shouting my girl's name. I teased you rotten; I'm afraid, almost letting you catch me but then sprinting off at the last second and hiding in the garden shed. Then Mum met Nicholas Garnet. They fell in love and married. Naturally, Nicholas didn't want your grandfather to call anymore, which ended our relationship. Nicholas and I never clicked, so I joined the Navy when I was old enough, leaving them with their two children, May and Mike. When Mike had his accident, they summoned me to return home to care for him, which I did and have been there ever since."

What was your girl's name?" I asked, knowing the answer.

"April. Mum had a thing about associating birthdays with a date or event."

"What happened to May?"

"She immigrated to New Zealand and never kept in touch. I'll explain why later. What you must be interested to hear is why I raped the Swedish girl?"

"It's why you are here."

"Joining the navy helped me identify as a woman. It was men only in those days, and let me tell you, being shut into a confined space with several hundred testosterone-charged machos for months on end was a life-changing experience for a pretty boy. I've never had so much attention before or since. Eventually, I settled into a steady shipwife relationship with a junior officer until I returned home to care for Mike."

"What started the stalking?"

"Being home again, I found some of my mother's clothes in the attic, started dressing up, and then walked about the house. I added make-up and plucked enough courage to shop and walk about town as a woman. It was a liberating experience, and probably the first time I felt comfortable in the skin I was in. Mike found this excruciatingly embarrassing and teased me about being mentally ill. How could I be a physical man but want to be a woman? How could I prefer sex with men when I had never tried it with a woman? He goaded me incessantly to try. If I still wanted to be a woman afterwards, he would accept me as I preferred to be, but only when I had tried it.

"Initially, I was reticent, but the more my inner voice nagged me, the more I decided to give it a go. I dressed up as a man and went to Chez Skinners and other pick-up joints, but as soon as I opened my mouth, women knew I was male and gay and preferred to be friends only, which wasn't moving me forward.

"You should try stalking them," said Mike. I assumed he was joking, but the more I considered the option, the more it grew. Living on Norman Avenue was perfect because lots of women cut through. One evening, I dug out your grandfather's old Leander hoody, wrapped a blue scarf over my mouth, and presented myself to Mike.

"Love it," he said. "When it was dark, I went out and waited behind a tree opposite the house. I'd been watching out the window for potential victims and spotted precisely the type I had in mind. Blond au pair girls. They were foreigners and unlikely to receive favourable treatment by the police. As my voice was distinctively feminine, I decided to remain silent and use lewd gestures to scare them into submission.

"With the first, I was more frightened than she was. With the second less so, and with the seventh, I'd reached the tonight or never stage. I hit her over the head and carried her into the graveyard, where I raped her before she recovered consciousness. And there ended my career as the Henley stalker."

"Why?"

"The easy part was I could now tell Mike, based on experience, that I preferred men. The hard part was living with what I had done to the poor girl. At times, I was praying for a knock on the door and being carted off to rot in prison. The guilt has eaten away at my sanity and health and continues to do so. Sharing it with you is the best therapy I've had. I've forgotten how often I left the house heading to the police station to confess. I almost turned to the church for help, but they didn't recognise people like me. What I want to do more than anything is write to the girl and offer my sincere apologies."

"It might make you feel better," I said. "But she was clear when responding to our request to bring charges against you. She put it in perspective, carried on with her life, and wanted nothing more. What was Mike's response to the rape?"

He respected my decision, and we settled into quite a sweet relationship where we still are, except I am too feeble to care for him. I could die any time, but I welcome it. I've lived too long with this debilitating guilt, and it will be a relief to be free from the constant accusations from my inner voice."

"I understand. It's a shame to go to one's maker carrying such a bitter load. Memories should be sweet, but those who live by the sword shall die by it."

"Profound but true and deserved."

"Has Mike inquired about a live-in carer for the two of you?"

"He's working on it. We've interviewed some Thai girls who are the current favourites."

"How will you pay?"

"Money isn't a problem, thanks to your grandfather. He purchased the house on Norman Avenue in my mother's name, and Nick Garnet made enough as a stockbroker to go and live in Menorca and provide us with a more than adequate income. After Nick and my mother passed, Norman Shannon helped manage our investments, which increased value under his stewardship."

"I'm pleased my grandfather made up for his sins."

"Your grandmother never forgave him but stood by him. In those days, it was what women did with errant husbands, especially those with money like your grandfather."

"I never knew he was wealthy. We didn't see much of it."

"He was a brilliant raconteur and was highly paid for motivational speaking and as a radio commentator for rowing events."

"I never knew. I wonder why my parents didn't tell me."

"Your father and his rarely communicated after the war."

"Why didn't I notice?"

"Too busy growing up, perhaps."

"What was the point of Mike describing the stalker to the police and me at Norman's funeral as resembling me?"

"He wasn't lying; at that age, we weren't so different, but he thought it would deter them from inquiring closer to home."

"Whereas it achieved the opposite. It sharpened my resolve to prove I wasn't the stalker and to identify the real culprit."

"Which you have now done. Dear nephew, I can

only apologise. I did warn him about the possibility, but he was trying to protect me. In some ways, he feels as guilty as me for egging me on."

"Then he will have to live with that. Thanks, uncle, for throwing light on the part of my life I knew nothing about. It explains a strange daydream I've had for decades. I'll report to the officer in charge of your case, and they will then discuss it with the CPS – Crown Prosecution Service. It's not for me to say, but I suspect no charges will be brought against you as the CPS will probably deem you unfit to stand trial."

"Thank you, nephew. It doesn't make me feel any better, but I have come to the same conclusion."

"What drove May to New Zealand?"

"The details are vague as I was barely five. It turned out Nick wasn't May's father. Your grandfather was. He paid for May to go and gave her some introductions from his rowing days to ensure she had a home and work opportunities. Oliver, somewhere on the other side of the planet, you have an aunt, and who knows how many cousins there are?"

CHAPTER 44

2024

I had no doubts my uncle had told me the truth. He was a dying man, and I was as relieved to be clearing the decks as I was to hear his story. Deathbed confessions are highly reliable, and why would he lie to me? What could he possibly gain? The idea was to depart this world with a clear conscience, not a turmoil of unresolved issues. Nathaniel may have gone unpunished by the justice system, but his self-flagellation had never ended. I touched my uncle's shoulder on the way out. After all, he was family, but I was unlikely to see him again.

"Goodbye, Oliver," he said as I opened the door.

"Goodbye, Nathaniel."

John was waiting outside. He indicated I should follow.

We collected some tea from the vending machine and headed to his office.

"Did you hear?" I asked as we sat down.

"A sorry tale."

"And your conclusion is?"

"Subject to confirmation with the CPS, I expect your uncle will be taken home later this afternoon. He'll need to sign a full confession, and hopefully, his doctor will confirm his frailty. We will also inform social services to ensure satisfactory care arrangements are implemented. Will you be heading off to New Zealand?"

"No, but I will try to track down my aunt May's or any descendant's address. With these online genealogy sites, it should be relatively simple, even for a fossil like me. John, thank you for your efforts in helping resolve this. The outcome wasn't bargained for, but it has tidied up almost everything."

"Shame we couldn't find Sara," said John, looking at me hard.

"Isn't it? I can live without knowing and can concentrate on the positives. A complete tribe of Matthews to garnish the planet for the next couple of generations."

"Not sure what they will inherit. We can only hope humankind gets its ducks in a row."

I finished my tea, stood and offered John my hand across his desk.

"Thanks again, John. Now, I need some time alone to absorb all this. I'll walk to the train station."

"I can't persuade you to accept a lift?"

"Thanks, I'll be fine.

Sitting on the platform at Twyford waiting for the Henley train, I felt terrible about not telling John of Jenny's diaries, but it was for the best. Knowing would only have given him a bigger problem.

I texted Inge Lise I was on my way.

Sending it was comforting. For the first time since my parents were alive, somebody else was as concerned about my welfare as I was about theirs. I thought back to the moment with Nathaniel when I learned that there was no sweetness and light between my father and grandfather. And how astonished I was that my parents omitted to mention my father's first marriage or my uncle and aunt. It was typical of their generation to keep matters under wraps. They didn't talk about the war or anything unsavoury, which was sad because their precious memories were vital in avoiding a repeat. They should have shouted them from the rooftops, not buried them under the mattress.

Inge Lise replied with hearts.

I glowed with pleasure. Finally, everything was taking shape. Better late than never for a life well lived. Now, I could go to my maker with a clean slate, but the problem was that now I wanted to live forever.

As the train rattled along, packed with youngsters heading for afternoon classes at The Henley College, a loud exclamation dragged me out of my preoccupation. I looked outside, and a group pointed at the deluge, making visibility through the windows impossible.

"April showers," they screamed.

I expected an instant reoccurrence of the dreaded vision.

And waited and waited, but nothing.

Paul S Bradley

"Thanks for the memory."

*composed by Ralph Rainger,
lyrics by Leo Robin (1938)*

Acknowledgements

Thanks to the staff of the Relais Hotel in Henley, Richard Wheeler, John Leathes, Fran Poelman, Elizabeth Francis, and my family for helping me through this challenging journey. Simon Thompson produced a moody front cover, and Gary Smailes persevered as my editor. The mistakes, as usual, are down to me.

The Author

Londoner Paul S Bradley has lived and worked in Nerja, Spain, for over thirty years, writing and publishing lifestyle magazines, guidebooks, and travelogues in English, German, and Spanish. On his retirement, he started writing books.

www.paulbradley.eu

Also by Paul S. Bradley

Cosy Mystery
The Andalusian Mystery Series;
Darkness in Málaga.
Darkness in Ronda.
Darkness in Vélez-Málaga.
Darkness in Granada.
Darkness in Córdoba.

Biography
Reinventing the Wheel, co-authored with
Judge Pat A. Broderick

Humour
The Fontainebleau: Based on a true story
co-authored with Robert H. Edwards

www.paulbradley.eu

Nostalgia Man
in Market Harborough

Without memory, we are nothing.

Paul S Bradley

Book Description

Nostalgia Man in Market Harborough is the second novel by Paul S Bradley in the trilogy exploring memory. Without memory, we are nothing.

Fresh from cracking the mystery of his youth in Henley on the Thames, retired Detective Chief Superintendent Oliver Matthews is asked by a former colleague in Market Harborough, Leicestershire, for help. An unstable inmate in nearby high-security Gartree Prison wishes to confess to unsolved murders from the 1970s, but only to the man who put him there, the young DC Matthews. Was the prisoner's memory playing tricks? Perhaps he thirsted for revenge, or could it be a genuine attempt to show remorse and provide closure to the victims' families? Despite the potential danger and imminent marriage to the recently rediscovered love of his life, Matthews can't resist yet another challenge to the misty recollections of his youth.

Prologue

My life was no longer my own, but I wasn't complaining. Gone were the many hours in my comfortable armchair with a pleasant cup of tea reflecting on unresolved mysteries of my youth. The recurring visions had stopped, but the voice inside my head was still there. Thankfully, it no longer nagged but supported my change of circumstances.

Finally, I was at peace with my seventy-six-year-old self and could move forward with a full deck. With this heavy weight lifted from my shoulders, I should be able to treasure my remaining moments with joy, sharing them with the love of my life and my extended family.

Other than an unknown distant aunt in New Zealand, my ancestry had no other gaps. In theory, I could depart this world tomorrow at peace with myself, except that now I wanted to live forever.

I had decades of catching up to do. My diet would undoubtedly be modified to facilitate such an extension. Even less lettuce and cucumber loomed ominously on the horizon.

What I had absorbed during my emotional roller coaster ride over the previous six months was that keeping the brain engaged with stimulating activity was a critical factor in sustaining good mental and physical health. Considering I was not the allotment type or keen on DIY projects, this left only one option. I was good at solving puzzles, particularly those involving false or distorted memory.

I wonder if this newly acquired knowledge might help others.

CHAPTER 1

2024

"Oliver, should I wear white?" asked Inge Lise from the tiny kitchen of my assisted living apartment in Market Harborough. She was making coffee. She drank gallons of it.

"Pink with polka dots would show off your blue eyes," I said, sipping my second and final cup of tea for the day. Bladder management, I called it.

"Pink with polka dots," she yelled. "What are you, some, oh, sorry, my love, I forgot, English humour. Seriously, should I wear white?"

"At the wedding?"

"Do you have a death wish?"

"Sorry, love, but you're asking a seventy-six-year-old man who has never been married to proffer advice on what to wear at our wedding, especially one with about as much fashion sense as Billy Connolly?"

"Billy, who?"

"Never mind, white would be perfect, but you would look amazing in army fatigues."

"I'll take that as a yes then," she said, sitting her

shapely curves down next to me on the cramped sofa, sampling her coffee and frowning.

"Not good?" I asked.

"It's English instant; at least it's hot and wet."

"Should we add a decent coffee machine to the wedding list?"

"I can't wait that long; I ordered one from Amazon. It'll be here tomorrow with some decent Arabic beans and a grinder."

"Don't order too much; we don't have the cupboard space."

"I'll be ordering so much more than a coffee machine, all of which will fit perfectly when we move into the house in Henley-on-Thames. Meanwhile, we can pile them up behind this sofa, barely big enough for a cat."

"Ok, ok, point taken, but we'll only be here another six weeks until we can complete on Norman Avenue. In the meantime, there are plenty of good cafes and eateries nearby, so Her Majesty won't have to dirty her fingernails in the broom cupboard of a kitchen."

"Don't we," said Inge Lise, shaking with laughter and almost spilling her coffee. "Sound like a married couple already?"

I reached over, touched her arm, gazed into her deep pools of blue and said, "I love you and would be honoured if you wear white."

She blushed and fluttered her eyelids.

"Are you ready for this?" she said.

"Of course, why even ask?"

"I'm worried the toll of last week might be too much for you."

"That's the psychologist in you speaking. Honestly, I'm fine."

"Then I respect your mental resilience. Discovering your father's and grandfather's lurid past and two more relatives on top of me and our son in such a short time frame would have floored most people. Are the police pressing charges against your Uncle Nathaniel?"

"No, he's too frail to stand trial, but he and his half-brother Mike Garnet have agreed to self-confinement in a local nursing home."

"Will you visit them?"

"I'm considering it."

"Nathaniel must know something about his sister's whereabouts. Would you like to search for her in Australia?"

"I'll look briefly at one of the genealogy sites, but I'd rather concentrate on us; we have so much catching up to do."

"Fair enough, but you were so determined to unravel your past that I assumed you wanted to see it through."

"When I set out on this quest to solve the mystery of my youth, my principal objective was to discover what happened on my last night in Henley and why I left with such a heavy sense of shame. I found those answers relatively early, and Jenny's diaries provided the final closure. Stumbling across you and our son was a complete fluke, but now we are together; all the rest has paled to insignificance. Yes, it was a shock to realise my father was married before he met my mother and as for my horny grandfather, he's been dead for so long, any youthful feelings I had for him evaporated long ago. In short, I achieved my objective and can now put it behind me and concentrate on you, the love of my life."

"Then we should make our wedding a big affair.

Start as we mean to carry on."

"We could, but as most of our friends are dead or dying, the list won't be impressive. Let's keep it to those who matter: immediate family and close friends. As soon as we've agreed on a date, we should reserve the appropriate rooms at the Red Lion, sorry, Relais in Henley. Are you happy for the reception to be in the hotel restaurant?"

"Perfect. Will you invite Nathaniel?"

"Hadn't thought, but no, it is our day to enjoy. His presence would be a distraction."

"Good. Have you decided what to do with the E-type and launch?"

"I'm inclined to dispose of them, less admin and fewer responsibilities, but I want to wait until our son Chris and the boys have at least seen them; then I'll decide."

"And we agree to keep this place and rent it out; I'll take care of whatever needs to be done?"

"Fine, but won't it interfere with your writing?"

"Now that I have you back, writing seems to have taken a back seat. Frankly, I'm excited about setting up shop with you and building a nest we can call home. I've been dreaming about it all my life, never contemplating I would. Yet here we are, and don't worry about the administration; I enjoy it."

"Just as well, I hate it."

"Then we are well suited, but don't expect to sit around all day being waited on hand and foot."

"I adore your Danish accent and amazing English, but it's feet."

"Whatever, but what will you be doing?"

"I have this rowing book to work on and am here to be chief chore assistant as directed."

"Good, but please don't let me turn you into a house mouse. I respect your independence, and while I can't wait to marry you, I don't want a henpecked husband to join me at the hip."

"What a relief. Then, promise me one thing."

"Go on."

"While browsing online catalogues, never buy his and hers anoraks."

We laughed so loudly I failed to hear the doorbell ringing.

I checked the monitor on the door phone and recognised a face I hadn't seen for a while. I pressed the speaker button and said, "Come on up."

"Who is it?" asked Inge Lise.

"An old colleague."

"From the police?"

"My former desk sergeant."

"What does he want?"

"A cup of tea for sure," I said, opening the door and waiting by the lift.

"I'll put the kettle on."

"Your English cultural education is almost complete," I said as the lift door slid open. Out stepped my old colleague, a huge, burly man in plain clothes. His brown hair was tinted with grey, and his prominent nose was gnarled. A faint scar decorated a cheek, and the dark brown eye on the same side twitched occasionally. Otherwise, he was as I remembered him except for the wily expression and slight limp.

"Well, well, well, Sergeant Stray, wot 'ave we 'ere then?" I said.

"Detective Chief Superintendent Oliver Matthews?" he asked with an expression so deadly serious that, for a moment, I delayed reaching out to shake hands. Then he burst into laughter.

"Had you there," he said. "And it's Detective Inspector nowadays."

"Have they lost the plot," I asked. "That's way above your skillset."

"It was my charm and good looks."

"What happened?"

"Three thugs jumped me when I caught them red-handed at a burglary scene."

"I hope they didn't escape."

"Two in hospital, all three now in Gartree High-Security Prison on a long stretch."

"Never mess with a Stray," I said.

"Especially a brown tabby."

We laughed, hugged, and slapped our backs. Now, I recalled his constant clowning, which probably accounted for his delay in advancement.

"Darling," I said as I closed the apartment door behind us. "This is George Stray. George, this is my fiancée, Inge Lise Oleson."

"Pardon me for saying, Ollie," said George. "But is the charming Ms Oleson vision impaired? I can't believe that after years as a confirmed bachelor, any woman would touch you with a barge pole, yet here you are about to join the ranks of blissful married couples."

"More grateful than blissful," said Inge Lise, handing over a mug of tea.

"He or you?" said George.

"Both," said Inge Lise.

"Do I detect a hint of an accent?" said George.

"Danish," said Inge Lise.

"Then I hope you won't be overextending your ninety-day allocation," said George with a straight face.

"Is that why you are here?" I said. "Enforcing Brexit."

George sipped his tea and regarded us both.

"Of course not," he grinned. "Just messing with you. All I can say, Ollie, is that you are a fortunate man. Just wait until I tell them at the station. They're never going to believe this. Now, can we sit down and talk business."

"Is this good for Inge Lise to hear?" I asked.

"No problem," said George.

We sat around the dining table, sipping our drinks. George put his mug down, looked at us both and said, "Do you recall Geoffrey Freer?"

"Vaguely, remind me?"

"He was one of your early successes, although it took you three murders before a lucky break caught him in the act."

"Nasty pervert," I said.

"Preteen girls were his speciality," said George. "Rape, torture, and then he strung them up on trees down hardly used country lanes. A farmer heard faint screams walking back from the pub and called it in. You were just in time to prevent his fourth victim from serious damage."

"He confessed straight away," I said.

"But only to those three," said George.

"There were more?"

"Two. Ollie, he is dying up at Gartree in the prison hospital and insists on telling you where he buried the other victims."

"I thought his modus operandi was to string them up?"

"His words, not mine."

"Why me?"

"For some reason, he trusts you and has intimated the bodies are somewhere near Great Bowden, where you used to abide before your expansive penthouse here."

"Great Bowden, but the other crimes were committed in Nottinghamshire. Wysall, I believe."

"Correct, but these were before he moved to Wysall when he lived in Harborough in a council house on Meadow Street. His younger sister Barbara is alive and abides in the same property."

"If I recall correctly, wasn't his mental health leaning toward the disturbed?"

"The shrinks deemed him sane enough to stand trial."

"But that was over fifty years ago. Are you sure this is kosher, and he's not seeking revenge?"

"You'll have to judge for yourself."

"When did you speak with him?"

"I responded to the prison governor's call this morning and went straight to Gartree."

"How did the prisoner seem?"

"Frail but alert and determined."

"How would you assess his memory?"

"He's not suffering from Alzheimer's, according to the prison doctor."

"I suppose I could spare an hour or two, but I have domestic commitments, and if this extends into a lengthy investigation, I will have to back out."

"No problem, I will work with you and can take over if necessary, but the man wants to confess. I suggest you hear him out. We should recover the bodies within a day or two, and you'll soon be free to wait at the altar for your beautiful bride."

"So, just a few days?"

I looked at Inge Lise with raised eyebrows.

"You do what you feel is right," she said. "It will keep your brain exercised and give me time to fill the lounge and gadgets for the new house."

"Oh dear," I said, disguising a grin. "When can we see Mr. Freer?"

"I can take you there now," said George.

Printed in Great Britain
by Amazon